FIVE THOUSAND YEARS AGO . . .

The lost continent we now call Atlantis was secretly colonized by space-faring Antareans. When Atlantis was destroyed, a small group of Antareans was left behind in sealed "cocoons" under the sea, while the rest of the colony was evacuated.

FIVE YEARS AGO . . .

The Antareans sent a probeship down to Earth to reactivate the cocoons. A group of older Earth dwellers discovered their secret processing room, which inadvertently prepared them mentally and physically for travel in deep space. A deal was struck between the earthmen and the Antareans: human volunteers were to replace the sleeping Antarean army on a journey to the stars.

FIVE MINUTES AGO . . .

A small Antarean craft landed on Earth. Aboard were four of the former Earth dwellers, a small advance group who had returned to prepare the way for others. Their mission, and the decisions they would make in the near future, would affect the sleeping cocoons—as well as the future of the human race . . .

Metamorphosis

Jove books by David Saperstein

COCOON
METAMORPHOSIS

METAMORPHOSIS

THE
COCOON STORY CONTINUES

a novel by
DAVID SAPERSTEIN

JOVE BOOKS, NEW YORK

METAMORPHOSIS

A Jove Book / published by arrangement with
the author

PRINTING HISTORY
Jove edition / November 1988

ISBN: 0-515-10026-9

Jove Books are published by The Berkley Publishing Group,
200 Madison Avenue, New York, New York 10016.
The name ''JOVE'' and the ''J'' logo
are trademarks belonging to Jove Publications, Inc.

PRINTED IN THE UNITED STATES OF AMERICA

10 9 8 7 6 5 4 3 2 1

To my mother and father,
Celia and Louis Saperstein.
They taught me to reach for the stars,
and must surely travel among them now.

And to the four women who took my creation,
my baby *Cocoon,*
and helped it grow and become . . .

Melinda Jason
Lili Fini Zanuck
Susan Schulman
Meg Blackstone

Acknowledgments

Roger Challop, MD
Director, Washington Heights Pediatric Group
New York Associate Clinical Professor of Pediatrics
Columbia University, College of Physicians and Surgeons

John Driscoll, MD
Director, Neonatal Intensive Care Unit
Babies Hospital
Professor of Clinical Pediatrics, Columbia University
College of Physicians and Surgeons

Ming-Neng Yeh, MD
Consultant in Ultrasound, Department of Obstetrics and
      Gynecology
Columbia University, College of Physicians and Surgeons

Captain Dick Pleasantdon
Boynton Beach, Florida

Captain Joe Klein
Boynton Beach, Florida

Capt. Alan L. Bean, Ret. U.S. Navy
Astronaut, National Aeronautics and Space Administration
      (NASA)
Retired from NASA June 1981

Mr. Robert T. "Terry" White
Public Affairs Specialist, NASA

Mr. Douglas K. Ward
Deputy Director of Public Affairs, NASA

Mr. John E. Riley
Chief of Media Services Branch, NASA

Ms. Susan Allison
My "out of this world" editor

Ms. Susan Schulman
Who did it again!

METAMORPHOSIS

FIVE THOUSAND YEARS AGO

The lost continent we now call Atlantis was actually once known as Antares Quad 3, a thriving center for interstellar trade, diplomacy and government. It was originally settled by a race of space travelers known as Antareans, who kept their presence secret from the then primitive inhabitants of planet Earth.

During this time a celestial accident occurred within our solar system as a large comet passed very close to the planet Saturn, tearing away a large portion of the planet. Most of this mass was catapulted into space, eventually forming a huge, hot spinning ball of planetary matter, set on a near collision course with Earth.

The Antareans, aware of this event, had sixty-three years to prepare an orderly evacuation of their colony. It was decided that an army, consisting of nine hundred forty-one Antareans, be left behind in sealed cocoons in a state of suspended animation for a time when they would be needed again in this quadrant of our galaxy.

As the evacuation of Antares Quad 3 was completed and the cocoons were safely stored deep within the continental bedrock, the whirling mass passed close to the Earth, changing the planet's orbit and destroying the entire Antarean continent. That chunk of Saturn eventually stabilized in orbit and became known to us as the planet Venus.

The cocoon army slept safely beneath the ocean awaiting the return of their fellow Antareans. Then . . .

An Antarean mothership, moored on the dark side of the moon, sent a probeship down to Earth to evaluate the status of their cocoons and then to begin the rejuvenation process that would restore the sleeping Antarean army.

But the human beings on Earth had advanced rapidly and although Antares Quad Three (Atlantis) was gone, a thriving civilization now occupied the land nearby the hidden cocoons. That area, known as South Florida, had become a gathering place of older humans who, after active and productive lives, moved, sometimes reluctantly, to this warmer climate.

The Antareans set up a processing facility in a partially completed condominium complex that they had purchased. They enlisted the help of a young Earth dweller, Jack Fischer, a struggling charter boat captain, to help transport the daily load of cocoons raised from the ocean floor back to the mainland for processing at night.

Four retirees, living in condos at the Antares complex, discovered the secret processing room, which was not in use during the day. Thinking it a health spa that was part of the facilities of their condo, they used the equipment and thus began an irrevocable metamorphosis that prepared them, both mentally and physically, for travel in deep space.

The Antareans then discovered that the unforeseen pollution of the air and oceans had damaged the cocoons. They were unable to rejuvenate their army properly with the equipment they had brought to earth. At the same time they discovered the four old men who had been using their equipment and found that because of their advanced years the processing had worked on their bodies and minds, adapting them perfectly for space travel.

A deal was struck, and the older Earthmen, after consulting with their wives, located nine hundred thirty-three more old people like themselves who were willing to leave their now unrewarding life on Earth to travel in deep space, replacing the still sleeping Antarean army. Thus the Geriatric Brigade, as the old Earth people called themselves, was born.

In a wild land and sea chase with the Coral Gables police and United States Coast Guard, the last of the brigade slipped over the side of Jack Fischer's boat, the *Manta III,* and swam beneath the ocean to the waiting Antarean mothership below. The spacecraft departed, leaving Jack and the bewildered group of pursuers behind. As the Antarean mothership soared away into deep space, a silent message was beamed back to the sleeping Antarean cocoons: "We love you . . ." And then . . .

FIVE MINUTES AGO

A heavy rainstorm moved across south central Florida, stalling just east of Miami Beach and halting all
small craft activity along the entire east coast from
Key West to West Palm Beach. The storm intensified,
closing airports and interrupting all outdoor activity.

Under cover of the storm's thick gray thunderheads
and heavy downpour, a small Antarean probecraft
landed and submerged in Red Lake, at the mouth of
the Red Lake Canal in Coral Gables. Aboard were
four Earth humans who had once lived in Florida and
one Antarean, the commander of the previous mission that had taken nine hundred forty-one Earth
dwellers into deep space.

This small advance group had returned to the
motherplanet to prepare the way for others of the
Geriatric Brigade, who had been away from Earth for
five years.

Their mission, and the decisions they would have to
make in the near future, would affect the sleeping
cocoons as well as the future of the whole human race.

CHAPTER ONE

Sheets of rain swept across the lush fairway, sending the last of the diehard golfers scurrying for shelter in their brightly colored personal golf carts. Jack Fischer watched the fleeing hackers with amusement from his vantage point behind the fabled eleventh green of the Boca Raton Golf and Tennis Spa. Most homes in this part of South Florida boasted a Florida room—a swimming pool and patio area totally enclosed, walls and roof, with fine screening that allowed the warm weather in but kept the insect hordes out. Jack had designed his Florida room so that a portion of it was covered by a solid roof section. Thus he was always able to find shade, no matter how sunny the day.

As the rain hammered down and the wind gusted, Jack peered out and grew momentarily concerned about the stability of the plastic bubble that covered his tennis court. He had built the court and then enclosed it in a pressurized air-conditioned bubble so that he could play in complete comfort, no matter what the weather was. It looked like it was withstanding the storm well. Sitting back on his chaise, he sipped a mimosa and flipped channels on the portable color TV until he found the local news. After watching a story about another local drug-related killing, followed by hollow, heartening words from the Federal Drug Enforcement Agency that they were "winning the war on drugs in South Florida," Jack perked up. The weather report was next, and if it was at all positive, he planned to visit with his friend Phil Doyle, who ran a sport fishing charter boat out of the

Boynton Beach Marina. They had talked about going out that afternoon, but as the weather showed no sign of breaking, Jack was certain the fishing would have to wait for another day.

The weatherman began his report. He told the TV audience that it was raining. Then he spent the next five minutes giving weather reports for the entire United States, including, Jack Fischer mused, the temperature in Oregon. The meteorologist, who arrogantly put "Doctor" in front of his name on TV, then announced that it was raining in South Florida, gave the current local temperatures in Miami, Fort Lauderdale and West Palm Beach, and told his fellow newscasters that he hoped for a better forecast on the evening program. Jack lifted his glass of orange juice and champagne in a toast.

"Here's to science. That was one hell of a forecast!" But then again, he mused, they never give a weather forecast in Florida, only a current report that anybody could know by just looking out the window. Perhaps it was against the rules of the Florida Chamber of Commerce? He got up, turned off the TV and stared out at the rain.

He had been uneasy all day, attributing the jumpy sensation to the depressing weather that had persisted now for two days. But there was more to this feeling than just the weather. At times over the past five years, after the fabulous adventure he had shared with the Antareans, a strange sensation of thoughts—voices inside his mind—would come over him. He would feel as though Amos Bright, the Antarean leader, and some of the old people who had gone off into space as the Geriatric Brigade were calling to him, actually speaking to him and greeting him from across the vast universal void. The contacts were always done with love, and although Jack had never quite mastered the art of telepathing his own thoughts, he was able to receive thoughts from others. It was comforting to know, or at least imagine, that his old friends were safe and alive; that from time to time they thought about him.

But today the feeling was different. It was close. Very strong. "Ah well," he said, and sighed aloud, "they promised to come back for me one day and that ain't anything shabby to have ahead."

Still and all, he was a lonely man. Keeping the secret of the Antareans and the Geriatric Brigade had been difficult. He was the first human to have contact with beings from another planet, and he could say nothing about it. He lifted his glass toward the leaden sky and, draining the sweet orange fluid, thought a silent loving toast to his faraway friends.

At the same time Ben Green and Joe Finley strolled through the main entrance of the now completed Antares condominium complex. They smiled inside, telepathing to one another rapidly, excitedly.

"I remember it all, Ben."

"Like yesterday. But look how it's changed."

"Yeah. They actually finished the place."

"Can you imagine living here now? Being retired, sitting by the pool, playing gin . . ."

"Dying of leukemia?" Joe Finley mused as they walked toward the A Building, passing the pool area. Their minds filled with memories of their last days on Earth.

"Pool's filled," Ben remarked, remembering the battle they'd had with the feisty manager, Ralph Shields, when they insisted on getting the pool filled and operating. Joe Finley glanced over toward the B Building.

"It's finished, Ben. The B Building is finished." Ben Green stopped to examine the high-rise condominium closely. When they had left the building was just a shell, partially constructed and sheltering the Antarean processing room that Ben, Joe, Art Perlman and Bernie Lewis had accidentally discovered. It was in that room, using the Antarean equipment they mistook for a health spa, that their own metamorphosis had taken place, forever changing them, expanding their minds and rejuvenating their aging bodies so that they could become the first human deep-space travelers.

"The place looks good," Joe remarked. "Neat."

"That it does, my friend. But a little too small for our purposes this time."

"That, Commander Green, is the understatement of the year!"

The rain began to let up and the sky brightened. Jack tried to telephone Phil Doyle at the Boynton Marina, but the storm had downed some telephone lines and he couldn't get through. He wandered into the darkened house, slightly high from his fourth mimosa sans food. The air was clammy, and as Jack went to kick up the air conditioner he passed his bedroom and heard the sound of running water. The hot tub was being filled. Cathy was still there. He went into his bedroom, a large room just off the Florida room that he had decorated like a South Sea Island hut. The ceiling was thatched grass, the carpeting a soft mat covered with skins and the furniture rattan and bamboo. His king-size waterbed was placed in the center of the room, covered with a zebra skin and white polar bear pillows. Underneath, black satin sheets added the final touch of fantasy.

Cathy Chung, a Eurasian of exceptional beauty and sexual prowess, sat in the redwood hot tub that was set off to the right side of the bedroom, surrounded by floor-to-ceiling sliding glass doors that looked out onto a secluded Japanese garden. She was nude. Her long, tapered legs stretched across the tub and were barely covered with the foamy water as it rushed in around her. She waved to Jack, beckoning him to join her.

"I thought you went home," he said, slipping out of his flowered shorts. "Want a drink?" He held up his mimosa. She shook her head and arched her back as the water rose. Her breasts seemed to float in the steamy water, showing large round, dark aureoles surrounding soft brown nipples.

"Jesus," Jack muttered to himself as he kicked his shorts away, picked up his drink and headed for the tub. At that moment Cathy slipped under the water and her long straight dark hair, more than shoulder length, spread out in the water like a black silk fan. Although they had spent the night together, Jack was aroused and hard by the time he stepped into the now completely filled tub.

As he reached for Cathy she grabbed his erect penis from under the water with both hands, pulling gently. He had no choice but to slip under the water with her, holding on to his mimosa as the sweet orange liquid blended with the bubbly hot water.

While Jack Fischer played and frolicked, Ben Green and Joe Finley entered the Antares condominium manager's office. A bright young secretary greeted them politely.

"May I help you gentlemen?"

"We'd like to speak to the owner."

"You mean the manager. This is a condo. It's owned by the, ah, occupants. You know, like retired people."

"Okay. The manager."

"There are no units available now." She reached for a clipboard with papers attached. "But if you'd like to leave your name and address or phone number, someone will contact you. We have several other properties and—" Ben cut her short.

"I'm sure you do, my dear, but we're interested in talking to the manager."

"He's not here."

"What's his name?" Joe Finley asked.

"Mr. Parker."

"Wally the Wonderful," Ben quipped. Joe laughed, recalling the battles they had fought five long years ago with Shields, the original manager of the condos, and Wally Parker, who was just the maintenance director at that time. In the end both men had fought a pitched battle that resulted in Parker being hospitalized and Shields jailed. It had all been a setup to distract them away from the processing room in the B Building.

"I beg your pardon?" the secretary said.

"Just a private joke. What about Mr. Fischer? Jack Fischer?"

"Oh." She smiled. "Now I understand. No. He used to be the owner, but when all the units were sold— that was even before me—like before I worked here? So he left. It was all like sold."

"Do you know where we might find him?" Ben asked pleasantly.

"No. I'm afraid I don't. He's somewhere up north . . ."

"New York?"

"No. Not that north. Like Lauderdale or Boca. Up there."

Ben and Joe thanked her and left the office. They would have to make another contact from the past. They trusted the Coral Gables banker John DePalmer, who had assisted Amos Bright in the original purchase of the Antares condos and who had handled all the financial transactions for the visiting Antareans, although he never knew their real identity. When they had left Earth five years ago they signed over the complex to Jack Fischer. Ben and Joe reasoned DePalmer would know where to find Jack. But in order to get that information, Amos Bright would have to make an appearance at the bank. They telepathed that message to Amos and their wives, who were waiting for them in the submerged Antarean spacecraft. They would all meet at the bank in Coral Gables.

As they walked through the grounds before leaving they glanced over at the pool again and noticed their old table, the one where they had sat day after day playing gin with Bernie Lewis and Art Perlman, watching their lives slowly come to an end. Or so they'd thought.

"A lifetime ago," Ben said.

"Light years actually," Joe answered. And that was true, for in the past five years they had actually traveled thousands of light years through the universe, sampling just a tiny portion of its wonders, meeting just a minute part of its population.

And now they had returned to prepare the way for some of their fellow human space travelers, who were returning to mother Earth to act out a ritual that was as old as life itself.

Time was short. They had to find Jack Fischer and gather as much help as they could at the highest levels possible, but at the same time they knew their mission, while of the utmost urgency, had to remain a total secret. Public exposure now could spell disaster of the worst kind.

CHAPTER TWO

When they had left Earth five long years ago, they had done so by choice. Nine hundred forty-one aged human souls chose to adapt their bodies for space travel and leave their home, their Earth, behind, perhaps forever. Some made the difficult choice of leaving families behind: grown children, grandchildren, great-grandchildren, sisters and brothers. They opted for a new and unknown life rather than live out the one they had on Earth with certain boredom and isolation in a society that venerated youth and physical appearance.

It was ironic that American culture attuned itself to physical fitness, diet and exercise in order to, among other things, live a longer and healthier life. When that was accomplished, however, when people did in fact live longer, they were shunted away to areas like Florida, Arizona and Southern California to "retire and live out their golden years."

The decision to leave Earth had to be made quickly by those who were fortunate enough to be approached by the organizers of the Geriatric Brigade, namely, Mary and Ben Green, Rose and Bernie Lewis, Alma and Joe Finley, and Bess and Arthur Perlman. But the secret had to be kept tight and secure. Those with families left letters behind, which Jack Fischer delivered personally. But for most—those who had been deserted, or put away in nursing homes, or left alone in the world to survive on meager pensions, Social Security or handouts, for the largest portion of the group—the decision involved only themselves. They would never be missed.

The Brigade was not an army to be trained for war. Rather it was to be used for education and training on other worlds. The initial mission was to go directly to Parma Quad 2, a large planet near the star we call Sirius the Dog Star.

The Parmans, a crystalline life form, had contacted the Antareans, and the Brigade was sent in answer. The Parmans, who had up to that point avoided contact with extraterrestrials, now wanted to venture into space. They offered a unique exchange: They would serve as navigators on Antarean spacecraft. Because they possessed the ability to draw energy from starlight, no matter how distant, they could lock on to any star and guide a craft to it. But more than that, they could convert the starlight to energy. The closer they drew to the star they focused on, the more energy they could convert, until space and time melded into one. The Antareans realized that with Parman guides on their ships they could finally achieve intergalactic travel.

The deal was struck and treaties entered into. But when the Antareans came to Earth to recover their cocoon army they found it damaged and unusable. It was then that they discovered older Earth dwellers could, because of the nature of the human aging process, be processed and transformed for space travel. Younger people, their bodies still aging and changing, could not take the processing. But nine hundred forty-one older Earth people leaped at the chance to become Earth's first space ambassadors.

As ambassadors they were among the best the Antareans had ever met. On the trip to Parma Quad 2, which would take several months, the Brigade adapted to their new life and newfound energy, while the Antareans aboard the mothership educated them. The humans were eager and bright students. In particular, the eleven who had chosen to be commanders proved to have an exceptional ability to absorb and process information as rapidly as any Antarean commander might.

They all brought wisdom and an appreciation for life that the Antareans knew was rare in the known universe. Some thought it was a result of the processing itself, while others in the Antarean crew felt that the expanded human brain usage, from slightly more than ten percent of capacity to nearly ninety percent, was the reason for the abilities now exhibited as the mothership hurtled toward Sirius and the Parman civilization.

The human commanders knew differently. Their race was oriented toward death as a fact of life. It was part of the deal, as Ben Green had told Amos Bright once. We are born and very shortly thereafter we learn we will die. Antareans were born under controlled conditions and died only when they chose to die, or if they were involved in some accident or disaster. An Antarean could live forever. A human certainly numbered his years and valued them. Now that mortality was changed forever.

Now aboard the mothership was a new race, never before seen in space. And amazingly, with their new immortality, the humans grew in their compassion for others as they learned of distant worlds with very different, but at the same time, very human problems. They asked endless questions of their teachers about the suffering of other life forms in the galaxy.

Amos Bright and the other Antarean commanders aboard the mothership were certain that their decision to invite these older Earth dwellers to join them had been a proper one. As Amos said to Beam, the female Antarean medical officer on the mission, "These Earth people are quite remarkable. They learn rapidly, but they always want to know more about the beings than the places. They have much love within them, and they want to share that with others."

"Perhaps we have brought them into space for another's purpose."

"You mean for the Master?"

"We all serve the Master. Perhaps He has willed that the time for these Earth people to join the rest of the universe has come. Perhaps they are needed."

"I feel that too. They will grow and come to understand much more than even we about the universe. They are a new race. I think we have been guided to bring them out from their planet to walk among others."

The Brigade had been welcomed by the Parmans. It was as if they knew that those they called integrators, those who would teach them about the known universe, would themselves be new to space travel. The two species got along famously, and the entire Parman orientation took less than two years. During that time several Antarean spaceships were adapted to use Parman guides in their propulsion and navigation systems.

When the orientation and integration process was completed, Parman guides were installed in the Antarean ships and, along with several human crew members, began intergalactic exploration. Many of the Geriatric Brigade chose to crew with the Antareans who remained travelers in our own galaxy, while some stayed behind as permanent ambassadors to Parma Quad 2.

So the Geratric Brigade was scattered throughout our own galaxy and beyond. Human influence was now and forever to be a part of the universal experience.

CHAPTER THREE

The shopping center in Kendall was busy as the storm ended and gray skies gave way to sunshine and patches of blue. The mall parking lot showed signs of the rain, with several areas still badly flooded from poor drainage. Shoppers, whom the rain had kept away, honked and fought for parking spaces near to the main mall away from the flooded areas.

Ben Green and Joe Finley made their way cautiously through the parking lot toward the blue glass and ceramic tile building that housed the Frist Bank of Coral Gables. An elderly couple in a 1973 Cadillac Coupe deVille that had seen better days raced through the lot toward a parking spot that was being vacated by another elderly couple in a new Buick LeSabre. Ben saw the Caddy pick up speed as another car, a 1982 Corvette convertible containing two teenage boys, headed for the same parking spot from the opposite direction. He reached over and pushed Joe Finley back as the Caddy roared into a flood pool of rainwater caused by the drain backup. A wall of spray spewed up into the air on both sides of the car, obscuring it from Ben and Joe's view. The splash was followed by the screeching of brakes as the Corvette tried to avoid the oncoming Cadillac—now behaving more like a motorboat than an automobile. As the teenagers swerved away, their car, with the top down and the radio blasting an irritating monotonous rock song, was deluged with warm dirty rainwater from the Caddy's wash. The two boys wound up stalled in the middle of the flood, soaking wet and cursing at the top of their lungs as the couple in the Cadillac slipped into the now empty spot, oblivious to the epithets being hurled at them by the teenagers.

"In some way I really miss Florida," Ben mused, observing the couple as they locked the car, gazed momentarily at the Corvette awash in muddy water above its hubcaps and strolled toward Burdine's.

"Just some senior citizens asserting their rights, out for an afternoon of shopping," Joe answered as they approached the bank building, which was sandwiched in between Harvey's, a classy home furnishings store and Loehmann's, a women's discount dress shop.

"Amos must be here," Ben told his friend. "The girls are at it already." Joe Finley looked ahead and saw his wife, Alma, firmly planted in front of the furniture store window, while Ben's wife, Mary, was carefully studying the latest New York fashions in the dress shop window display.

"You can take the woman away from the shopping, but you can't take shopping out of the woman!" Ben laughed as they waved a greeting to their wives.

If John DePalmer was surprised to see Amos Bright, he kept it to himself. Even though five years had passed, he remembered with absolute clarity every transaction he had processed on behalf of Mr. Bright. Of course Mr. DePalmer had no idea that Amos was an extraterrestrial, although he did suspect the man was not ordinary by any means.

At their first meeting Amos Bright had asked to speak to then Assistant Manager DePalmer in private. He had given the banker several million dollars' worth of diamonds, which DePalmer had taken to Amsterdam and Tel Aviv and sold for cash and a generous commission. He had bought the Antares condominium complex, then an unfinished construction project, for Mr. Bright as well. And he had staffed it, managed it and eventually sold it on behalf of the last owner, Jack Fischer, after Amos Bright had signed over the ownership to him.

Now as his old business associate sat across the table in the bank's private conference room, DePalmer studied Amos and the two elderly couples with him.

"These past five years have treated you well, Mr. Bright. You don't seem a day older than when we last met."

"Time passes; I try to keep in shape. Let me introduce Mr. and Mrs. Green and Mr. and Mrs. Finley. They're friends of mine, good friends. We have some business we'd like you to help us with—if you're still able to, shall we say, approach things with perhaps some unorthodox methods."

DePalmer smiled and greeted the two couples. If only Mr. Bright knew how unorthodox things were now in South Florida. The banks were loaded with cash, mostly as a direct result of the drug traffic. But now that the federal government was cracking down on money laundering, the larger operators were moving their cash offshore, using the same "donkeys"— human carriers who brought drugs into the country— to take millions of dollars in cash out. Recently twenty employees of a South American airline had been detained with more than seventy million dollars in cash on them collectively. Since the maximum amount allowed out of the country per person is ten thousand dollars, arrests were made and the money was confiscated. With that kind of pressure, DePalmer was sure that the large dealers would be seeking the bank's anonymity again in the near future.

In the past John DePalmer had not been in a position to deal with drug money, and actually he was not sure he could go through with it now if the opportunity presented itself. He had friends in the banking community who had laundered money for huge fees. They hid their profits in Swiss accounts, but deep down they knew they belonged to the ruthless dealers they served. DePalmer was still his own man, but he wondered if he could resist.

The interest rates had fallen, the condo market was overbuilt and oversold, depositors had withdrawn huge sums to seek better returns through the stock and bond markets and he had several marginal loans that were now in doubt. Business wasn't great, and his bosses were down on him, pressing for a better bottom line.

As those thoughts raced through DePalmer's mind they were read by Amos and his four companions, all of whom were full Antarean commanders. They silently approved of DePalmer's honesty and agreed to help the man as best they could.

"We have two things we'd like to accomplish today, John," Amos began. "The first is to locate Jack Fischer, the young man to whom I signed over the Antares complex."

"That's no problem. I speak to him from time to time. Nice young man, although with all his wealth I think he'd want to make some more growth investments than he does."

"Living the good life, is he?" Ben Green asked.

"Very much so. Wine, women and song, as the expression goes. Not to tell tales out of school. I like the young man. He just seems so . . . so lost, so aimless."

"Well," Alma Finley said, "maybe we've come along at the right time. I think we've got a business proposition for him that he just can't refuse." They all smiled. DePalmer laughed nervously.

"Let me write down his address for you, and phone number. It's unlisted, but I'm sure he'd want Mr. Bright to have it." DePalmer wrote both down on a white pad, tore off the paper and handed it to Amos Bright. "You said two things, Mr. Bright."

Amos reached for the small leather case he'd kept tucked under his arm and placed it on the table. He unzipped it, opened the first compartment and withdrew a thin black Lucite box. Placing the box on the table, he looked up at Mr. DePalmer.

"I still like to use the same currency we began our business dealing with," he said as he unsnapped the box, revealing more than fifty Class-D, blue-white, six-carat diamonds, each worth more than fifty thousand dollars on the wholesale market.

"They're beautiful. And perfect as usual."

"Thank you. We'd like to sell these, however you think best, open a few accounts, obtain some credit cards and the services of a first-rate travel agent."

"I can arrange that," DePalmer said as Amos Bright slid the case of diamonds across the table to him. He looked down at the stones just one more time and then snapped the box shut. "We can open the accounts now and a complete line of credit. My estimate is at least two million, probably two point five after these are sold. Our corporate travel department will handle those needs for you."

"Excellent," Amos answered. "Each of us will want an account. Divide the money evenly." He stood up as did the others. DePalmer knew the meeting was over.

"If there's anything else you need, Mr. Bright, anything, you know I'm at your disposal. You still have my home number?"

"Yes. We'll be in touch. Thank you, Mr. De-Palmer."

They left after the accounts had been opened. Amos returned to the submerged spacecraft to advise those on Antares that they had landed safely and that plans were underway.

Mary Green headed for Miami Airport to catch a flight to New York. It had been more than five years since she had seen her daughter, Patricia Keane, and her three grandchildren. A reunion with them was a joy she had anticipated from the time they'd left Antares, but her reunion would also be a test to see how a family might react to a returning space traveler. Their acceptance of her story would affect others who wanted to—who had to—return themselves.

Alma Finley hired a car and driver to take her to the Fort Lauderdale airport, where she would get the first flight out to Washington, D.C. She was going to call on an old friend and ex-boss from the days when she was an editor for NBC network television news. Caleb Harris was now the Washington Bureau Chief for the entire NBC news network. Alma hoped that Caleb would believe her fantastic story and use his influence to arrange a meeting with the President of the United States.

At the same time Ben Green and Joe Finley, having rented a car, drove north on I-95 toward Boca Raton for their own meeting with an unsuspecting Jack Fischer. Jack was about to be folded back into the world of Antarean visitors from outer space and the Geratric Brigade he'd helped to organize, process and leave the Earth five years ago.

CHAPTER FOUR

The rain had stopped. While Ben and Joe made their way along the crowded Interstate, Jack Fischer was saying goodbye to Cathy Chung in the driveway. He helped her put down the tattered roof of her bright orange VW Beetle.

"It's gonna clear up," he said, looking at the fleeting rain clouds as they gave way to patches of blue.

"Then you'll be with Doyle, huh?"

"I think so." He opened the door on the driver's side for her. She started to get in, then stopped and gave him a long, tender kiss.

"You're a sweet man, Jack Fischer. Sweet but flighty."

He laughed as she jumped into the car, started the ancient engine and backed out of his driveway, gears grinding and brakes squealing.

"I'll call you later," he shouted after her, knowing his words were lost in the air rushing around her oval face and long black hair as it fluttered in the wind. "Later . . ." Jack turned and went back into the house to try to reach Phil Doyle again.

A block away, parked under a drooping poinsettia tree, Detective Sergeant Matthew Cummings, in his last year with the Dade County sheriff's office, sat in his Olds Cutlass munching on a box of Fruit Loops. When the Oriental girl in the orange VW drove past him he slid down in the driver seat, trying to hide. Cathy was concentrating on an old Stones tune and noticed nothing. After she passed Cummings put aside his snack and attentively watched Jack's house.

The ritual of spying on Jack Fischer had been a part of Detective Cummings's life for nearly four years, ever since all charges against Jack had been dropped after the strange disappearance of scores of old people from the South Miami area.

The worst part of Cummings's frustration was that he, along with several Coast Guard vessels and helicopters, had chased Jack Fischer's and Phil Doyle's boats, loaded with old people, out toward the open sea in an area known as the Stones. It was obvious that the old people were being tossed into the sea, but when the police and Coast Guard had tried to stop them and make an arrest, their vision had somehow been obscured, the helicopters had malfunctioned and, except for Cummings, no one seemed to have a clear memory of what had happened.

When the area was cleared the old people were gone. Fischer and Doyle were there, outriggers spread with bait in the water as they fished the calm night sea. Above them, unnoticed, an Antarean mothership loaded with hundreds of volunteer human senior citizens was but a flashing speck in the clear Florida night sky. And the most fantastic human experience ever recorded, travel into deep space, had begun.

Cummings had pressed charges against Fischer and Doyle—kidnapping, transporting illegals, smuggling and even murder. There were people missing, but no evidence they had been on Jack's or Phil's boat. The eyewitnesses, mostly Coast Guard pilots and sailors, could not swear that they had seen these old people aboard. It was all confusing and vague in their minds. They had been in pursuit of two sport-fishing vessels, the *Manta III* and the *Razzamatazz,* and a small helicopter. The weather became foggy and an electrical disturbance caused their instrumentation to go haywire. No one could actually swear to the fanciful story that Cummings told to the Coral Gables district attorney.

Jack Fischer, Phil Doyle and Madman Mazuski, the

helicopter pilot who swore he was fish spotting for Jack and Phil, were brought in and questioned. By then the Antares condominium complex was in Jack's name, and he was a man of financial means. He hired a top lawyer and things cooled down.

Eventually, in an embarrassing confrontation in the DA's office, Sergeant Cummings began to testify about the old people jumping over the side in an act of mass suicide. His credibility became strained when the detective began to talk about a huge underwater craft that emerged from beneath the sea as a dense fog suddenly appeared. The DA looked at Jack's lawyer apologetically. When the Dade County detective began to describe the craft as a "spaceship that took off into the sky" the DA halted testimony and asked to speak to Cummings alone. A week later the charges were dropped. Cummings was assigned to a desk for a year, along with his partner, Coolridge Betters.

But whenever he could, especially while Jack lived at the Antares complex, Cummings kept an eye on him, convinced that the greatest mass murder in the history of the nation had taken place, and Jack Fischer was responsible. After the condos were sold and Jack moved to Boca Raton, Cummings would still make the long trip north whenever he could. Someday, he swore, Jack Fischer would make a mistake, and he would be there to nail him.

Something in the air, a tingle down his spine, told him that today might be that day. Moments later, as Ben Green and Joe Finley pulled into Jack's driveway and got out of their car, Detective Sergeant Cummings knew his vindication was at hand.

"I'll be goddamned," he gasped, sliding down once again, his balding head and bloodshot brown eyes barely visible above the dashboard. "It's two of those old farts that were on his boat. They jumped over the side, but they're back. Alive. It's going down again—I can feel it. Okay, you old fuckers, this time I'm gonna be ready for you!"

Ben and Joe heard Cummings's thoughts and made a note to deal with him later. Right now they had more pressing business with their old friend, Jack.

As they approached the front door, Jack hung up the phone. He had reached Phil and told his friend he'd be at the dock in a half hour.

Something turned him around as he walked to his bedroom to dress for fishing. Something pulled him toward the front door; then the doorbell rang. He shuddered and slowly opened the door. Before he saw them, he knew who was there.

Ben Green smiled broadly across his ageless face. "Hello, Jack. How the hell are you?"

"Good to see you again," Joe Finley added quickly, extending his hand in greeting.

"Oh my God!" Jack knew they were there, but he couldn't believe it. "Is it really . . . are you two who I think you are . . . who I know you are?"

"In the flesh," Ben answered.

"May we come in?" Joe asked, feeling Cummings's inquisitive eyes burning a hole in his back.

"Sure . . . sure. Christ, you guys look great!" The two men stepped into the house. Jack closed the door and stared at them. "I never thought I'd see you guys again. Well, not so soon anyway. So, how is everyone? Jesus, you've actually been out there? What's it like? Where did you go? How's Amos and Beam . . . and . . ." He stopped abruptly, realizing that he was babbling and the two old men were staring at him with broad smiles on their faces.

"Let's sit down, Jack," Joe suggested, "and we'll tell you everything."

They went into the living room, and as the two older men sat on a white silk couch Jack went to the bar and poured himself a stiff scotch on the rocks.

"You guys want one?" he asked.

"No thanks," Ben said.

"Maybe a beer?" Joe asked. "It's been a while since I had a cold brew."

"No beer out there, huh? Sounds like a good

business to open." Jack reached into the bar refrigerator. "Heineken?"

"Perfect."

He brought the beer over to the couch and settled in an easy chair nearby, taking a slug of his scotch.

"You live alone?" Joe asked, taking a long draw on the frosty green beer bottle.

"Still a bachelor."

"What about Judy?" Ben asked.

"Judy? Oh, Judy Simmons. Yeah . . . show biz. She did these commercials and someone in New York saw them and made her a great offer to work up there. I haven't heard from her in . . . God, almost two years, but I heard she was in Los Angeles doing TV shows."

"She was a nice girl. How's your brother?"

"Arnie's fine. He and Sandy moved to Atlanta last year. They have a little girl and another on the way." Jack smiled at the two men, reading their thoughts, knowing what was coming next. "I can hear you guys thinking. I thought I forgot how to do that . . . telepathing."

Joe put down his beer and fixed his gaze on Jack. "So are you?"

"Lonely? I guess so. Since we finished the B Building and sold it all off there isn't anything for me to do down at the condos. But I keep busy. I fish with Phil on the *Terra Time*. I gave him that boat. I still have the old *Manta III*. I can't seem to be able to part with the old bucket."

Jack had drained his scotch. He stood up to get another. "I can't get over you guys just walking in like that." He reached the bar fully aware that both men were concentrating on him, blocking their thoughts from the telepathic abilities he had developed while working with the Antareans on their last fateful visit to Earth five years ago.

Jack had been a struggling charter boat captain in Coral Gables. The Antareans, disguised as humans, had enlisted his boat and his help in locating, raising and processing their cocoons: casings containing

Antarean soldiers in suspended animation, left behind thousands of years before when the continent we call Atlantis was destroyed by a passing comet.

The pollution in our oceans had damaged the cocoons and the Antarean rescue party was unable to revive them. It was at that time that Ben, Joe and two of their friends, Art Perlman and Bernie Lewis, discovered the Antarean processing room. Thinking it was a health spa and part of their condo facilities, the four men used the equipment and changed the course of human history forever.

The Antarean cocoon-processing equipment, though deadly to young earth bodies, worked wonders on the aging humans. They were cleansed, strengthened and transformed into perfect specimens for deep-space travel. These four men became the core of the Geriatric Brigade.

Before their departure, the Antarean leader, Amos Bright, signed over the ownership of the Antares condominiums to Jack and promised to return for him one day when his body had aged sufficiently to be processed.

Now, five years later, as Jack sat with Ben Green and Joe Finley, he knew that although he had abused his body somewhat, it still was only thirty-five and not yet ready for the Antarean processing room.

"So you guys here for a visit? Vacation? Maybe pick up some back Social Security checks?"

"No," Ben began, "we're an advance party. Joe and I came with our wives and Amos Bright on a probecraft. The others, well, some of the others are following on an Antarean watership."

Joe Finley stood up and walked to the large picture window that faced out on to the golf course. A foursome of two elderly couples was playing the eleventh hole. Joe watched the ponderous, creaky golf swing of the man closest to the window. He was well into his seventies. The man's wife sat in their golf cart shouting words of encouragement and praise as his golf ball skittered along the plush fairway and stopped fifty yards ahead. Out of the corner of his eye, Joe Finley also noticed Detective Sergeant Matthew Cummings hiding behind a hedge of newly planted brush bottle pines that bordered the fairway.

"Does that cop hang around here much?" he remarked, turning back toward Jack and Ben.

"Cop?"

"Cummings. From Coral Gables," Joe answered.

"The one who chased us that last night," Ben chimed in.

"Oh, that cop. Is he out there?"

"He's spying on us," Joe said.

"Yeah, well, he comes around a little now and then. He was a mess after you guys left. They arrested us, you know. Phil and me and the Madman. But they couldn't make anything stick. The Coast Guard guys were totally confused and then when old Cummings and his partner—what was his name?"

"Betters," Joe said quickly.

"Yeah, Coolridge Betters. Well, they both started yapping about kidnapping and murder. For a while it was a little sticky but DePalmer got me a first-class lawyer. Eventually old Cummings began to mutter about you guys going over the side and the Antareans and the mothership, so . . ."

"So they certified him and dropped it all?" Ben said, smiling.

"Not certified, but put him on the back burner. He retires soon. He's over the hill—" Suddenly Jack realized he was sitting in a room with two men who were considerably older than Cummings. "Sorry about that, guys."

"That's okay, Jack. We've come to realize that over the hill is an earthly term. It's all relative." Joe smiled kindly at Jack.

"I can dig that," Jack said. "You guys look like you're gonna live forever."

"In a manner of speaking that might be true," Ben

remarked, "and if you recall, Amos promised to come back for you when your time came."

"I think about it every day."

"Good," Ben continued, "because now we need your help once again."

"If you guys want to use the condos again, that's a problem. They're all sold."

"No, Jack," Joe Finley said, sitting down next to the ex-charter captain, "the condo complex is way too small for our needs this time."

"This time we're going to need more than a few charter boats and a processing room," Ben added as he sat down on the other side of the young man, clapping his arm around Jack's shoulder. "And now I'm going to tell you the damnedest story you ever heard."

Jack took just a moment out from listening to Ben and Joe to call Phil Doyle and say he would be by later with a big surprise. He then sat down between the two space travelers and continued to listen to their fascinating tale. When they finished, Jack sat silently for a moment. Then a wide grin turned into laughter as he let out a whoop and danced around the room.

"This is absolutely great! I'm with you all the way. When do we begin?"

Joe and Ben relaxed and smiled. "We already have," they said in unison.

CHAPTER FIVE

Mary Green's flight to New York's La Guardia Airport had been uneventful. There was a moment, however, shortly after takeoff from Miami International, when she realized that it had been years since she put her life in the hands of beings other than the Antareans or the Parman guides. She sat, feeling the DC-10's powerful engines propel them forward, knowing that a human being was flying the airplane with a rather primitive technology compared to the transportation she had used for the past five years.

The idea that she could lose her life in an earthly plane crash, no matter how remote the chance, drove home the absolutely complete adaptation she had made to life in deep space. She loved her life more now than she had ever imagined, but being back on Earth, in the relatively frail human aircraft, gave a sense of mortality that she had not experienced for a long time.

At the same time Alma Finley was preparing to depart on her flight to Washington, D.C., from the Fort Lauderdale airport. The women communicated with one another, sending comforting thoughts across the Florida skies. They eventually accepted their fate and had a good laugh about it.

Still, each of the women monitored the cockpit on their respective flights, chiding one another for doing so, but feeling more at ease being able to listen to trouble-free "pilot talk" from takeoff to landing.

Now in the midafternoon light, with the late spring

sun overhead, Mary Green walked along the peaceful, tree-lined street two blocks from her daughter's home in Scarsdale, New York. She had asked the taxi driver to drop her off a distance from the house so that she might approach it quietly.

Birds sang. A black squirrel chased a gray one across the street and up a ponderous oak. The only car that passed was a Mercedes station wagon loaded with two preschool kids, a yellow Labrador retriever and a harried young affluent mother. Mary's thoughts drifted back to another such tree-lined street where she and Ben Green lived in Westport, Connecticut, before they retired to Florida. It had been a good life, she mused, but then, in a very real sense, she had been reborn, and in these past five years she had walked down some very strange streets that were light years away.

Now she was home on mother Earth. It was May, warm and blooming—azaleas, rhododendron, the last of the tulips and the first of the marigolds. She breathed deeply of the sweet spring air whose perfume filled her expanded and enhanced brain with awakenings long forgotten and recently remembered. Her absolutely unabashed joy at being alive quickened her pace unconsciously, moving her along quickly until she was only a few short steps away from the home of her daughter, Patricia.

She stopped now, unsure of how it would be to suddenly appear after so many years . . . after such an abrupt departure. Ben had written the letter they had left behind for the immediate family. Jack Fischer had delivered it, as he had delivered all the other letters left behind by the members of the Geriatric Brigade who had families on Earth they cared about. So many had no one. So many had been abandoned, shunted away to South Florida, turned out to live on inadequate Social Security or, in the worst cases, welfare. During their travels in space, as the members of the Brigade got to know one another, horror stories were told by these elderly space travelers of beatings and neglect.

But in the case of the Green family, things had been different. Theirs was a solid, loving family that supported one another. Mary was sure that after the initial shock of seeing her mother alive, Patricia would welcome her with open arms.

In their letter to the family, Mary and Ben had written of their love for their children and grandchildren. They explained the wonder of the great adventure they had been offered by the Antareans, of the chance to live a long, full and useful life. Without knowing what really faced them in outer space, they had speculated on being among the first humans to meet beings from other planets, other galaxies, and how honored they felt to be chosen to walk among the stars. The letter was filled with love and kindness and a hope that the family would understand and be happy for Mary and Ben.

Now as Mary approached the large Tudor set back from the street with the driveway hidden beyond a row of hedges, she noticed the front door of the house was open. She stopped and looked off to the right beyond the hedge and saw her daughter, Patricia Keane, unloading grocery packages from the tailgate of a new Volvo station wagon. The woman, a forty-year-old clone of her attractive seventy-two-year-old mother, slammed the tailgate shut, lifted her packages and began walking through an opening in the hedges toward the front door. Mary Green stood still, hoping Patricia would not notice her. But she did.

For a moment Patricia Keane was frozen in her tracks, unwilling and unable to believe her eyes. Mary reached out to her daughter telepathically with comfort and love. "Yes," she thought, "it's me. I've come home." Pat dropped the groceries and flew across the neat, freshly cut lawn, weeping tears of joy, thrilled to overflowing that her mother was home.

The women embraced as Pat sobbed and laughed and cried, unable to let go, afraid that Mary was just some apparition that might vanish if she loosened her grip.

"Darling," Mary said after a minute had passed. "Please. I've come seventeen light years to see you, and you're squeezing the breath out of me."

"Oh . . . oh Mother," Pat said as she loosened her hold and stepped back, keeping her hands on Mary's shoulders. "It is you? Oh God, how we all missed you. Dad? Where's Dad? Is he okay?"

"He's just fine. He's in Florida. You'll see him soon. He sends his love."

"Mom! Oh God . . ." Pat just couldn't contain her emotions. She hugged her mother again and cried until the tears streamed down her tanned cheeks. A moment later, after Pat realized they were out in the street, both women walked hand in hand to retrieve the scattered groceries and then disappeared into the house to catch up on five years of separation.

Ben Green, now in Jack Fischer's car headed toward the marina at Boynton Beach, felt all of his wife's emotions telepathically, as did all of the commanders. They realized the Green family would be a test case—a measurement of how the other families might react to the sudden reappearance of the geriatric space travelers.

CHAPTER SIX

Alma Finley's flight to Washington, D.C., had been delayed, and when she finally landed at National Airport it was four P.M. The rush of business people trying to get out of the nation's capital, as well as those arriving to do business the next day or returning from forays out among the population, turned the small terminal on the Potomac into a madhouse of brief-case- and garment-bag–toting humanity. She called Caleb Harris and advised him that she would be late. He told her he'd wait and they agreed to meet in a small watering hole they once frequented long ago. It took her the better part of an hour just to locate a taxi and get clear of the airport traffic.

As she sat in the battered, dirty taxi, she was exhausted and hot. Although it was May, the tempera-ture was close to eighty degrees Fahrenheit, and D.C. humid. The cab was not air conditioned. How far this is, she thought, from the advanced technology she had become accustomed to on Parma Quad 2, or the Antarean mothership. Even the diminutive probeship was luxury class compared to her transport during this short journey from Florida to Washington today.

"Now you sure you want the NBC on Michigan? 'Cause we got that NBC place over on Kentucky too," the black cab driver asked.

"Yes, I'm sure."

"That's executive people there. I know 'cause my sister, she works over there, and they go home pretty early. About five for sure, and with this traffic and all, we won't get there till maybe five-thirty." The man was honestly concerned.

"I know," she answered softly, "but they expect me. I called ahead."

"That's smart." He turned up the ramp leading from the parkway onto the 14th Street Bridge.

Off to the left, Alma gazed at the Jefferson Memorial and felt a twinge of homesickness, recalling her days as a reporter on a local New York television news program. It was there that she met Caleb Harris. He was a senior editor for NBC. They'd met at a New York Emmy Awards dinner long ago, just after her divorce and before she'd met Joe Finley. Harris fell for her and they had a brief love affair. When she realized it was just part of her loneliness, that she didn't love him, the affair ended. But they remained friends, with Caleb Harris eventually offering her a network reporting job after he had become NBC's New York network anchor. Now Caleb Harris was Washington Bureau Chief for NBC and a senior vice president of the network as well. He had become a grand old man of broadcasting and political commentary.

When she called from the airport he'd been coy on the telephone. "So you came to seduce me again after all these years?"

"Now how could an old woman like me seduce a famous TV personality like you? You must have your pick of the typing pool these days."

"There's never been anyone like my Alma." He laughed.

"You're damned right," she answered. "Now let me find a cab in this madness so we can get on with this seduction."

"Are you okay?" he asked, genuinely concerned.

"I'm fine. Let me go and I promise you an evening you'll never forget."

"Now you're talking, sweetheart. Bring it on . . ."

They sipped gin and tonics and munched on a mixture of peanuts and pretzels at a tiny corner table. The bar, a gathering spot for young network news people, was busy. Once in a while one of them threw a curious glance in Caleb's direction. If their eyes happened to meet, Caleb's icy gaze exorcised the intrusion immediately. He enjoyed the power, especially when Alma noticed it.

"You are beautiful beyond belief. Jesus that sounds like the worst cliché . . . but I swear you don't look a day older than when I last saw you. What is it, fifteen years?"

"Twenty, sweetheart, and you're very kind."

"I'm very honest too. That Florida climate must agree with you, Alma."

"Well, let me be honest too. I've been away from Florida for a while."

"Traveling?"

"Oh yes. You would definitely call what I've been up to traveling. Could I . . . ?" She pointed to her empty glass. He signaled to the attentive waiter for another round. Alma then slipped a thought into Caleb's mind. The newsman frowned, then turned, and in a loud voice called to the waiter.

"No limes this time, Jimmy." He turned back to Alma, an expression of disorientation on his face. "You did say no limes, didn't you?"

"No, but I thought it."

"What is that supposed to mean?"

"You asked me what I've been up to and I said traveling. I want you to just listen to me. Don't get up, don't humor me and whatever you do, don't make a scene. What I'm about to tell you is probably the news story of the century, perhaps of all time. And before I begin, you have to promise me you will keep it completely confidential, except to those I designate."

"Sounds heavy." Caleb mulled over the idea that Alma Finley might be a bit senile. He recalled his own mother's bout with an illness late in her life that today had a name. Alzheimer's.

"There's nothing wrong with me," Alma said, reading his thoughts.

"Who said anything about that?" The waiter arrived with their drinks, cleared the empty glasses and quickly departed.

"You thought it."

"How do you know?"

"You thought about your mother too."

"Jesus, Alma, what the hell is this?"

"One hell of a story, Caleb." She took a sip from her drink and began. "Let me go right at it. For the past five years I've been on four different planets, one of them in another galaxy."

"Oh Christ—" But before Caleb Harris could go any further, Alma began to transfer images of Parma Quad 2, Antares, Subax-Rigel Quad 3 and Hillet in the Alphard Galaxy into his cerebral cortex. After the initial shock of feeling Alma totally in control of his mind, she calmed him and he began to enjoy the trip. It was, as Caleb later described to the President, a multimedia light and sound show, but it filled all the senses, not just visual and aural.

Fifteen minutes later he was huddled in the narrow hallway next to the men's room, a pile of quarters stacked on the scarred shelf of the pay phone, using every ounce of clout he possessed to arrange a meeting with the President of the United States immediately.

He returned to the table smiling like the Cheshire Cat. "Fifteen minutes. Margo McNeil said she went out on a limb for you, not me. He'll give us fifteen minutes at seven-thirty tomorrow morning. Then he's off to Camp David."

"Honey McNeil?"

"She's Press Secretary now."

"She remembered me?"

"Quite clearly. She said you were one of the few people who took time to talk to her when she first came to the network from Chicago."

"She's very bright. Didn't she have a thing for Malcolm Teller once?"

"People always like to gossip. Who's to say?" Caleb shrugged and smiled.

"So you still take care of your own, is that it?"

"I never approved of digging into personal lives as long as it didn't affect the job."

"And us?" Alma asked softly.

"We were discreet, weren't we?" he said, reaching across the table to hold her hand.

"Yes," she answered. "And now how about a quiet dinner someplace private. There is another part of this story that needs telling before tomorrow's meeting. It's critical that we convince President Teller to help us."

"Well, all you have to do is get inside his head the way you did mine and—"

"No," she said quickly. "I can't do that. It's not allowed. Only in an emergency."

"It seems to me whatever you need of him, it's important. Critical, you just said." He signaled for the check.

"But if I let him know what I can do . . . eventually it will frighten him; frighten those around him. Imagine having these powers in a negotiation or at a summit?"

"They would be invaluable. Overwhelming. I understand." The waiter brought their bill and Caleb signed it. They stood up and walked out the front door into the warm spring night.

"Is that little Lebanese place still open over on 17th Street?"

"Still there, pillows and all." He hailed a taxi. Before they got into the cab, Caleb Harris held Alma with both hands, firmly grasping her elbows. "Thank you for coming to me, for trusting me."

She smiled and touched his weathered, handsome cheek. He heard nothing as she then stepped into the cab, but her friendship swelled deep inside his sometimes cynical heart.

Seventeen light years away, in the system surrounding the star called Scorpius on the planet known as Antares, an enormous Antarean watership, crewed with a full complement of crystalline Parman guides, small specialized Antarean medical and flight teams, forty-two humans and four off-planet human-oids, cleared the gravitational pull of Antares. One of the Parman guides locked on to a tiny speck in the firmament: Earth's sun. The watership began to accelerate. The rite of return had begun for its special human passengers, taking them on a journey that many now believed had been decreed by the Master eons before humankind ever appeared on Earth.

CHAPTER SEVEN

Because Jack Fischer and Ben Green went to Boynton Beach in Jack's car while Joe Finley drove his rental car back down to Red Lake, Detective Sergeant Cummings was forced to make a quick decision. He chose to follow Jack and Ben, and while he noted the make, model and license plate of Finley's car, he couldn't help but feel frustrated in not knowing where the lone old man was headed.

The Boynton Marina is just south of the Boynton Inlet, a cut of water that connects the inland waterway with the Atlantic Ocean. Boynton Beach, a retirement community along Florida's eastern Gold Coast, has its share of affluent homes and high-rise condominiums. With the phenomenal growth of South Florida, towns such as Boynton Beach, Delray Beach, Lantana, Boca Raton and West Palm Beach have blended into one long, heavily populated retirement/resort town, each with a marina, condo developments, sandy beaches, shopping centers and a variety of restaurants ranging from expensive French chic to Pizza Hut.

Cummings kept his distance behind Jack's silver Lincoln Town Car. His pulse quickened as he saw the car turn east off the main highway US 1 and then turn left into the marina. As he jockeyed for position to make the same turns, his radio crackled alive with the voice of his long-time partner, Detective Coolridge Betters.

"Car fifty-eight. You out there, Matt?"

"Dr. Betters, I presume?" Cummings answered after quickly snatching the radio mike off its mount.

"What's up, Sarge? I got a message to get back to you pronto."

"Go to channel four."

"On my way." They both switched their radios over to a little used frequency that was usually clear.

"Take this down, then grab an unmarked and see if you can pick up the trail," Cummings said as he swung his Olds Cutlass into the marina parking lot. The sight that filled his eyes caused his heart to noticeably skip a few beats. "Jesus Christ," he muttered.

"You want me to look for Jesus Christ?"

"What? No. They're here, Coolridge. By God they're here!"

"Hey Matt, what's up?"

"Fischer—"

"Not that again. You've got ten months to retirement, man."

"Listen to me, partner. They came back today. The old guys came back."

"What old guys?" Betters's voice deepened, more serious now.

"The old guys that were on the boat that ran you off the canal and made me the laughing stock of Dade County. Only now they're here, and they've contacted Fischer and he's taken them to the marina."

"In Boynton?"

"Bingo, Sherlock. I'm looking at Fischer, Doyle and one of the geezers. The big one who went over the side last."

"What's goin' on?"

"Another snatch I'll bet. One of them is headed your way. Maybe to the Gables, to that Antares condo place they used last time. He's driving a new dark blue Electra, a rental. Florida plate is ARM-335782. He left Boca about twenty minutes ago so if you stake it out on I-95 in North Miami, maybe Ives Dairy Road, you should pick him up in another twenty."

"You want me to grab him?"

"Hell no. Just track him and see where he lives and who he sleeps with."

"You okay, Matt?"

"I haven't been this okay in five years, partner. We're gonna get them this time and shove it right up that DA's blowhole."

"Yeah, well, just take it easy and don't jump the gun."

"I'm cool. This time I'm gonna have the proof and nail these mothers. Now get on it and give me a ring when you pick up the trail."

"You got it, Matt. I'm outa here!" The radio clicked off. Cummings knew their conversation could have been monitored, maybe recorded. He only hoped that friendly ears hadn't made much of it and would let their lack of formal police radio talk without the mandatory "roger," "over" and "out" pass as just two over-the-hill, about-to-retire cops chatting about the good old days.

Ben Green had also monitored the police conversation while Jack looked for Phil Doyle aboard the sleek forty-eight-foot Hatteras *Terra Time*. He sent the information along to Joe Finley, who exited from I-95 and drove south along Route 1 to his rendezvous with Amos Bright at the submerged probeship. Detective Betters would have a long, unfruitful wait on the Interstate.

"Well, I'll be damned," Phil Doyle exclaimed as he came out onto the fantail of the *Terra Time* and saw Ben Green standing on the marina dock. "Jack said a surprise, but I never expected—"

"Keep it down," Jack whispered to Phil. "We don't want the world tuned in to this reunion."

"Yeah. Sure. So come on aboard, Mr. Ah . . ." Doyle had forgotten Ben's name.

"Green. Ben Green." The old man jumped spryly aboard the luxurious fishing boat.

"Right," Phil said. "You want a drink?"

The weather had become sunshine and fair skies.

The marina was quiet. By May most of the boats that winter in Florida have left for their summer homes in Chesapeake Bay and Long Island. One fishing boat, the *Downtime,* which moored next to Doyle's boat, had just returned to dock. The catch consisted of barracuda, two good-size dolphin fish and a thirty-pound snow grouper. The mate, a shaggy young man with a red beard and bare chest that was covered with fish scales, glanced up from his fish-cleaning chores to notice Ben come aboard his neighbor's boat. Doyle noticed the curious look.

"That's a hefty snow grouper you got there, Billy."

"He goes over thirty."

"Where'd you get him?" Doyle asked as Ben and Jack entered the main cabin behind him.

"On the reef up north."

"You sure you didn't drop a hook down on the six-hundred-foot wreck?"

Billy looked away. He was embarrassed. The regulars who fished these waters knew certain spots that would always produce big fish such as the snow grouper now being butchered on the dock next to Phil Doyle. It was an unspoken code that those spots were left alone as much as possible so that when charter customers, paying as much as five hundred dollars a day to fish these waters, had bad luck, the charter captains could go to the special spots and pick up a good fish or two. This insured return business and good word of mouth which was the life blood of the dwindling charter fishing-boat business. In this instance, Doyle was certain that the young mate had dropped a heavy line down to the wreck at six hundred feet just off the inlet. It was one of the few places that snow grouper still inhabited in these waters. The fish would bring five or six dollars a pound, maybe more if Billy could sell it in small chunks to the old people who came down to the dock to buy fresh fish from time to time. If not, he would take the grouper steaks and sell them to a local restaurant.

"Well," Phil called over to Billy, satisfied that he had distracted the nosy young man from speculating about who Ben Green might be, "I'm sure glad to hear that. Maybe a good sign that the fishing's coming back."

"Maybe," Billy answered, knowing he'd been let off the hook and grateful to Doyle for that gesture.

Below deck, Jack sipped a cold beer and lounged on one of the two sofas that lined the main cabin wall. Ben, now momentarily in telepathic contact with his wife in Scarsdale, enjoyed a frosty Pepsi in the spacious galley.

"That kid is a royal pain in the ass," Phil remarked as he entered the posh carpeted cabin. He smiled at Ben Green and sat down next to Jack.

"It's nice to see you again, Phil," Ben said as he enjoyed the emotions Mary sent him while she was reunited with their family seventeen hundred miles to the north.

"So what's up?" Phil asked, looking from Ben to Jack and back to Ben. "I mean the last time I saw you, Mr. Green, you and a bunch of your buddies were cutting one hell of a trail into the wild blue yonder."

"They're back on a mission, Phil. We're gonna help them."

"Doin' what?" He squinted for a moment, then narrowed his glance at Ben. "We gonna gather some more old folks up for you?"

Ben laughed at Doyle's description of their last meeting. "No. Something quite different this time."

"Yeah." Jack grinned. "This time the flow is in the other direction."

As Ben and Jack related their plans to Phil Doyle, Detective Cummings waited patiently in his car, watching the *Terra Time* and waiting for his partner to pick up Joe Finley's trail. The late afternoon sun would set and night come upon the sleepy marina before Cummings realized no one was on the boat.

What he didn't see was the submerged Antarean probeship, arriving after dark with Amos Bright and Joe Finley aboard. It parked silently underneath the *Terra Time,* picked up Ben, Jack and Phil as they quietly slipped over the side, boarded the probeship through an open hatch and headed to the dock in Boca Raton where Jack kept his old charter fishing boat, the *Manta III.* They had a full night's work ahead to prepare the equipment so that Amos might examine the Antarean cocoons left behind on their last visit. Now, if things could be arranged, the watership speeding toward this part of the Milky Way Galaxy might fill its fluid storage compartments with an army that had been asleep for five thousand years.

CHAPTER EIGHT

Mary had hours to spend alone with Pat before two of her grandchildren, Pat's daughters Cori and Beth, returned home from school. Cori was the youngest, a student who had wanted to be a doctor for as long as anyone in the family could remember. Beth, on the other hand, lived in an adolescent dream world in which school was a bore and a waste. Tall, slender and quite beautiful, Beth bore a remarkable resemblance to Mary in her younger days. The oldest daughter, Cynthia, was just completing her third year at Emerson College as a communications major.

Mother and daughter sat in the breakfast nook of the spacious modern kitchen, sipping coffee, holding hands and trying to catch up on five years of separation.

"And how is Richard doing?" Mary asked after she had heard all about her three granddaughters' progress.

"They love him. He'll be a full partner in two years. The market is booming."

"Market? I thought he was a lawyer."

"He is. But he's been specializing in corporate mergers, so he spends a great deal of time with underwriters and bond people. It's all very complicated."

"Is he happy?"

"He loves his work."

"And you, darling?"

"Me? I'm fine, Mom, honest. I've been thinking of going back to work, or maybe school . . ." Pat got up and brought more coffee over to the table. "You know,

Mom," she said as she poured more coffee into their mugs, "when you had gone we were told there had been some kind of accident . . . that several people had drowned and were missing. We didn't understand what had— Why in the name of God did you do it? How could you just go off like that and not say anything?" Pat was angry. Her eyes filled with tears as she remembered their grief when they'd thought Mary and Ben had died.

"You got our letter. Mr. Fischer brought it to you."

"Two months later."

"I'm sorry, dear. There was no other way. It had to be a secret."

"The letter was almost worse. You were out there," Pat said as she gestured toward the sunny window with a southern exposure. "We couldn't talk . . . we couldn't . . . when would we ever see you again?"

"I'm here now."

"But it wasn't fair. Not to me or Melanie—"

"How is your sister?" Mary asked, interrupting.

"Fine. Off on another of her expeditions. The Great Barrier Reef this time. She's a Ph. D. now. Marine biology. Something to do with sea mammal viruses."

"Anyone special?"

"Every day it's someone special. One man? Not my sister."

"I'm sorry we left that way." Mary stood up and walked to the sunny window. "No, that's not true. I'm not sorry . . . we're not sorry. We made our decision selfishly. It's our life. In the end we understood that, and we hoped that you might too." Pat stood and moved to her mother's side.

"When we read the letter and Mr. Fischer explained about the cocoons and the Antareans, we were overjoyed to know you two were alive. It's just that it was like you were dead . . . because it seemed we would never see you again. Can you understand how frustrating that is? To know you and Dad were out there someplace and we couldn't know . . ." Mary took her daughter's hands and held them to her breast. She then telepathed a soft, calming love to Pat.

"Do you feel our love for you?"

"Yes, Mother. It's wonderful."

"Have you felt that way during the past five years?"

"Many times. It was as though you and Dad were here with us. The girls, especially Beth, said so often, 'I have this feeling that Grandma and Grandpa are still with us, all around us, and that they love us.'"

"We do. And those feelings, the way you have my love now, is what we send to you from across the universe. We are with you, my dear Patricia. We will be with you always." The two women embraced. It was then that Pat noticed the enlargement near the base of her mother's skull.

"What's this?" Pat asked, gently touching the rounded ridge that ran along Mary's spine and up onto the top of her head. Most of it was hidden by Mary's hair.

"An implant," Mary answered, stepping back from Pat and turning so her daughter might get a better view of the enlarged brain.

"They did this to you?"

"I volunteered. It had to be done to those who wished to command."

"Why? What is it, this implant?"

"There are some things that we are not allowed to tell. If you can wait until the family comes home, Michael too, then I'll tell you as much as I can. What happens here, with my family, with you . . . well, a great deal depends on how you react to our new ways, to the things we've seen and done."

For the first time Patricia Keane realized that her mother, once a quiet, even at times subservient wife, mother and homemaker, was now extremely alert, strong and in control of the situation. The absence of five years had changed Mary Green in a way Patricia didn't understand. For a fleeting moment the word *alien* passed through Pat's mind.

Yes, my child, Mary thought to herself. *We are home on our mother planet and at the same time we are aliens among our own kind. We are a new race. But where do we really belong?*

Later that evening when Cori, Beth and Michael Keane got over the initial shock of seeing Mary, they enjoyed a family dinner seated around the mahogany dining table that had been a gift from Ben and Mary to the Keanes when they had moved to Florida. Mary explained that their words and thoughts could be sent across vast distances, and that she and Ben had always sent them love. That was what they'd felt. She told them of their decision to become commanders. Cori, the fifteen-year-old, examined the cerebral implant carefully.

"And this expands your brain function to full capacity?" the teenager asked.

"Even beyond that. We can combine our thoughts, our wills and energy. We are eleven commanders, but when we join telepathically, even across light years, we become one hundred times more powerful."

"Can you speak to Dad now?" Pat's husband, Michael, asked.

"I am! He sends his love and is glad to see you are all looking so well and grown up. He can't wait to give you all a big hug."

"He can see us?" Beth asked incredulously.

"And hear you, and if I touch you then he feels that touch."

"Then here's a kiss, Grandpa," Cori said as she got up and kissed her grandmother. Everyone laughed until Cori, suddenly startled, gasped. "Oh. It can't be. But I just felt someone kiss me back."

"Grandpa did that," Mary told her youngest granddaughter. "And this is for all of you." One by one, each at the table had the sensation of Ben Green gently kissing them on the forehead. Michael even touched his balding pate as his father-in-law sent him a greeting too.

"The others, where are they?" Pat asked.

"Alma and Joe Finley are here with us. The other seven are on a mission."

"Mom," Pat asked finally, "you and Dad wrote in the letter that you would be gone . . . perhaps forever. You said you would live a long, fruitful life out there. Mr. Fischer said the Antareans seem to live forever. Why did you come back? I mean now . . . so soon?"

Mary looked around at her family, knowing the moment had come for her to make a decision. On the probecraft they had discussed it over and over again. It was a judgment call that depended on how the family responded to Mary's return. She wanted desperately to tell her family about their mission, but she feared the knowledge she would impart might be an impossible burden for them to carry in secret for as long as they lived on the Earth.

"Before I answer you, and I promise I will, let me tell you a bit about our adventures out there as you call it. Let me tell you about some of the things I have seen and the beings I have met. Afterwards, if you insist, I will tell you why we have come home to our Earth."

On the watership flight deck, commander Ruth Charnofsky, formerly of lower Collins Avenue and now in her ninety-first year of life, stood alongside commander Frank Hankinson. He had once been a newspaper publisher in St. Louis, Missouri, and although he had opted for commander status, his wife Andrea had not. The watership was approaching light speed as Ruth and Frank watched the Parman guides change shift. Far ahead, irrevocably locked on to, the Earth's sun was their distant beacon home.

"Home," Ruth said.

"Was or is?" Frank answered.

"A good question," she mused as her thoughts went far out to the great red giant star Rigel and the planet, Subax-Rigel Quad 3, which had been her home for the past three years. But more than the planet and its great red sun, her thoughts were of her new husband, mate and friend Panatoy, the tall man from another world with whom she had shared her life these past three years in that inhospitable place. The man she loved as dearly as she had her first Earth husband who had died decades ago. Panatoy now slept below, suspended in his special atmospheric chamber, awaiting the watership's arrival on Earth and the revelation of the awesome secret they carried on board. She could picture his strong, graceful body, glowing with the bluish pigmentation of his people that had come to seem so beautiful, so *right* to her.

CHAPTER NINE

Manta III was still in good shape. Jack had enough money to buy any yacht his heart desired, but this old charter boat was his love. He kept it docked along the Intercoastal in Boca Raton, just south of Yamato Road.

During the night while Detective Cummings kept his vigil near *Terra Time,* the Antarean probeship slipped out of the Boynton Beach Marina and headed south, submerged beneath the Intercoastal Waterway, to Jack's dock in Boca Raton. They moored the probeship directly underneath the broad-beamed *Manta III* and proceeded with their preparations for diving the next morning.

It wasn't until well after midnight that Cummings suspected he had been duped. Interior and running lights had been left on aboard *Terra Time.* Now they clicked off simultaneously. A timer? Cummings speculated. He got out of his car and cautiously approached the luxury Hatteras yacht. There was no sign of life. Only the gentle lapping of water against the sturdy dock pilings and fiberglass hull broke the eerie stillness of this moonless tropical night.

Cummings boarded the boat, flashlight in hand, his detective's badge conspicuously pinned to his crumpled tan sports jacket. The last thing he needed was to be taken for an intruder. Charter captains had the reputation of being very touchy about unauthorized passengers aboard their boats. The door leading to the main deck cabin was open. Cummings clicked on his flashlight and played the beam around the cabin.

"Hello. Anybody home?" he called in a friendly voice. No answer. He moved into the cabin and strained to hear sounds of people sleeping below. Again, total silence. The *Terra Time* was empty. Somehow, Jack, Doyle and that old man had slipped away.

Earlier that evening Coolridge Betters had radioed to inform his partner that the rental car and elderly driver, as described, had never made it to Ives Dairy Road on I-95. Both cops agreed that Betters should head down to the Antares condo complex in case it was being used as a base again. Cummings had not heard from Betters after that.

Instead of trying to raise Betters on their special prearranged radio frequency, Cummings found a pay telephone on the deserted dock and called his partner's home. The aging black detective answered on the fifth ring.

"Hello?"

"Coolridge, it's Matt."

"Yeah? Oh, hey man, listen, I'm sorry about not getting back to you, but my radio just went down suddenly right after I got to the Antares condos."

"You see the old guy?"

"I did. Well, not exactly the guy, but I found that rental down on the Red Lake Canal, just below the condos. Damned near the place they tossed me out onto that lawn five years ago."

"But you didn't see the guy?"

"Nobody. You want to stake out the car?"

"Not now. It's just you and me. We can't be spreading things too thin."

"How'd you make out, Matt?"

"The fuckers gave me the slip."

"They took the boat out?"

"No. But somehow they got off without my seeing them."

"Maybe they went to Fischer's boat."

"He still have that old tub?"

"I think so. He keeps it up in Boca somewhere. I can't remember the name—"

"*Manta III,*" Cummings blurted out. "I'll never forget that name and the sight of those old people going over the sides and stern of that boat. It makes me sick to this day."

"Yeah, well, we can get on the horn in the morning with the Boca PD and see if it's registered there."

"You do that. First thing. I'm gonna get me a motel in Boca for the night. I'll call you at seven."

"You want me to meet you up there?"

"Not right now. Let's keep an eye on that condo. After I check out the *Manta III* we can talk. Okay?"

"Okay, Matt. Get some rest."

"Not till those creeps are in the lockup."

Betters heard from Cummings precisely at seven A.M. He had already spoken to the Boca Raton police, who confirmed that Jack Fischer kept a thirty-eight-foot fishing boat, *Manta III,* docked near the U.S. Army Corps of Engineers facility on the Intercoastal Waterway.

"I'm on my way," the senior detective said. "I'll radio when I get an eyeball on the boat."

A half hour later Matthew Cummings reported to Betters in a disappointed voice that the *Manta III* was not in its dock. When he'd asked around, the fuel barge attendant had recalled seeing the *Manta III* leave just before dawn, nearly two hours previously. The attendant, a grizzled old toothless Greek, who smoked a crooked, foul-smelling DiNoble cigar, chuckled when Cummings flashed his badge and asked for more information.

"Do you have a more precise time that they left?"

"Coupla hours. The sun no for to come yet."

"Did you see who was on the boat?"

"Dark. Hey, it's night before the sun she come."

"Which way did they go?"

"To the ocean. Through the inlet up to the bridge." And then as an afterthought he added, "He take that old tub out pretty fast. I guess he for to have trouble keeping up with the submarine."

"Submarine?" Cummings repeated. "There are no submarines in the Intercoastal."

"Maybe." The old Greek chuckled again. "Maybe I just make imagine."

Matthew Cummings knew he had lost them for the time being. He radioed to Betters and asked his partner to go up to Boynton Beach and keep an eye on Doyle's *Terra Time* while Cummings waited for the *Manta III* to return. They had to return to one of the boats, Cummings reasoned, unless they had a submarine like the old barge attendant had claimed. But that was ridiculous. Cummings dismissed the thought.

One hour after a spectacular Florida sunrise, the *Manta III* was on site over the Stones. While Jack and Phil stayed above, keeping an eye out for intruders, Amos Bright, Ben and Joe detached the probeship from the *Manta III*'s hull and guided it beneath the calm Gulf Stream waters, homing in on the chambers constructed five millennia ago in the ocean floor below.

After locating the precise coordinates, the Antarean and his two human commanders left the probeship through the pressurized hatch and swam freely toward the first chamber location. They located the doorway and carefully uncovered the seals that protected this section of the sleeping Antarean cocoon army. Crystal-clear water allowed sunlight to penetrate and illuminate the reef. The seals were intact and undisturbed, exactly as they had been left five years ago. Amos located the chamber locking marker and, slipping an oblong metal device from the leg pouch on his wetsuit, he inserted the sharp end into the marker and activated the mechanism. The chamber door slowly slid open, hardly stirring the sandy ocean floor around them.

The chamber below was undisturbed. Hundreds of cocoons, snugly nestled against one another on racks, glowed with a faint red light at the tip of each. Each rack held fifty cocoons, and in this chamber there were three racks. Ben, Joe and Amos entered the chamber, each swimming down along a rack, checking to see that all of the cocoons were viable. Satisfied, the men paused for a moment and thought a prayer for their sleeping companions.

Afterward they resealed that chamber and went on to check out the three remaining chambers. Everything was in order. Later that evening, after they returned to the dock and had hidden the probeship, Amos Bright would send a message to the Antarean watership, now only weeks away from its earthly destination.

"Our brothers and sisters are well and asleep. They await your arrival and the great day of awakening. We send them your love."

Back at the dock in Boca Raton, a restless, unshaven Matthew Cummings was buoyed for the first time in nearly a day when he caught sight of the *Manta III* chugging up the Intercoastal toward its mooring. This time, in the light of day, Jack kept the broad-beamed fishing boat down to four knots. This allowed the probeship, attached to the *Manta's* hull, to ride low in the water and therefore out of sight. Cummings backed away from the dock, hiding in the shadows cast by a copse of palm trees. The old Greek watched the detective hide himself. Then he saw the *Manta III* coming in. He muttered to himself, still chewing on the cigar stub. "That submarine is under the boat. I can see. Well, if Jack stops for to get gas, I tell him. If not, then I just watch."

But Ben, Joe and Amos didn't have to be told that Cummings was there. They had tuned in on his presence moments before. Their problem was not how to confront the Coral Gables cop, but when.

CHAPTER TEN

Amos Bright's message was joyfully received aboard the watership by all who were awake and functioning. The six human commanders were gathered for conferencing when the news arrived that the cocoons were safe.

Bess and Arthur Perlman, Bess's sister Betty Franklin, Bernie and Rose Lewis, Ruth Charnofsky and Frank Hankinson all sat around the oval obsidian table that contained a data screen upon which they now studied a detailed map of the western coastline of South Florida. The huge Antarean watership groaned slightly as the Parman guide farthest forward adjusted its crystalline alignment to compensate for a momentary change in the far distant Sun's ultraviolet radiation.

Antarean waterships had been named for their function, which was to carry liquids, usually under extreme pressure, to planets and Antarean colonies within our galaxy. They were not constructed for intergalactic flight. The three huge storage tanks, each capable of holding hundreds of millions of gallons of pressurized fluids, were overwhelmingly the most prominent feature of the vessel. The tanks, attached by service walkways to one another, trailed out behind the flight deck and crew quarters, which were dwarfed by the size of the containers. At times these tanks carried water to arid planets. Many of the customers who bartered for the Antarean water were dependent upon waterships for survival. The Antareans, respected and ancient travelers, held the trust of the water users.

At other times the modular tanks were filled with liquid oxygen, hydrogen and nitrogen, and transported to planets or colonies without natural atmospheres of their own. The Antareans were gifted in their ability to create and maintain entire atmospheres around such planets or under specially constructed domes. Millions of living beings depended upon Antarean technology and honesty. Failure of either could mean a disaster of major proportions.

This particular watership had three tanks. Two of the huge containers were filled with exotic mixtures of life-support gasses from four diverse planets, while the center tank was filled with liquid oxygen for ballast. It had been recalled from the Rigel Quad 3 system, where it was replenishing atmosphere, to Subax, an ice planet near the red giant star Rigel.

Ruth Charnofsky, now a citizen of Subax, studied a detailed map of the underwater topography near the area of the Stones. "The closest place to park the watership, as far as I can see, is here," she said, pointing her remarkably smooth, tapered finger at a spot on the ocean floor some three miles from the Stones.

Bernie Lewis leaned in to see the location. "That's the old wreck off Boynton. It'll mean moving the cocoons a long way underwater." His hand swept across four miles of ocean.

"We have the flight crew and the probeship," Bess Perlman said.

"That's manpower and time. It'll take weeks to move all the cocoons," Art Perlman chimed in, "and we won't all be able to help."

"And I'm sure Ben and Joe will get that nice young man Jack to help us again." They all smiled at Bess's optimism.

"We'll have to make do," Ruth Charnofsky said, a certain finality in her voice telling the others that she had come to a decision. Her age and her keen, concise manner of taking action when discussion had come to an end, made her the natural leader among the human commanders. "How we proceed will also depend on where Amos, the Greens and the Finleys eventually find the facility we need," she continued.

"That will be the key," Bess Perlman agreed, shifting in her chair uncomfortably. She was not feeling well. Everyone in the room sensed her discomfort.

The problems they faced were indeed unique and unexpected. Five years ago, when the elderly humans who chose to travel with the Antareans underwent the physical transformation required for off-planet life, no one had anticipated or completely understood all the effects of Antarean space/body/mind processing on human beings.

As it turned out, stopping the aging process was only the beginning. In addition, a complete cleansing of blood and bone marrow, organs, and the lymphatic and respiratory systems removed all disease and damaged tissue. This process was dangerous to younger humans, which is why those who chose to leave the planet had to be seniors of at least sixty-five to seventy years of age. And the human reaction was unique in Antarean experience, in that the aging process not only stopped, but slowly, at first imperceptibly, reversed.

Beyond physical cleansing, repair and reconstruction, an expansion of the human brain's capacity to near full potential was also begun in the processing room of the Antares condo five years ago. The commanders had consciously undergone additional mental enhancement with cerebral transplants, a device that brought their mental capacities up to Antarean commander level. But the expansion of total brain capacity, thought to be perhaps ten percent in most humans, increased to nearly ninety-three percent even for those who did not become commanders.

All of these first human space travelers had weathered the journey to Parma Quad 2 well. They spent two years living within the Parman society, teaching and being taught, acting as ambassadors for the Antareans, and generally integrating themselves and the Parmans into the fascinating and limitless universe which contained a multitude of life forms, societies and civilizations.

It took another two years of travel, with many intergalactic side trips, before it was evident that one special aspect of the processing was unique to the human race. Reproductive systems that had stopped functioning twenty to forty years before had quietly begun to work again. All of the space travelers, male and female, could become sexually active if they chose to do so.

Not long after that another unique effect became evident, and one that was not surprising among people who had not had to think about pregnancy for decades. As the watership hurtled toward Earth, twenty-eight of the women aboard were pregnant. Couples who already had great-grandchildren were about to become parents again, and new couples had been formed.

Four of the expectant mothers had taken off-planet mates. Rather than separate these couples, those who required special environments had been suspended in special sealed containers developed by the Antareans, with the required gasses, light spectrum and nourishment for that particular race and species. Very much like the Antarean cocoons now resting on Earth's ocean floor, the containers could theoretically function indefinitely, preserving the precious life they supported.

Precious life were the key operative words throughout the universe. It was, in fact, the primary reason why this watership now raced toward Earth. The birth law, like most universal laws living beings adhered to, was unwritten and simple to understand.

"All new life to come is a gift. Whenever possible,

the birth of new ones is to be accomplished upon the homeplanet of the mother, or the egg bearer, or the divider. The highest priority of passage is to be given to any and all travelers who ask to be taken to homeplanet for the purpose of giving birth. This right shall be denied to no life form."

This watership was now on that sacred mission.

CHAPTER ELEVEN

The President sipped his black coffee and smiled cordially at the attractive woman now seated across from him. She looked relaxed and comfortable settled in the pale blue armchair. Her forest-green dress blended perfectly with the chair and dark blue carpet, both emblazoned with the presidential seal. They had been introduced by Caleb Harris and Margo McNeil, the President's attractive Press Secretary. After the amenities were over both had left the Oval Office. The President was now alone with Alma Finley. He quietly admired her good looks as he mused to himself, "This woman is at least fifteen years older than I am and is just about the sexiest female I've laid eyes on in weeks."

President Teller, a Democrat from the Deep South, was sixty-three and the first president to be divorced while in office. His wife had waited until his first term was over and the official party announcement made that Malcolm Teller would seek a second term before she filed for divorce. Her grounds were adultery. She made the proof a public campaign issue. To the chagrin of the Republicans, now controlled by the Evangelical Right, and Teller's enemies in his own party, the public, always with the underdog, perceived the President as a wronged man. Since it had been widely rumored that both Teller and his wife led separate private lives, his wife's denuciation came as no surprise to the Washington press corps and the public. He was a man caught by a wife whose own sexual activities and proclivities could never stand the scrutiny of a public investigation. This was just not fair play. Margaret Simpson Teller wrung her hands and bemoaned her role as the betrayed wife. The voters chuckled to themselves. The spokesmen for the white Christian Right and their Evangelical television preachers were as voices in the wilderness. The media didn't buy it. Mainstream television didn't bite. Only the sensationalistic rags picked up on the story, much to the embarrassment of the Grand Old Party.

Malcolm Teller was reelected in a close, hotly contested race. Now, with his place as a two-term president secure, he openly dated the most beautiful and interesting women in the world, inviting many of them as house guests to the White House. The nation, with a large majority brought up in the turbulent sixties, seemed almost to regard their President's womanizing as patriotic. Telling stories about the sexual appetites of past presidents, long kept secret by a protective and elite Washington press corps, now became a popular parlor game.

"Women are my friends," Teller proclaimed when questioned about his rumored affair with the attractive fifty-three-year-old shapely blonde, blue-eyed Prime Minister of Sweden. "And when they are also as brilliant, important and attractive as Prime Minister Johanssen, then," he continued, "I say let the courses of nature and national interest converge and go forward hand in hand!"

He was comfortable with women and secure with himself. But there was something unnerving about Alma Finley.

"I think you're attractive too, Mr. President," Alma said softly a moment after Margo McNeil had closed the Oval Office door firmly behind her.

"I beg your pardon?" he answered, wondering if his carnal thoughts about this woman were somehow showing on his handsome, suntanned face. "Did I say something I didn't hear?"

"No," she laughed gently, "you didn't say a word. But you thought it now, didn't you?"

"Thought what?" He was instantly uneasy. Margo had insisted that he see this Mrs. Finley as a personal favor. They were supposed to spend the weekend alone at Camp David, which he knew she was looking forward to, so it had surprised him when Margo asked that they delay their departure. He was sure this had originally been a fifteen-minute appointment, but when the Press Secretary introduced Mrs. Finley she inexplicably remarked that she and Caleb Harris would be back in thirty minutes.

"You were thinking I'm a sexually attractive woman, and you were surprised you felt that way because of my age."

"How in the name of . . . are you a . . . one of those mediums?"

"No."

"Well, I guess my press notices proceed me. Good guess." He stiffened. Alma put down her coffee cup and settled back in the comfortable antique armchair. As she did, the President, seated on a matching divan across from her, leaned forward, his dark brown eyes focusing on her calm, intelligent face. He concentrated his attention. "Now what exactly can I do for you, Mrs. Finley?"

"You can listen to me for fifteen minutes, Mr. President. I'm going to tell you the very best story you've ever heard."

And she did.

The weekend at Camp David was cancelled, as were most of the presidential appointments for the next few days. The Secretary of Defense, Gideon Mersky, one of Malcolm Teller's oldest friends and closest advisors, was summoned to the White House. He arrived to find Caleb, Margo, Alma and the President huddled in a meeting in the Oval Office. He promptly joined them. In a few minutes, after Alma was persuaded in the interest of saving time, to tune in to the Secretary's thoughts, he was convinced she was telling the truth. He became extremely enthusiastic and excited.

"Mal," he began, addressing the President in familiar terms, "do you realize what this means to the country? Imagine having a woman, no . . . what did you say, four people? . . . right, four Americans—capable of listening in on our enemies' most secret thoughts . . . of telepathing information securely all around the world . . . of having the experience of . . . what shall I call it . . . alien technology. It boggles the mind, Mal. It's absolutely sensational."

"It's not! We're not to be involved that way." Alma was firm. She allowed her annoyance to permeate the minds of the others in the room. With the exception of Gideon Mersky, the others understood and were sympathetic to Alma's concerns. But the tough Defense Secretary, a brilliant man, shrugged off Alma's concerns.

"Mrs. Finley," he said in a matter-of-fact tone of voice, "I understand you are under certain . . . restrictions, shall we say? I can live with that. I can live with the fact that you have made promises—sworn allegiances—to other planets, governments, whatever. But unfortunately, or perhaps fortunately, you are now back on, as you put it, homeplanet—the land of your birth. You are an American citizen under American law. It may well be that you will have to decide your loyalties either to America or to these Antareans, who I might point out, although welcome, are still in this country illegally."

The room was silent. Alma neither sent her thoughts nor received theirs. She reached out to Ben, Joe and Mary. In an instant they communicated, discussed and concurred.

"Then we have nothing more to discuss, Mr. President. Thank you for your time. Thank you, Caleb, Margo; I'll be going now."

"Wait a moment," the President said. He turned his attention toward the Defense Secretary. "Gideon, perhaps you haven't grasped the total situation here."

"I've grasped it all right. This woman, these people want us to help them. Fine. All I've said is that we could use their help as well."

Caleb Harris couldn't contain himself anymore. "You're an idiot."

"What you think of me is of little consequence, Caleb. I'm here to speak as the Secretary of Defense, as an advisor to the President, as the person with the mission to keep this country free and strong, and as an American."

"Did it ever occur to you that this situation might go beyond those rather parochial boundaries?"

"There's nothing parochial about being an American—"

"Let's stop this immediately!" The President was on his feet, angry. "I apologize for this, Mrs. Finley. Gideon here means well, but he's a bit of a zealot. I don't think he's quite grasped the enormity of the situation, or its importance in the context of human history."

"Oh, I understand Mr. Mersky's position. It's very natural, very human. In fact, one of the most interesting conversations, or rather confrontations I should say, that we humans had was regarding our ideas about nationalism. The Antareans, who have been travelers for over one hundred thousand years, have carried the code, the unwritten laws, to many parts of our galaxy and beyond. When we few humans, who had lived on this little speck of blue in the endless reaches of space, first stepped out into the universe, one of the first attachments we lost, and oddly clung to at the same time, was our citizenship of Earth. The dichotomy of our feelings was immediate as we watched our homeplanet dwindle and finally disappear into the black void. The strange thing was that none of us ever referred to ourselves as Americans again. We were of Earth, or bipedal called human or warmblooded mammal dweller from Quad 3. But never American. I suppose it would be like someone at a world conference of nations proclaiming he was from Yonkers or Keokuc or Sacramento. Too small . . . provincial . . . parochial. In deep space we don't talk of such things. We know the scope of our vast universe, the variety of life and civilization out there. It would be futile, and honestly quite arrogant, to ever hold nationalism as more important than the preservation of life, one single life, no matter what its origins or physical appearance.

"I . . . we simply don't live in caves anymore, Mr. President, and though I don't wish to appear superior to you in any way, you, almost everyone on this planet still does. I think we made a mistake coming to you. I think we may have made a mistake trying to bear our young on homeplanet." She stood up and prepared to leave. "It is not too late to intercept the watership and have it return to Antares. The cocoons are well hidden, safe and viable. The Antareans can come for them another time."

"Please, Mrs. Finley." The President reached out and took Alma Finley's hand gently in his own. "Please just wait a moment. I want you to stay. I want to help you. There will be no strings attached." He glared at the smug Defense Secretary. "I will personally vouch for the safety and secrecy of your mission. The government of the United States and the powers of this office are at the disposal of you and your friends. Please, stay."

Alma knew the President was sincere. She reached to obtain a sense of Mersky's mind. She stared at him. He returned her stare. He was a tall, gaunt man with a shock of dark curly hair that cascaded unruly, blending with heavy eyebrows and a salt and pepper beard. Black penetrating eyes were his most dominant feature. They burned with laser intensity once they locked on to another person's gaze. Then he was in her mind. "I don't know if you can hear me, Mrs. Finley. I am not sorry about what I said, but I will apologize if the President asks me to. However, I want you to understand that I will do whatever he asks or orders me to do. And I will do it with all my strength and energy. That I pledge to you!"

The corners of Alma's mouth curved upward slightly. Her gaze softened. "Thank you, Mr. President," she said aloud, still staring at Gideon Mersky. "And thank you, Mr. Secretary. I am sure you will be a tremendous asset to our mission."

The tension in the room abated. They all sat down again, relaxed and eager to begin planning for the watership's arrival and the events that would follow as the mothers-to-be of the Geriatric Brigade neared term.

CHAPTER TWELVE

Before dinner Patricia Keane had called her oldest daughter, Cynthia, a junior at Emerson College in Boston, and told her to come home. When she heard why, Cynthia rushed by taxi to Logan Airport and caught the last Pan Am shuttle to La Guardia Airport. Being the first-born, Cynthia had a special relationship with her grandmother Mary. When she arrived at the Keane home she leaped out of her father's car and rushed into the large Tudor house. Mary Green was in the kitchen helping Patricia clean the dinner dishes. Cynthia rushed in and hugged her, tears flowing, squealing for joy.

"Oh Grandma . . . it is you . . . oh God . . . how I missed you . . . how I love you . . . oh . . . I'm so happy . . . I do love you . . ."

Mary stroked her first-born grandchild's hair and held her tightly to her bosom. Cynthia had been a girl of fifteen when she last saw her. Now she was a woman of twenty. The measurement of time passed, of family missed, was most apparent in the changes she saw in Cynthia.

With everyone gathered, they settled comfortably in the screened-in family room. It was a warm May night. Where to begin?

"Let me start by telling you about the night we left this planet. So much was happening around us. The others, most of the members of our Geriatric Brigade, were being shuttled out to the submerged Antarean mothership. Eleven of us remained behind in the processing room because we had chosen to become commanders. Our bodies had already been processed.

What was then required was a surgical procedure, a cerebral implant." At that point she once again showed them the bump on her skull.

"Did it hurt?" Lisa asked.

"Not at all. But we had to remain quite still for about an hour so the implant could root itself to our cerebral cortex. While that happened we began to learn how to combine our minds and think and act as one. The power of it was awesome. Finally we could wait no longer. The police were coming because they thought someone had kidnapped a bunch of old people and were torturing them, or worse. We boarded two boats that the Antareans had and made our way out to the mothership. The Coast Guard was all around, helicopters, cutters, speedboats, police boats . . . chaos. The Antareans kept our pursuers at bay while we slipped over the side into the ocean."

"You jumped into the ocean at night?" Cori interrupted. "Weren't you afraid of sharks?"

"No, dear. We were afraid of nothing. The mothership was far below, more than four hundred feet down, white and glowing. We swam toward it without breathing. Air was not necessary. It seemed but a few strokes and we were there. A round portal opened below us and we swam, no floated, through a wonderful substance, like a membrane. It allowed us through but kept the sea water out. My first impression of the mothership was that it was bright and warm. Safe. The others—the old people we had gathered from all over the country, from the abject poverty of Collins Avenue, from degrading nursing homes, from our old friends who hadn't moved to Florida—they were all there. We eleven were their leaders. Everyone was warm and safe."

The Keane family sat enthralled by Mary's story. She continued, describing the takeoff, the journey away from motherplanet Earth, the long weeks of learning, training for their new lives, and finally their arrival on Parma Quad 2. She then went on to tell just a bit about that planet where they'd spent nearly two years, and other places that she and Ben had visited as crew members on the Antarean mothership.

From time to time, when Mary wanted to make a point or clarify a location, they were able to step outside into the backyard and stare up at a star-filled sky. Mary identified certain stars as systems she had visited with Ben and the Antarean mothership after leaving Parma Quad 2. There was unbelievable wonder, even in the eyes of her cynical Wall-Street–hardened son-in-law when, quite casually, she pointed out a star and said, "We were there just about seven months ago on a survey measuring the rate of expansion of the Talican planetary system. Then we returned to Parma Quad 2, there." Her finger swept across the midnight sky to the Dog Star, Sirius.

"That seems like quite a distance," Michael said, tracking the vast expanse of universe between the two stars.

"From here it is," Mary answered. "Up there it's a little closer. Of course, with the Parman guides we travel pretty fast. It depends on their star fix and the rate of ultraviolet absorption they set."

"The speed of light?" Cori remarked. She was a straight-A student, quite the opposite of her sister Lisa, whose one dream was to live in Beverly Hills and be a movie star. School was a waste of time for Lisa, and she looked forward to her graduation as an inmate serving hard time in the Federal penitentiary looks forward to his day of release.

"Of course," Lisa answered unexpectedly. "They have to travel that fast or they wouldn't be here."

"It means," Michael Keane injected, "that we are looking at stars before Grandma was there. Actually hundreds of thousands of years before, because it takes the light from those stars that long to reach us here."

"Then how did Grandma get here before that light

if she traveled at the speed of light?" Cori asked. No one answered. Mary laughed.

"I said we travel fast, but I never said at the speed of light. No, light speed would take too long. The Antareans, with their Parman guides, can displace space. In effect, they bend it. Something like using the shortest distance between two points by moving those points closer together and then traveling along the new distance created."

"Like making a short cut," Cynthia suggested.

"Yes. Something like that. A short cut that they build and then use. Not one that existed before. Light moves in a relatively straight line, and for some trips light speed is adequate. But the Parman guides take light, starlight that is, and project it back across the universe after absorbing it from the most distant stars. When they project that light, they project the space-craft as well."

"Does it hurt?" Cori asked.

"Does what hurt, darling?"

"To travel that way?"

"No. But without the processing we had back in Florida five years ago, it would be impossible for us to travel in space at all. And more interesting than that is the fact that the Anterean processing only will work on old humans. You young people will have to wait until your body ages if you want to go out there." She gestured up toward the starry sky again. They all craned their necks and filled their eyes with the wonder of the universe above them.

"My God," Lisa said. "There are so many stars, so many places to go and see. Will you see them all, Grandma?"

"Maybe not all, but your grandpa and I plan to keep on traveling for as long as we can." They walked back to the family room filled with awe of Mary Green's adventures. Patricia was tired, exhausted from the strain of the day's events. The girls wanted to talk some more, to hear about the planets and the living beings Mary had seen. They kept their grandmother up for several hours after Pat and her husband had fallen sound asleep.

For the first time since joining his law firm, Michael Keane called his office and reported he was sick. It was a lie. He stayed home with the rest of the family as they sat enraptured by Mary Green's stories about her travels in space. The two younger Keane daughters, Cori, fifteen, and Lisa, seventeen, had hardly slept. They awoke with more questions for their grandmother about the beings she had met: how they lived, did they have music, how they dressed, what their schools were like, what they thought about humans. They pleaded with their mother to let them cut school the next day. Patricia Keane had no choice but to agree.

It was Friday, another sunny spring day. They gathered around the breakfast table, a wrought-iron glass-top affair with matching upright chairs that were as uncomfortable as they looked. Patricia Keane loved the set and no one dared complain. The sun poured into the large kitchen. Mary tried to help with breakfast but the girls insisted on serving her. She was the guest.

"You're an ambassador, Grandma," Cori announced as she served grapefruit halves topped with maraschino cherries. With a flourish she placed a grapefruit in front of Mary and began to sing, "Hail to the Chief."

"That's for the President, dummy," Lisa chided her younger sister.

"Well, maybe Grandma will be president of a planet one day," she answered, giving Mary Green a kiss. "I love you, Grandma."

"I love you too, darling. I love all of you." Mary sat back in the hard metal chair and looked at her family. Had she missed them? After five years, what did they really think about her return? It was part of her mission to explore these feelings so as to help the others returning make decisions regarding contacting their own families. Last night she had told them some of her adventures in the broadest terms.

There was no way of knowing how detailed she should be. It pained her to reach into their minds from time to time to see what effect her stories and her presence had. There was love, there was genuine happiness for her return. They were relieved that she and Ben were alive and well. But underneath those very human feelings there lurked another, almost buried thought. Grandma was different. Grandma knew so much, had seen so much, was in some undefined way superior. She had not aged. She was strong and healthy and nearly eighty years old. There was a separation between them, and it frightened Patricia. And deep within his mind an emerging idea gnawed at Michael Keane's id. Alien, he thought. Mary is an alien . . . not of this world. She speaks of other worlds as though they were her home, and of other creatures—beings—as though they were her kind. What has she become? Who is she?

A large plate of toast, Lisa's chore, was the last item to be brought to the table. It was nearly all burned. Cynthia complained, knowing her protest would fall on deaf ears.

"The toast is burned," she said as she passed the scrambled eggs to her father. Lisa grinned impishly.

"It's good for your teeth that way," the seventeen-year-old actress-to-be said.

"You sound like a commercial," Cynthia answered sarcastically.

"You think so? You really think so?" Lisa was suddenly serious. "I'm going to see an agent in New York next week. She's Leslie Blackman's agent and she gets her lots of work."

"Leslie Blackman is beautiful." Cynthia threw the final dig, she thought, but it rolled off Lisa's back like water off a duck.

"Maybe, but I've got character. Right, Grandma?"

"You were always a character, dear."

"See!" Lisa then took a piece of toast and scraped off the charred top until the piece was half its original size. Everyone at the table burst into laughter. Lisa played it to the hilt, slowly buttering the toast, taking a large bite and then rolling her eyes in delight.

Mary caught herself laughing, filling up with old feelings: pride in her family, love for her grandchildren, the sense of being an older generation observing and enjoying the renewal of life. But she *was* an alien. She watched her family and felt guilty. Perhaps they should have stayed behind five years ago. The grandchildren had grown, matured into wonderful girls, women. Her other daughter, Melanie, was halfway around the world in Australia, a marine biologist, a stranger. How much had she missed? Was it really worth it? At that moment Ben Green reached her mind and quelled her doubts. "Yes, my darling, it was, it is worth everything. What we have to do is important." And then their thoughts melded as one and they recalled their son Scott, a casualty of Viet Nam, a statistic, a name engraved on a long, silent, dark, brooding strip of black marble in Washington, D.C. With that thought, and the potential for starting a new family that Ben and Mary knew they now had, the decision was taken.

Mary had not revealed the total reason for their return to Earth. She told her family it was to bring the cocoons back to Antares. But, because it was such a new and wondrous event, she mentioned nothing of the pregnancies, including the fact that she was certain she too was going to have a baby.

CHAPTER THIRTEEN

At that time there were 1,158 satellites and much space hardware of one sort or another circling the globe in a variety of orbits and distances from the Earth. Their purposes were as varied as science could devise. Of this large number of extraterrestrial hardware, only thirty-seven had the capability of noting the entrance of the Antarean probeship that carried the Greens, Finleys and Amos Bright into the atmosphere. Only seventeen of those had the capability of instantaneously relaying information on the intruder back to their Earth stations. Six belonged to the United States, five to the Soviet Union, two to Japan and one each to India, England and Israel. The probeship entry was so fast that by the time these satellites locked in on it the ship had blended into the electrical storm and appeared as just another electrical anomaly. However, because it was classified as an extraordinary event, what little data they had gathered was studied by these governments. Since the occurrence had terminated over American soil the extremely secret Defense Intelligence Agency, the DIA, had the task of deciphering the event. Heavy weather eliminated the possibilities of visual sightings and most of the local Florida airports were closed down, making radar contacts few and inconclusive. Within two days the final DIA report simply stated: Electrical Atmospheric Disturbance—EAD/close file.

A probeship is a relatively small, very fast craft, about the size of a railroad car, and highly maneuverable. A watership, on the other hand, is a large visible craft, especially if it has three huge high-pressure storage tanks in tow. To bring that craft to Earth undetected was another matter.

They temporarily used the President's office as headquarters for the operation.

The first order of business was to identify and recruit a small and highly specialized group of people who would share Alma's secret on a need-to-know basis. With jackets off and sleeves rolled up, the President and his Secretary of Defense worked on a list of trusted people who would be part of the inner circle. Caleb, Margo and Alma plotted out a schedule of events based on information Alma had, which was updated by her husband, the Greens and Amos. Data from the watership flowed through all the commanders' conscious minds.

Landing the watership secretly was the first problem to be solved. Gideon Mersky took charge of that aspect of the operation. He would put together a team of his brightest think-tank people and give them a hypothetical problem. It might even be possible to initiate the solution without involving many people.

The medical aspect of the operation was to be overseen by the new Undersecretary of Health, Dr. Mohammad Kahwaji, a board-certified neurosurgeon of Pakistani heritage. He was somewhat nervous to be called to the President's office on short notice. The doctor was a deliberate man, known for this eclectic approach to problems. It was for this reason that he was chosen. No one could imagine what complications these pregnancies might hold. The women were, to put it simply, old. Could their bodies take the strain of birth? After being processed for space travel and being exposed to a variety of atmospheres, gravities and exotic foods, what effect would all that have on the babies? When he was told of the four interplanetary matings with off-planet beings, the little brown man just frowned, sat down and shook his head slowly.

"You ask me to design an obstetric and pediatric facility for patients that by all rights should be under the care of a geriatrician. And then to prepare for circumstances we, I, cannot begin to fathom." He smiled slyly. "But, you know, it is interesting. I think we must be anticipating all eventualities. So we will need a large facility, perhaps many. There will be housing for the couples, prenatal care, and of course a complete obstetric department. Then I will want pediatric intensive care units ready with delivery and operating rooms, a surgical staff—both gynecological and geriatric." He chuckled. "That's a specialty I imagine is rare—a gynecological geriatrician." Everyone in the room joined in his amusement. "Then the nursery. That will require a specialized staff as well—"

"I think we'll need engineers and chemists too," Caleb suddenly chimed in. "Those four mixed marriages, or whatever you call them . . ."

"Matings," Alma corrected him.

"Yes, well, from what we've heard it's possible that the babies might be—I don't know—I hate to say it, but not human. They might need a special environment."

"The watership is bringing atmospheres," Alma said.

"Yes," Doctor Kahwaji stated, "but Mr. Harris is correct. We will have to design and build environments, if not for the babies then for the nonhuman parents. And the babies might have special requirements different from either parent. Yes, engineers, chemists, biologists—I think most of the sciences will be required."

"Can it be done?" the President asked.

"I believe so, Mr. President," the Undersecretary answered in his best surgeon's manner. "The problem will be to keep this a secret. You know many of the best scientific minds in this country—and frankly I think we should settle for nothing but the best—well, some of those people have a different point of view from us about government, or at least about your administration." Gideon Mersky looked up from writing on a yellow legal pad.

"I don't think that's a problem. When those folks, and I don't care what their politics are, find out that they're going to have the opportunity to work on some real live extraterrestrials, I think they'll go along with whatever we ask."

"And afterward?" Caleb asked.

"After what?"

"After the babies are born, after we don't need these scientists, doctors and engineers anymore. What then?" Everyone in the room looked at Alma.

"We will have to cross that bridge when we come to it," she said wistfully. "Right now I think we have to find the best people and the best facility. The welfare of the mothers and the babies should be the only criteria."

"I agree," President Teller said. "We'll just have to educate those folks somehow." Dr. Kahwaji turned his attention to Alma Finley.

"Can you tell me anything about the changes you experienced while these Antareans processed you?"

"After the processing—that was here on Earth— we all experienced euphoria. I never felt so well, so healthy. *Clean* is the word that comes to mind. Clean and pure. We were disease free. My own husband's leukemia was completely cured. People that came to us crippled with arthritis, palsy, heart disease—they were all made well. My friend Bess had, has, a sister, Betty. She was a stroke victim, confined to a bed in a miserable nursing home. With my own eyes I saw her transform and become alive again." Everyone in the room had stopped their work as they listened to Alma relate her story.

"We eleven, the commanders, had to make an additional adjustment to the implants. But the real change was within ourselves, within our psyches. It took nearly four months, Earth time, as best we can figure, to reach Parma Quad 2. That was a period of adjustment and learning. We all believed that we had done the right thing, leaving Earth, that is. And physically we were prepared for the rigors of space travel. But as we pulled away from our planet, as it grew smaller, a profound silence swept through the whole group, nine hundred forty-one strong. In what seemed like a few moments we felt the mothership slow down. There, outside the membrane we had entered through, was the planet Saturn. It was glorious, like an orange ball whirling within a kaleidoscope of rocks and debris of all manner and shape and color."

"Our Voyager took some great pictures of Saturn," Gideon Mersky remarked.

"Yes, of course, Mr. Secretary, but you have to see it in person. It's enormous. Or at least we thought so until we visited some other planets. And I hear that in the galaxy Hydra there are planets with moons the size of Saturn."

"And it cost us five hundred million dollars to look at photos of what this woman casually observed," the President mused.

"Not so casually," Alma continued, "and many were still not convinced they had done the correct thing. It was an uneasy time. The ship had picked up speed again and we settled into our quarters. It was interesting that for such a large ship there was a very small crew. Only five Antareans on the flight deck plus the seven that had been on Earth. Of course there were three pairs of Parman guides, but they remained outside for most of the trip. Only toward the end, when we were approaching Parma Quad 2 and had learned the rudiments of their language, did we understand how intelligent and advanced they were."

"So you went to school on the ship?" Caleb asked.

"Yes. It was hard work, but fascinating. Then, oh maybe two weeks out, we slowed again and actually came to a stop. You can imagine our excitement when we looked out and saw three other spaceships. I'll call them that, actually they were Zeridian science vessels from the area of our galaxy we call Pleadies. Amos Bright, our leader, invited some of the Zeridians aboard to meet us. They were bipedal mammals from a water planet. By our standards they were short, perhaps three feet, no more than four. They greeted us by touching and smiling. It was a wonderful time for everyone. You see, we had become so familiar with our Antarean crew that they didn't seem alien to us anymore.

"Meeting the Zeridians brought that into focus for everyone in the Brigade. It was as if we had stepped through Alice's looking glass into a totally new dimension, a startling new way of seeing things, others, ourselves. Even though we were millions of miles from Earth, for the first time as a group to the very last person aboard, we were changed forever. We were part of the greater universe. And we were accepted by its inhabitants."

"Everywhere?" Margo McNeil asked.

"Everywhere I've been with the Antareans," Alma answered.

"But," Dr. Kahwaji interrupted, "what I am really driving at is to understand what physical changes you have experienced. Changes that might affect a fetus."

"I don't know," Alma answered.

"You had no physical examination out there?"

"Never."

"Then we will have to plan accordingly," Kahwaji said to the President, "for every eventuality."

The phone rang. Dr. Caroline Macklow from the National Oceanic and Atmospheric Administration, NOAA, had arrived and was in the outer office. The Press Secretary went out to get her. Dr. Macklow, a Ph.D. specializing in oceanic pollution, was fifty years old with wispy gray-brown hair, a face that appeared too small for her owlish green eyes and a smile that was disarming. She was tall, nearly six feet, and carried her large frame upright like a statue—a clothed female David. She entered the room and immediately paid her respects to the President. Within a few moments she had met everyone, was sworn to secrecy and brought up to date on the historical events that were about to happen. Dr. Macklow's expertise would be valuable in the salvaging of the cocoons.

And so the day wore on. The team grew. Two of Gideon Mersky's whiz kids, as he liked to call them, Phillip Margolin, a military analyst he recruited from the Rand Corporation, and Alicia Sanchez, a project supervisor at NASA, were assigned to work as a team on the problem of masking the watership's arrival and landing.

Dr. Michelangelo Yee, the President's medical advisor, was brought in to coordinate the personnel for Dr. Kahwaji, whose background and contacts were in the scientific community.

The chief of the White House Secret Service detail, Benton Fuller, was briefed by the President and asked to hand-pick three other agents who would remain loyal and keep their mouths shut.

Caleb Harris and Margo McNeil schemed of ways to keep the inquisitive press at bay.

The Undersecretary of the Navy, Captain Thomas Walkly, one of the highest-ranking black officers on active duty, was brought in to coordinate the naval activity in the area of the Stones before, during and after the arrival of the watership.

By the end of the day the White House group had grown considerably and had taken some firm decisions.

The watership had to be screened as it approached Earth. Its size and configuration made it easily detectable, even by unsophisticated radar.

A medical facility that already existed was required for the returning mothers- and fathers-to-be. After some discussion it was agreed the recently completed wing at the NASA Space Medicine Center in Houston, Texas, could be effectively sealed off without attracting attention.

Dr. Kahwaji would discreetly contact some of his colleagues in the academic world. They all concurred that approaching private industry would be a mistake. He had good friends at the Albert Einstein Hospital in New York, the Massachusetts Institute of Technology, the University of North Carolina in the Research Triangle and Stanford University in California.

The logistics after landing would be handled by the Navy under the command of Captain Walkly. The returning humans and a few Antareans would be taken by a small guided missile frigate to Elliot Key, a small uninhabited and inconspicuous island south of Miami. From there speedboats would ferry them to the Florida mainland, landing approximately twenty miles east of Homestead Air Force Base. From that point trucks would transport them to Homestead and a waiting C-5A MATS cargo plane for the final leg of their journey to the Houston Space Center.

Everyone worked well into the night, with meals being brought in from the President's living quarters by his personal staff. By three A.M. everyone was beat, but they had made great progress. Alma thanked them all. She would remain in Washington to coordinate their activities with her fellow commanders. Caleb offered her his bed for the night; he would sleep on the sofa. The President suggested she be a guest in the White House. Alma declined both offers graciously, stating she preferred the privacy of her hotel.

After they had all left, Malcolm Teller and his Press Secretary had a drink alone in the Red Room, a baroque sitting room with a deep red carpet, plush red velvet Louis XIV chairs, black marble cocktail tables. The walls were covered with red flocked wallpaper and mundane oil landscapes by obscure artists of the late eighteenth century. They discussed and marveled at the events of the day as they sipped twenty-year-old Chivas Regal.

Neither was tired, but rather stimulated by being a part of such an historical event. The stimulation eventually led them to the President's bedroom, where they made love in Abraham Lincoln's bed.

CHAPTER FOURTEEN

A week later the Antarean watership entered Quad 3, Earth's quadrant of our Milky Way Galaxy. In a few days the Parman guides would change over to light speed and, keeping our moon between them and earth, make their final approach.

The idea to use the watership had come from Chief Commander Ruth Charnofsky. After learning of the human pregnancies she circumvented the normal chain of command on Subax, a planet steeped in military tradition and strict obedience to unwritten common law, and contacted Amos Bright directly through the other commanders. It might have taken weeks had she gone through the proper channels. Her mate, Panatoy, concurred with her decision.

The plan was simple. Contact all the pregnant humans and gather them on Antares. Then, using the watership, initiate a round-trip mission. Bring the humans home for birth on the motherplanet and return the earthbound cocoons to Antares, where they could be processed and rejuvenated. She convinced Amos Bright that it was foolhardy to leave the cocoons on Earth any longer than absolutely necessary. "There is an unstable, primitive political environment there," she argued, "that could erupt into nuclear holocaust at any time, endangering the cocoons, perhaps destroying them."

The destruction of those nine hundred twenty earthbound Antareans would be a great loss to their race, who inhabit a planet that cannot support life on its surface. Antareans are underground dwellers who capture the heat and energy from their planet's core. All food and water is artificially created without benefit of natural sunlight or atmosphere. After creating a thriving civilization hundreds of thousands of years ago, the Antarean race made the decision to apply their energies and efforts to the exploration of space.

Now, after millennia upon millennia, they were known throughout the universe, and more than one thousand races and civilizations were known to them. They revered and cherished life, having progressed genetically to the point where their life span was indefinite. They were a limiting society, which meant that new life could not be created unless an old life died. Each death had to be confirmed and the body, or any remains, returned to Antares. From that inert tissue material the Antarean gene splicers and *invitro* scientists would extract and manipulate genetic matter that, in effect, re-created the dead Antarean. The new life would have no memory of its parent or its parent's memory. But it would be a clone, a replicate of the deceased, and a valued member of Antarean society.

More than five hundred Earth years would pass before a new Antarean reached adulthood. During that time it was educated, trained and permitted to work on the motherplanet, far beneath the barren, forbidding surface of Antares. After this apprentice period the new adult was allowed to begin space travel and exploration on one of the eighteen hundred Antarean space vessels now in operation throughout the universe. There were at this time two hundred thirty-six thousand Antareans alive. At any given time more than fifty thousand of them were either traveling in space or serving on distant planets.

Ruth Charnofsky's idea was accepted immediately. A grateful Antarean high council granted her citizenship on Antares, an extremely high honor for an off-planet person.

The human expectant parents were gathered as planned. Now, as they began the final leg of their journey home, Ruth, swelling with her Subax– human baby in her womb, pondered just what this baby might be, or become. Ruth was ninety-one years old and until five years ago, had barely survived on her meager Social Security checks.

Now she was a strong commander and citizen of a planet other than her own. She had traveled among the stars, witnessing sights and wonders only dreamed about by her fellow humans. And she carried a child. She contemplated this embryo. What was this baby? Her mate, Panatoy, might be called an animal by the bigoted cretins on her own homeplanet. She knew him to be a kind, thoughtful and loving male. As good and tender a man as her late husband, whom she had buried more than thirty years ago.

What would their baby be? Human? Subax? And what might the three other mixed matings produce? For that matter, what would the fully human babies, about to be born to elderly parents, look and be like? What genetic changes had the processing they had required for space travel wrought? This was all new ground, reaching into the unknown. But wasn't that what she had seen and heard throughout her travels in the universe? Blending and mixing . . . changing. For unlike the Antareans, who opted for controlled genetic reproduction, most of the life forms in the universe reproduced by means of ovum and sperm: the exchange and blending of chromosomes and genetic material within a DNA common to uncountable species. Exchange and blend. Diversification. And yet, so much that was similar. Humanoid was the predominant species: warmblooded, mammalian, bipedal with a relatively constant brain size and nervous system configuration. There were wonderful variations arrived at by natural selection, climate and solar spectrum. In other advanced civilizations genetic manipulation had flourished, producing incredible varieties of humanoid life.

The animal and plant kingdoms stretched across the universe as well, with millions of species and varieties that were also constantly changing. Blending. Becoming.

And beyond that, civilized intelligent life forms of crystalline design and others that thrived in gaseous vapor clouds.

It was also believed, but not yet confirmed, that another life form existed within the electrically charged solar winds and nebulae from which new galaxies and solar systems were formed as others aged and disintegrated into the void.

A myriad of life spread across the vast, unending expanse called the universe. Yet, if you opened your heart and mind to this endless dwelling place, as Ruth Charnofsky had when she fell in love with her blue Subax, it was hard not to see that some grand plan was at work here. What appeared haphazard was, in fact, of purposeful design. New blendings begat new races and they in turn developed further.

Hurtling along at inexplicable speed toward her motherplanet, Ruth Charnofsky contemplated this new life form within her body. She had but one desire. To give birth and nurture her child. This was the plan. This was the ultimate universal purpose.

CHAPTER FIFTEEN

Nobody would ever suspect that the modest log cabin set deep in a grove of tall spruce on the rise above the Beaverkill River was, in fact, the think tank for Operation Earthmother, as the project to aid the returning elderly space travelers was called by the very few people who knew about it in the Department of Defense. Upon close inspection a trained eye might notice that aside from the usual white satellite dish sported by all the recreation homes in this area, this cabin had an additional black mesh dish hidden some hundred yards to the north in among thorny blackberry bushes. Its purpose was to receive and transmit high-speed encoded data from the DOD's space computer main-frame facility at the Pentagon.

The misty rain that had begun at dawn continued to midday. Alicia Sanchez, a tall, thirty-two-year-old NASA project manager who sported a Master's from MIT in astrophysics and Ph.D. in quantum mechanics earned on the other coast at Stanford, parted the kitchen curtains and peeked up at the low, moisture-laden clouds. It showed no sign of clearing. Her gaze then traveled down to the river where, at the edge of a deep pool on the far side, her partner and cohort for the past eight days, Phillip Margolin, cast a fly to trout feeding peacefully along the riverbank. On the third cast a two-pound brown trout rose for his perfectly cast fly and within ten minutes Phillip had netted the sleek spotted fish. Alicia watched from behind the curtain as Margolin carefully removed the fly from the trout's lip and easily returned the fish to the crystal-clear river. She experienced a mild rush of adrenaline, which told her she liked him even more upon witnessing that gentle act from the tough computer expert.

Smiling to herself, she turned from the window, walked out of the kitchen and sat down at the computer terminal in her work area. Her two assistants, Martin LoCasio and Oscar Berlin, both assigned to her from NASA headquarters in Houston, had gone into Roscoe, the closest town in this upstate New York resort community, to get the Sunday papers and to buy something for dinner.

It was hard to believe that only eight days had passed since she had been secretly flown to Washington, introduced to the Secretary of Defense, to Phillip Margolin, an aide to the Secretary and a Ph.D. himself in chemistry, rocket sciences and computer analysis. Eventually she met the President himself. The briefing they had regarding Operation Earthmother was held in the Oval Office. It was there that she'd met Alma Finley and heard the whole fantastic story of the pregnant women from the Geriatric Brigade.

She keyed up the latest computer reentry model, which they had developed and refined last night, and began to run it against the parameters Joe Finley had supplied this morning. He's a really nice old man, she thought to herself as she leaned back, craning her neck to see in to the screened-in porch where he bunked. He was still sleeping on the daybed they had moved out there for him. She and Margolin had spent hours pumping Finley about his travels in deep space. As they listened to his tales of planets and civilizations, it became apparent their education was inadequate to grasp the idea of a universe teeming with life. Finley kindly and quickly put the matter straight, reminding them that not too many years ago he was a taxi driver in Boston, struggling to get a fading acting career on track.

"We've spent our entire existence on this planet under the assumption that we were alone in the universe. Our assumed self-importance and self-centeredness has closed our minds, most of us that is, to the idea that we might be just one little populated planet in a universe of living beings on millions of planets. Give the idea some time, you'll eventually understand how wonderful it is to be part of a living universe and how foolish it was to deny that for so long."

After he'd put them at ease he then insisted on sleeping out on the porch even though it was damp and chilly. When they protested he told them about the weather conditions on Parma Quad 2, where the temperature differential was a full ninety degrees hourly and the humidity a constant state of supersaturation. "It was like living inside a steam bath that froze every hour on the hour, then thawed out for a while, then froze again. This porch is a delight for me."

Satisfied that Finley was still sleeping comfortably, she went back to running the model against her own program, which tracked the moon's position relative to South Florida on the day projected for the watership's arrival. The initial results looked promising, but the rapidly approaching deadline worried her. According to Finley, the watership could be in position on the moon's far side in less than two weeks. They were scheduled to present a viable plan to the Secretary and President in two days.

A half hour later Phillip Margolin came through the back door into the kitchen on the run. He still wore his wet hip boots, tracking mud and sand across the cabin floor. The door slammed behind him, startling Alicia Sanchez, who looked up from the computer's video screen. The noise also awakened Joe Finley, who cocked one eye curiously open toward the energetic DOD scientist.

"We missed a key element last night," Margolin announced as he carefully placed his bamboo fly rod against the wall behind Alicia's computer terminal.

He tossed his hat, a dirty plaid affair covered with flies, spinners and a manner of feathered trout lures, onto the nearby Early American knotty-pine sofa. Without further comment he slid a matching chair over next to hers and proceeded to clear the work she was doing off her TV screen, pecking furiously at the computer keyboard.

"Never completely accept all givens as immovables."

"I beg your pardon!" she said, grabbing his wrist firmly. "I happen to be in the middle of something." She was three inches taller than he, and a black belt karate expert besides.

"Just give me a second. I think I know how we can do it!" He made no attempt to free his wrist nor fight her grasp. He just looked at her, allowing his piercing dark brown eyes to speak for him. She understood that passion and intelligence that lurked behind that gaze and eased her grip. He slid his hand out of her grasp, proceeding to enter and move data rapidly. Joe Finley, now fully awake, came into the room and watched Margolin as he furiously and precisely restructured the reentry model.

"What's up?"

"Phil's on to something more exciting than a trout —he says." There was mild sarcasm in her voice.

"You look like you've got something going here," Joe remarked as he moved closer to the terminal.

"THE answer," Margolin stated firmly. "But it's going to mean parking two of the watership's tanks, probably the ones with the atmospheres, on the far side of the moon. Then we have them configure the third tank this way." He keyed in the program and a three-dimensional model of the watership with one of her storage tanks nestled close up and crosswise against her stern came onto the screen. Phil Margolin keyed in another command and the model began to rotate, revealing its rising above what appeared now to be the moon's surface. The Earth was far off in the background. "With this configuration we can mask the entry all the way from the moon and create the shadow we need with the reentry of the space shuttle *Remembrance*."

"What about the atmospheres?" Alicia asked. "They'll need them in Houston sooner or later."

"I'm hoping they can manufacture what we need there. The three tank configuration is too large for what we have available for masking now. Perhaps the probeship can shuttle down whatever gasses are necessary. What about it, Mr. Finley?"

Joe Finley, who had arrived at the cabin a few days after Sanchez, Margolin and their assistants had set up housekeeping, studied the video screen. He understood what Margolin had in mind, but it would require conferencing with the others.

His wife, Alma, was still in Washington coordinating the arrival of the watership with the efforts underway by a special Navy Seal unit, under the command of Undersecretary Walkly, to prepare a clear and secure ocean area near the Stones.

Mary Green had ended her family visit in Scarsdale and returned to Florida. Shortly thereafter she and her husband, Ben, flew to Houston, where they met with Dr. Kahwaji to help prepare the hospital facility.

Amos Bright, Jack Fischer, Phil Doyle and their chopper pilot buddy, Madman Mazuski, worked out of Boca Raton aboard the *Manta III,* preparing the cocoons in their chambers for transport to the watership after it had been safely landed and hidden beneath the South Florida seas.

After studying the plan Joe Finley concurred. "This way we are sure to bring the watership down totally undetected. We'll let Doctor Kahwaji know about the atmospheres. I'll have Amos contact the watership right away."

"It will mean bringing in more new people," Alicia said.

"There's no choice," Phillip answered.

Joe left the room to have privacy while he contacted Amos Bright and the Greens. Margolin watched the old man carefully. After Finley was out of sight he looked up at Alicia, who was standing beside him now.

"They do it telepathically, you know."

"I know."

"All across the galaxy."

"All across the universe."

"I'd love to know how to do it. How about you?"

"Are you kidding? I'd give my right arm . . ." Their eyes met and Margolin, a tough, dynamic scientist, who had been all business since they'd arrived at this mountain retreat, smiled warmly at his attractive Hispanic partner.

"Keep the arm. It suits you," he said softly as he touched her right arm.

"Huh?" She blushed. Did he know she'd been attracted to him the moment they'd met in Washington?

"The arm." He squeezed her gently.

"Oh, that arm. I meant the other one." She smiled at the diminutive but forceful man seated at her computer. Her eyes went to the screen. "We still won't have a final deployment configuration for the first screen until we fix a firm point of entry." He released her arm but continued to look directly up at her pretty dark-complected face.

"That won't be determined until the last minute, for both screens I imagine." She looked back down at him again.

"Is something wrong?" she asked.

"Wrong? What could be wrong? The fishing is great and we've licked the problem. Quite the opposite."

"You're staring at me."

"You're beautiful, so I'm staring at you."

"Thanks a lot. We've been together for eight days. How come I suddenly got beautiful?"

"The work is almost finished here."

"That's how it is? Business before—" She didn't finish the sentence because he stood and was very close to her now.

"Pleasure?" He smiled. She stepped back.

"You make me uncomfortable; we're working. Mr. Finley . . ."

Margolin's demeanor changed abruptly. He was all business again. "Of course you're correct. I apologize."

"That's not necessary."

He sat down and began to work again. She sat next to him and watched as he refined the model and began making printouts of the proposed trajectory for the watership's trip from the moon to rendezvous with the space shuttle *Remembrance*.

"Thank you," she said softly.

"For what?"

"For saying I was beautiful."

"You are. It's a fact." He tried to keep a business edge to his voice. She leaned over and gently kissed him on his cheek.

"So are you, hotshot," she said. A flush of redness appeared on the nape of his exposed neck, but he said nothing.

A few moments later Joe Finley returned to say that the atmospheric tanks could be secured on the moon's far side and that the burgeoning group now firmly ensconced in the new wing of the Space Medicine Center would add some physicists expert in the physiological and thermodynamic properties of exotic gasses.

He had other news, sad news, about one of the passengers aboard the watership, but he kept that to himself.

CHAPTER SIXTEEN

When Joe Finley had contacted the watership, it was Ruth Charnofsky who gave him the bad news. The first woman to become pregnant had miscarried. The fetus was badly deformed. The parents were both commanders, Bess and Arthur Perlman.

The Perlmans had requested that the other commanders not be told about the tragic event. Bess blocked her emotions and withdrew into her own private world. The six other commanders aboard, including her husband, could not enter her mind to comfort her. She was distraught, weeping at times uncontrollably. Rumors of what had happened spread through the watership to the other expectant parents. A wave of fear permeated the ship. All of the pregnant women began to wonder whether their own babies would be carried to term.

Art Perlman knew he had to somehow break down the barrier behind which Bess had retreated. Physically she recuperated from her ordeal. Her body mended quickly. But after four days her mind still remained shielded, keeping out the others. Keeping the pain of her loss to herself. Ben wondered if that might be nature's way—that the female work out the loss alone. He rejected the idea and doubled his efforts to console his wife.

They had conceived the baby on Prima Maugur, a giant moon in the Pasadian System near the blue dwarf star known to us as Mira in the constellation Canis Major. This was a system where everything was giant-size. The moons, planets, comets and asteroid materials were all of a grand scale. Gravity, even on that moon colonized by Antareans, was enormous compared to Earth. Perhaps that had caused the eventual abortion of her baby.

But the child was deformed, and that raised questions in everyone's mind about the viability of pregnancies in human women of their age. It was true that their reproductive systems had been rejuvenated, but were they functioning normally?

Art Perlman originally was convinced the miscarriage had something to do with their being commanders. Somehow the genetic changes, or perhaps the cerebral implant itself, made normal reproduction impossible for them. Beam, the Antarean medical officer who had been on the last mission to Earth and who was now aboard the watership, assured Art that was not the case. If anything, she maintained that the changes they experienced as commanders probably made them fertile before the other men and women in the Geriatric Brigade. It was true that Bess was just about the first to become pregnant. Ruth Charnofsky was second, and she too was a commander. But all signs showed that Ruth's pregnancy was proceeding normally even though her mate was not a human.

Now, after spending time alone with Bess, holding her hand and speaking softly to her in their dimly illuminated cabin, Art Perlman finally grasped the deeper reason for Bess's behavior. During their marriage on Earth they had no children. That had been a deliberate decision that Bess made after she discovered her husband's involvement with organized crime. He had been a high-level, but outside, accountant and lawyer for the mob. He was never indicted, arrested or prosecuted. But his name was always in the newspapers and on radio and television. He had been called to testify at every congressional crime hearing, beginning with the Kefauver Committee in the early 1950s. Bess, whose father had been a renowned judge in Brooklyn, refused to have children —to give her husband and his kind an heir to train to

continue in his dirty work. She never knew that her
father was on the mob payroll, and Arthur never told
her.

Having an inheritance of her own and a full-time
job as a saleswoman in a high-priced dress shop in
downtown Brooklyn, she never accepted what she
called blood money from her husband. Even when her
widowed sister, Betty Franklin, was confined to a
nursing home after having a stroke, Bess paid for her
care, never bending to accept her husband's money
even though they had retired to Florida years before.
Betty was also a commander now. But she understood
her brother-in-law and his past. She knew about her
father's involvement. Once she had been taken from
the home and processed by the Antareans, Arthur
Perlman had asked her to keep the secret from Bess.
She agreed.

After the Perlmans had spent that bitter childless
life together and were confronted with the opportunity to leave the Earth with the Antareans, Bess believed
they were embarking on a new life, a new beginning.
She convinced herself that her God, the One the
Antareans called Master, had given them a second
chance. Her pregnancy was a confirmation of that
belief. She was convinced it was a sign that Arthur
had finally been forgiven for his earthly sins and life of
evil. Now, after the miscarriage, she withdrew into a
shell, into the old way of thinking. This loss was
another punishment for her husband's crimes. Retri-
bution from an angry God.

After knocking, Beam walked quietly into the cabin. It was a spacious room decorated with a mixture of
artifacts collected from Parma Quad 2, Antares, Prima Maugur, Hillet—a planet in the Alphard system
—and a few keepsakes they'd carried away with them
when they left Earth five years ago. Bess lay on the
bed, her back toward her husband and the Antarean
visitor. Beam wore her human skin covering, that of

an attractive thirty-year-old blonde, blue-eyed Caucasian. Now that they were approaching Earth, where she would have to wear it almost constantly, especially among the staff being assembled in Houston, she was wearing it often aboard the watership so as to stretch out any folds in it and make sure it was completely molded to her body.

So many years had passed since he had seen Beam's covering Art almost didn't recognize her when she entered the room.

"Hello, Commander Arthur. How is Commander Bess?"

He stood up to greet her. "Hello. She's resting. Do I know you?" Then he reached to her mind and laughed. "Beam! I'd forgotten. I'm sorry."

"You didn't remember!"

"Now I do. It's funny but I just never think of you this way anymore, only as an Antarean."

"But I do make an attractive human, don't I?"

"Of course. Those young doctors are going to chase you all around the hospital."

"Well, we'll see about that. Anyway, this time my human skin is thicker," she said.

Bess, who was not asleep, listened to the conversation. She and Beam were old friends, good friends. She had been one of the first to discuss what being an Antarean female was like with the bright medical officer. In a society that cloned their kind, Beam still admitted there was a deep inner force within many female Antareans that drove an urge to bear young, to be a mother.

Beam walked to the side of the bed and reached out to Bess with her hand, touching the older woman on her head, stroking her long loose hair. Beam recalled vividly the moment when Bess had begun her processing all those years ago in the Antares condominium in Coral Gables. Her hair had been white then. As the rejuvenation process progressed, Bess's hair had become darker and darker until it took on a sheen and chestnut color that was now spread out on the bed pillow. Bess responded to her gentle touch and allowed Beam to feel her pain for an instant.

"I am so sorry, Bess," the young Antarean whispered. "I am here to share your grief, to help." The human female commander did not respond. Her husband left the room. "Bess? Will you speak to me?" No response. "It is very important that you listen. Will you at least do that? We cannot find your mind, we cannot find a way to tell you what has happened. Will you listen?"

"Yes." The voice was faint. A whimper.

"Thank you." Beam paused, choosing her words carefully. "We are all so sorry for what happened. The baby was not right. That is the Master's way for many. But now we have so many aboard who are to be mothers soon. They have heard what has happened. They are worried. They are concerned. This is not good for them, for the babies that are coming." Bess turned slowly; her tear-filled eyes, swollen from crying, looked up at Beam.

"I can't do anything about the babies that are coming."

"Yes you can. You can help Commander Charnofsky and your own sister Betty. You can help me. We must calm the women, we must assure them that everything will be good . . . that this is right, that this is the Master's work."

"Losing my baby was the Master's work."

"Perhaps. Who is to say? All I believe is that these babies that are coming are of a new race. An important race. All Antareans believe that their birth was preordained eons ago. It is our mission to do all we can to insure they survive and thrive."

"Mine didn't," Bess answered bitterly. She sat up, taking a tissue from the nearby night table and blowing her nose.

"I know. I am sorry. It was not right. The next will—"

"There will be no next!"

"Who is to say? Would you have believed it possible at all five years ago? Have you not traveled among the stars and looked upon the Master's great work?" Beam was a deeply religious Antarean, trained that way because as a medical officer she would be close to many Antareans when they died. It was part of her duties to certify an Antarean death so a new one might be born. Many times death, which could be voluntary and usually was, had to be administered by a medical officer.

It was the sovereign right of an adult Antarean to request his or her own demise. For a race that revered life, and for whom there was no limit to the time they had to live, they also respected the decision to end life as a rational and personal right of every adult Antarean. They did not look upon death as a finality, but rather a moving-on to another level of existence. Their bodies, their flesh, was renewable. The proof was that the clone that replaced the dead Antarean looked exactly the same as the original. But the life force within, the spark that they said came from the Master, that which we call soul, that they believed was unique unto each individual. That was what moved on to another level of life, or existence, to a place within the Master's grand plan.

Bess wiped her eyes and accepted Beam's words. Her Antarean friend was correct. The time for self-pity and recrimination was over. The births to come were important and had to be nurtured.

"I'm sorry," Bess said. "I've been selfish." She opened her mind and heart. Immediately the consciousnesses of the other commanders, some from across the solar system, rushed into her brain and brought comfort and strength. Strongest of these was her husband. She silently called to him. He entered their room and crossed over to the bed. Beam was on her feet, backing away, as Art and Bess embraced. Just as Beam closed the door behind her, allowing the

Perlmans their privacy, so did the other commanders disengage their minds from Bess's, leaving her alone with her husband to mourn their loss together for the first time.

Later that night two of the women went into premature labor within an hour of each other. They knew each other; they were friends. Actually both couples were originally from St. Louis and had been recruited for the Geriatric Brigade by Andrea and Frank Hankinson. The Hankinsons were the first people recruited by Ben Green, Joe Finley, Art Perlman and Bernie Lewis after they had made contact with the Antareans back in Florida five years ago.

After Parma Quad 2, Frank Hankinson, who was a commander, led a group of his friends to live and work in the Alphard system which is located in the constellation we call Hydra. It is a six-planet system with the dwarf Alphard as solar source. Two of the planets, Betch and Hillet, are populated. A humanoid life form evolved on Betch, which is a seasonal water planet about twice the size of Earth.

The Antareans established relations with the Betch civilization thousands of years ago and, because the Betch were not space travelers, helped them colonize Hillet, a less hospitable planet devoid of humanoid life or civilization. Over the millennia the Antareans changed the atmosphere and weather conditions on Hillet, warming the surface, increasing the rainfall, thus causing agriculture to flourish. With a stable food supply the population increased. Now, although the Betch and Hillet histories record the colonization, the Hilletines consider themselves a race apart from their motherplanet Betch and, in fact, have their own language, technology, religions and governmental forms. The relations between the two planets are cordial, but neither are races that travel in deep space. The Antareans provide the only transport between the planets.

It was on Hillet that Frank Hankinson, his wife and

three other couples, all from St. Louis, settled and worked as teachers and ambassadors. And it was there that these two women became pregnant.

Arthur Perlman watched his wife administer to the two women in labor. His heart went out to her, but she was strong, using her telepathic abilities to soothe the anxious mothers-to-be. Frank entered the labor room, which had been hastily prepared by Beam's Antarean medical team, woefully inexperienced in the matter of human birth. Although his wife was not pregnant, they had come along on the trip because he was a commander. She was not. During the trip they had discussed the idea of trying to have a baby, but after seeing Bess miscarry they decided to wait until there was more data regarding birth among the other older human women.

"I'd hoped we could have made it to Earth before this," Frank told Art.

"Even at the speed our Parman guides move us, nature will have her way," he answered wryly. "Babies will be born in their own time, no matter how many light years we travel." Bess and her sister Betty were with one of the women, Julia Messina, a stout, dark-eyed woman with short black hair that offset an oval olive-complected face, typical of her Sardinian heritage. Julia's husband, Vincent, a fireplug of a man whose leathery skin bore witness to his years in the construction trades, hovered nearby, his brow furrowed with concern. Both sisters concentrated on the couple, keeping their minds relaxed and positive as Julia's labor intensified.

The other couple, Lillian and Abe Erhardt, were calmer and fatalistic about their baby. Ruth Charnofsky, herself pregnant some five months, and Rose Lewis, also a commander, were present to care for Lillian, who as a much younger woman some forty-five years before had given birth to twin boys in the back seat of a taxi. Her husband, then a young Marine corporal fighting against the Japanese in

World War II, was ten thousand miles away across the Pacific on a tiny island called Iwo Jima. Now they held hands and offered their appreciation to Ruth and Rose, whose telepathic abilities helped to ease the labor pains.

"So far so good," Art said to Frank. He smiled at Bess. "I think we're serving no purpose here."

"Women's work, huh?" Frank commented, understanding Art's desire to leave.

"I suppose. It's certainly not mine anyway." He was nervous himself.

"Well, everyone looks like they've got things under control." Frank waved to his St. Louis friends, the Messinas and Erhardts, and left the sterile room with Art Perlman.

The babies were born within seven minutes of each other. The Messinas had a girl, the Erhardts twin boys once again. The first humans born aboard an Antarean spaceship—any spaceship for that matter—were perfectly normal and healthy, if a little premature. But they didn't appear premature. They looked full term, fully developed, strong, alert and hungry. All their fellow passengers and the Antarean crew greeted the babies with cheers and love. Their arrival and condition gave everyone on board a tremendous emotional lift and quashed the fears of the remaining expectant parents. The sight of the mothers, both in their midseventies, nursing their infants was truly something never before seen in the universe.

The cries of the newborns echoed throughout the watership as it now sped past Jupiter, slowing imperceptibly again as the Parman guides tuned their solar absorbtion rate. Their arrival on the far side of Earth's single moon would take place within the week.

CHAPTER SEVENTEEN

"I think it's time we reeled in those two fish," Secret Serviceman Benton Fuller remarked as he adjusted his chaise to catch a more direct exposure to the late afternoon sun.

"I agree," answered Gary McGill, a special FBI agent in the Greater Miami area. His job was to coordinate security clearances for presidential visits to the southeastern United States. He had come to be good personal friends with Benton Fuller, which is why the Secret Service chief of the White House detachment had requested that McGill be brought into Operation Earthmother. "The last thing we want is a couple of loaded pistolas floating around out there just waiting to go off."

They were at McGill's home, a modest pastel-pink stucco house located adjacent to a canal that ran west out of Perine. The local claims to fame were the Parrot Jungle and Monkey Jungle, tourist attractions that brought mobs of visiting grandchildren into the area twice a year when the schools up north closed for winter and spring vacations. But now Perine was just a sleepy South Florida town and the perfect headquarters for Operation Earthmother. The house next to McGill's had been taken over by Undersecretary Captain Thomas Walkly and his staff of three. From there they were coordinating the real activities of Operation Earthmother with the special naval maneuvers supposedly designed to interdict drug traffic in the waters between the Bahamas and Florida's east coast.

The two policemen, relaxing beside McGill's swimming pool, were discussing the status of Detective Sergeant Matthew Cummings and his partner, Detective Coolridge Betters. The watership was scheduled to arrive within five or six days, and the two Coral Gables cops were going to be in the way.

"I'm amazed they've kept this all to themselves," McGill continued. He wore a bright-flowered Hawaiian bathing suit and sipped on a Bloody Mary diluted from melting ice. Both men were in their late forties, tall and trim. They worked hard at keeping in shape and took their jobs seriously. In South Florida, with the burgeoning drug trade claiming the lives of all manner of law enforcement people as well as traffickers, Special Agent McGill knew the value of having his reflexes and muscles toned and sharp.

Likewise, given the responsibility of protecting an American president in the armed camp called the United States of America, and a world filled with terrorists intent on becoming martyrs for their causes, Agent Fuller kept himself in top shape, although these days as he neared fifty the task became more and more difficult. He turned over onto his back and reached for his own drink, a gin and tonic.

"Those two have an agenda all their own. I checked out their files. They were involved with our 'visitors' the last time they were here. In the end there was a DA who made them look real stupid."

"Yeah," McGill interjected, "I checked that out myself right after you called me. I think you're right. They've been onto that Fischer guy and his buddies like flypaper."

"Mr. Bright is concerned. He doesn't want anything to happen to those cocoons out there."

"I hear you. I agree. How do you want to do it?"

"I'm not sure, except I know I don't want the Coral Gables Sheriff involved. The last thing we need is a local yokel knowing what we know."

"That would be a circus. You want another?" McGill asked, motioning toward Fuller's empty glass.

"No thanks. I think the best way is to involve the two of them in the pickup."

"The Navy exercise?"

"I'll have to fly it by Walkly."

"He seems to be wound a little tight these days."

"He's okay. Just military. He doesn't want his end to screw up."

"Assuming he says okay, when do you want to move on them?"

Agent Fuller thought for a moment, considering his available forces. In the end, after pressure from the Secretary of Defense, he had been authorized to brief only three of his most trusted people, two men and a woman, on the extraordinary events that were unfolding. They were now spread out. One man was with the President, another with Mary and Ben Green in Houston, and the female agent was assigned to Alma Finley. She would be arriving with her husband, Joe, soon. But for now, it was going to be up to McGill and himself to take care of the two snooping detectives.

"I think ASAP." Fuller looked up at the sun turning golden as it sank lower in the western sky. There would be no more suntanning today. "As a matter of fact," he said, raising himself out of the comfortable chaise, "I expect there's no time like the present. Let's get showered and dressed and pay the good Captain Walkly a neighborly visit."

The same setting sun turned the waters of the Inland Waterway into a rich golden liquid that reflected onto the crisp white hull of the *Manta III* in its Boca Raton mooring. Jack Fischer, Phil Doyle and Madman Mazuski lounged on the fantail, sipping beers in full sight of Detectives Cummings and Betters.

Below the waterline of Jack's broad-beamed sportfishing craft the Antarean probeship was alive with activity. Amos Bright transmitted new data regarding the cocoon chambers to the watership. At the same time he coordinated a conference between Alma

Finley in Washington, Joe Finley in Roscoe and the Greens in Houston.

The Margolin–Sanchez team had solved the approach diversion problem for the watership to Joe's satisfaction. Amos concurred and forwarded the basic outline for the plan on to the watership flight deck. Joe Finley planned to leave the Catskill cabin as soon as the team packed up. He would return to Washington and join his wife for the presentation to the President in a few days.

The Greens reported progress with the Space Hospital facility and medical teams that were being assembled. The problem of manufacturing four different atmospheres for the off-planet fathers was under study. The engineers were requesting a molecular and subatomic breakdown of the inert gasses for the Subaxian chamber. There was some problem in keeping Panatoy's atmosphere stable under the pressure and temperature conditions required. Amos passed on their request to the watership. It would take a few hours for the reply.

Everything seemed to be progressing well. They were all aware that their movements in Florida had been monitored to a certain extent by the two aging detectives. Amos had met with Benton Fuller two days ago when he arrived in Florida from Washington. He had not heard from the Secret Service agent since then and was acutely aware that both Cummings and Betters were always nearby.

"We finished preparation of all the cocoons today. Jack and his friends have been invaluable."

"Are those cops still around?" Ben Green asked.

"That they are," Amos said.

"Persistent, huh?" Alma remarked.

"Obsessed, I'd say," Amos answered. "Agent Fuller said he'd take care of it, but so far they're still watching."

"Have they followed you out to sea?" Mary asked.

"Once last week. They rented a helicopter."

"Rented?" Ben questioned.

"One of those that take people for rides out in the Everglades, I think. But they had engine trouble and had to turn back."

"That was convenient," Joe said, laughing. They all understood that Amos had caused the engine trouble.

"But," Alma said, "that's a sign they haven't said anything to their superiors. Otherwise they'd have used a police aircraft." The others agreed.

They were right. But barely. Matthew Cummings and Coolridge Betters had not shared their suspicions with their fellow police officers or the District Attorney. They had, however, hired an old friend who was an ex-underwater cameraman, now the owner of a small engineering company that manufactured underwater housings and lights for professional motion picture cameras. The man, a German named Hans Leiter, had hidden underwater near the Boca Raton outlet to the ocean late one afternoon. He used a special underwater camera and high-speed film as he photographed the *Manta III* below her waterline. As predetermined, Leiter gave the undeveloped film to the two detectives. He'd seen something lashed to the hull of the *Manta III* through the murky Intercoastal water, but he wasn't sure what it was. He suspected it had something to do with drug smuggling, and when you lived in Miami the less you knew about those things the safer you were.

That afternoon Cummings had received prints of the film Leiter had taken underwater. Although both detectives had no idea what the probeship actually was, they had reached the same conclusion—that it was a high-speed submarine to be used for smuggling. It wasn't much, but they had decided that since the old men and women had disappeared and they were getting nowhere, it was perhaps time to bring in help.

Jack, Phil and Madman Mazuski were aware that the two detectives from the Coral Gables sheriff's office were watching them. The white one, Cummings, was in his car at the corner of the marina parking lot. The other, the black cop Betters, was across the waterway on a houseboat moored at the private dock of a high-rise condominium.

"Like living in a fishbowl," Jack remarked after he spotted Betters watching them through binoculars.

"Mr. Bright should have fixed that chopper to ditch. That would have discouraged them." The Madman gulped diligently on his fourth beer.

"And brought an investigation down all around us," Phil said. He had ceased taking out the *Terra Time* each day as a ploy to keep one of the detectives occupied. "That Betters is a smart old cop. He caught on that my boat was just a diversion after the second day. Even if Cummings is a stubborn bastard, we're just not sure they haven't left some information around somewhere . . . just in case something happens to them."

"Jesus, Phil, that's so goddamned TV melodramatic. You've been watching too much *Miami Vice*," the Madman said, his hands gesturing toward the houseboat.

"Phil's right," Jack Fischer said, "and Amos agrees. We can't take any chances. That's why he just gave their helicopter a little problem. But I wonder how long those two are going to be satisfied just watching."

"Why don't the old guys and Amos just get into their heads and scramble their brains?" Mazuski chuckled.

"Because it's not their way," Jack responded. "But they'd better do something soon. The Finleys are due back soon, and I don't think Cummings will hold off again after they show up."

At that moment a blue Ford Taurus pulled into the parking lot and stopped in the spot next to Matthew Cummings's Olds Cutlass. The detective paid little attention to the driver of the new car as he got out, locked the door and then went to his trunk. Probably a boat owner, Cummings surmised by the man's casual nautical dress. Had he seen the similar car parking in the condo lot across the waterway, with a similar-looking, similarly dressed man getting out and approaching Coolridge Betters on the houseboat, he would have thought differently. He glanced away from the Taurus and refocused his attention on the fantail of the *Manta III*.

The next thing he knew the passenger door of his car was open and the nautical man was leaning in presenting his United States Treasury Department ID that identified his visitor as Secret Service Special Agent Benton Fuller. Across the Intercoastal at the same moment, Detective Betters was staring at a similar ID belonging to FBI Special Agent Gary McGill.

Cummings had chosen the "quiet" place where they could talk without attracting attention. He'd radioed over to Betters, who by that time had been briefed by McGill, to meet at Marty's Cozy Nest on Biscayne Boulevard in North Miami Beach. It was a twenty-four-hour strip club featuring teenage addicts and a steady clientele ranging from truck drivers to businessmen in suits to horny retirees.

Betters and McGill drove down to the club on US 1 while Cummings and Fuller took the Interstate, I-95, and arrived a good twenty minutes ahead of the others. Fuller was shocked at Cummings's choice of a meeting place.

"You call this quiet?"

"I say we can talk here undisturbed. I know the owner. He's a retired fruit and vegetable man from Philly." Without asking, Cummings walked to the rear of the dark, smoke-filled strip joint and settled into a booth. He gestured for Fuller to be seated across the blue marbleized Formica table. A tall, glassy-eyed, bleached-blonde girl with bare silicone-filled breasts, wearing nothing but a checkered apron and a sequined G-string, came over to the table.

"Hiya, Sergeant. I ain't seen you in a coon's age."

"How's it going, Midge?"

"It's goin' . . . it's comin'. Where's your buddy?"

"He'll be along. Get me a Coors. You want something?" he asked Fuller.

"Coke."

"In a glass or on a glass?" Fuller looked confused. Cummings laughed.

"He wants a Coca-Cola."

"Then he should say so," she muttered, doing an about-face so that her ample buttocks, still wet with perspiration from her performance on the runway, brushed against Benton Fuller. Cummings enjoyed the federal agent's discomfort. It was why he'd chosen to come to this place. Like many local Florida policemen he wasn't impressed with the federal law enforcement people. They were supposed to come into Florida to close down the drug traffic, but they kept their information and operations to themselves, placing little trust in local police departments. The feds' theory was that the drug kingpins had the local police on their payrolls. In many cases that was probably true, but it gave a bad name to all the police. The honest cops resented it. Deep down inside when Cummings had suspected the old men and Fischer were in the drug business, he dreamed about a major bust without the feds. Now that they had shown up he was certain he would lose the collar and they would take all the glory.

"Is there a telephone here?" Fuller asked.

"Next to the toilet."

"I've got to call someone to meet us. Does it have to be here?"

"This is safe. You wanted quiet and safe."

"He's a naval officer."

"Tell him to leave his sailor suit home."

Fuller got up and went to the phone. There were just a few customers in the club, and they were gathered at the bar that served a dual purpose as a dance runway for the strippers. As Fuller walked away, one of the girls, a dark Cuban named Carla, was doing her act on the runway. One of the other girls, also Cuban and named Marta, watched as Fuller got up from the table and walked toward the telephone at the very rear of the club. Marta got up from her stool at the bar and threw a questioning glance at Cummings. The cop smiled and gestured for Marta to follow the man. She did, thinking she was about to make a few extra dollars on a slow afternoon.

While Fuller was making his call, and, Cummings hoped, having difficulty with a Cuban hooker who wasn't used to taking no for an answer, the drinks arrived, as did Betters and McGill. Midge was setting the drinks down as the two men came into the club. She smiled a warm welcome at Betters.

"You want a bourbon?"

"Neat. Some branch water on the side. How about you, Gary?"

"Coca-cola. Ice."

"At least this one's local," Midge said, moving her act away toward the bar. Betters and McGill sat down opposite one another.

"Where's Fuller?" McGill asked.

"On the phone. He said he had to call a sailor."

Betters looked at his partner questioningly. On the ride down neither detective had learned exactly what was going down. All they had been told was that Jack Fischer, his friends and the old people were now under federal surveillance and that the federal government required the cooperation of the two Coral Gables cops.

There was a sudden ruckus from the rear, excited raised voices and the distinct sound of a man's voice saying, "Hey, back off." A moment later Marta came stomping past the booth, her bare breasts bouncing with each angry strut. She stopped across from the table and glared at Cummings.

"That ain't no John. That's a *maricone* . . . a fruit. He don't want no woman." She continued her angry march back to the bar, then disappeared behind the bar into the backstage dressing area. Benton Fuller returned to the table.

"Some trouble?" Cummings asked innocently. Betters fought to keep a straight face.

"Goddamned hooker tried to grab me back there. Right in the middle of a phone call."

"To Walkly?" McGill asked.

"Yeah. I told him to meet us here."

"And how to dress, I hope," Cummings interjected.

"Uh huh. He'll be up in forty minutes."

"Alone?"

"Of course."

Midge returned with the rest of the drinks. She placed them gently on the table. "Will that be all for y'all gentlemen?" she asked, now sporting a sweet Southern voice.

"Let me pay for this," Fuller offered, reaching into his pants pocket. Betters, who was sitting next to him, stopped him, but it was too late. "Holy shit!" the Secret Service agent exclaimed, "my money's gone!" Before he could do anything, Detective Cummings grabbed Midge's wrist.

"You move your ass on the double back there and tell Marta I want this man's money NOW!" He spun her with one swift movement and slapped her rear end hard.

"Not to worry, Mr. Fuller, your money will be back in a moment." It was.

Amos Bright came up through the galley of the *Manta III* and joined the three men as they watched the final rays of the sun disappear in the pink and blue cloud-streaked western sky.

"The cops left," Jack told him.

"I know. Our people from Washington are with them now."

"Does that mean they're out of the picture?" Phil Doyle asked.

"In a manner of speaking," Amos answered. "Let's

just say that the next time we see them it will be under new and different circumstances."

By the time Captain Walkly had arrived, dressed in jeans, a Grateful Dead T-shirt and torn dirty sneakers, Cummings and Betters had been filled in on most of the operation. It was big, bigger than they had imagined. The old people were "world-class" drug kingpins from Hong Kong. Jack and his friends were involved in the largest narcotic shipment the Federal Drug Enforcement Agency had ever tapped into. It was going down within the next week. From this point on the movements of the old people, Jack, his friends and the submarine operator would be monitored by the feds and the United States Navy. That was where Captain Walkly figured in the operation, which, they were told, was code-named Earthmother. He arrived in time to tell his part of the story.

"We were worried about you two," he began, after Midge had brought him a Coors Light and a round of drinks on the house for the others. She began to apologize for Marta again, but Betters told her to forget it and to get lost.

Walkly continued, "Because the key to the operation is that submarine attached to the bottom of the *Manta III.*" As he spoke he examined the photos of the probeship that Cummings and Betters had obtained. "To think that they might have seen the diver who shot these . . ."

"They didn't. He's the best," Cummings said proudly. He must be, Walkly thought to himself. Amos Bright hadn't picked him up telepathically.

"Well, in any case, from here on in we can't take any chances. You two will stay with us until the operation goes down. I've cleared that with your boss."

"I don't know about that—" Betters started to object.

"That's it!" Walkly was firm. "I've got several ships moving into the area—nearly eight hundred men, plus choppers with sea sleds and a nuclear submarine. Nothing is going to screw this up—nothing!" His manner was a little overbearing.

McGill spoke up. "Besides, we need you boys. You're familiar with both their boats and that chopper pilot of theirs."

"Mazuski," Cummings muttered. "He's a drunk and a menace."

"Well," Fuller said softly, "after we nail their asses the only thing he'll be flying is a steel prison cot." Walkly's eyes had drifted over to the runway where Midge was now performing. "Isn't that right, Captain?"

"Sure," Walkly answered, turning his attention back to the group huddled in the booth. "That's for damned sure. I need you two aboard the chase boats to make positive ID on that *Manta III* and the *Terra Time*. As a matter of fact, I want you men to make the arrests when the time comes."

"You mean that?" Cummings asked. Betters was wary.

"You guys were on to these rats five years ago, and they slipped out of it." Fuller sounded sincere. "We know how much heat you took for that mess. You guys deserve this part of the collar. We'll have our part of it too, as will the Navy."

"There's plenty to go around," Captain Walkly said as he watched Midge's pendulous breasts sway and slide to the music. "Plenty . . ."

CHAPTER EIGHTEEN

Everything appeared normal at the Lyndon B. Johnson Space Center, NASA's sprawling headquarters and training facility thirty miles southeast of downtown Houston, Texas. Since the terrible accident that destroyed the space shuttle *Challenger* shortly after takeoff, and with it the lives of seven heroic American astronauts, NASA had fought a long hard struggle to regain the confidence and support of Americans in their space program. This had been done, and the Johnson Center was now a beehive of activity. It was not uncommon for two or three missions to be in various stages of preparation at one time. The launch schedule of shuttles alone had reached more than one per month.

There had always been a space medicine center in Houston. In the mid-1980s a specialized facility had been opened in San Antonio, Texas, with the specific mission of applying the knowledge and experience gained in space medicine to benefit more Earthbound humans.

Then, as America prepared to begin manned flights to planets within our solar system, the Johnson Space Medicine Facility was reactivated and expanded. It was in the recently renovated hospital wing of Building 11 that Dr. Kahwaji had set up his now burgeoning facility designed to accommodate the expectant parents of the Geriatric Brigade.

Approximately five days before their extraterrestrial guests were scheduled to arrive, the chaos that the twenty-one doctors representing seven specialties—

eighteen engineers of various talents, twelve chemists, ten physicists and scores of support people, ranging from hard-hat sheet-metal and foundry laborers to surgical pediatric nurses—could cause as they interacted suddenly calmed.

Mary and Ben Green, who had arrived a few days before, met with the entire staff in a secure auditorium next to Mission Control. They were the first actual "aliens" the staff had seen. Everyone was curious. Many of the top scientists and doctors who had been wooed by Dr. Kahwaji, Dr. Yee and the President had serious doubts that this operation was what they had been told. Some were convinced there were military reasons for their work. For others the details of Operation Earthmother seemed too fantastic to be true. There were also grumblings of covert political activities being the real reason for the secrecy and security surrounding the project. This undercurrent became acute when four atmospheric temperature-controlled chambers were ordered on a crash basis. Overnight several new engineers, chemists and physicists arrived, taking over most of the second- and third-floor areas that had previously been set aside for staff living quarters. No one was told what their mission was, and so the rumors flew.

But now they all understood. This was real. As they listened to the Greens talk, the entire group sensed they were about to become an extremely privileged group of humans.

"It was a natural thought, and many of us, scattered across this and other galaxies, had it simultaneously. When we learned that birth on motherplanet was an important part of the universal unwritten laws, we experienced a closeness, a oneness with life out there as we had never felt before. Mary and I are here as witness to the great news. We are not alone in this universe. We are all part of something wondrous, something alive and ongoing." Ben Green had captured the audience's attention. Not one person stirred; they hardly breathed.

"This is our motherplanet," Mary continued. "And we are coming home to have our young. You have all done a magnificent job. Some months ago, as we all gathered on Antares awaiting the watership, some of us had serious doubts about how much help we might get upon our return.

"It was the Antarean leader, Amos Bright, who settled our doubts. He pointed out that we, the Geriatric Brigade, had responded and aided his race without reservation on their last voyage to Earth. He saw no reason why our fellow human beings would not respond in kind and aid us. He was correct. Unfortunately you will not meet him on this voyage, as he is tasked with the responsibility of returning the cocoons to their Antarean home."

"That which you have done and will do," Ben said, "in the weeks and months ahead, will be recorded as one of humanity's finest moments. You are hosts to the first visitors from deep space. We are deeply grateful to all of you and we bless you."

They both then telepathed to all the other commanders, who in turn singly and collectively reached out to each individual in the audience with thanks. The resultant swell of goodwill and love passed from the commanders to the expectant parents aboard the watership and beyond, throughout the universe, to all the other members of the Geriatric Brigade.

And then it was time to get back to work with new purpose.

The overall plan for the facility was the cooperative brainchild of Dr. Kahwaji and the eccentric Sino-American obstetrician-pediatrician Dr. Michelangelo Yee. Dr. Yee, whose seventy-six-year-old arthritic hands were no longer able to perform the delicate fetal surgery he had pioneered, was still the incontestable leader in the exciting new field. He was, as Dr.

Kahwaji stated, "beyond the leading edge. Yee is even far beyond the twilight zone of fetal medicine."

The facility for Operation Earthmother was three stories high. Each floor could be sealed off, and sections on each floor could also be isolated by impenetrable plastic shielding. It contained the most up-to-date medical and environmental technology available.

Everything was designed and centered around the moment of birth. The top floor contained examination rooms, including ultrasonic machines and amniocentesis facilities. Dominating the floor were the operating-delivery rooms. They were built in groups of three in the center of which was a pediatric intensive care unit capable of servicing nine infants at a time. Three state-of-the-art incubators, complete with life-support systems and isolation chambers, were available in each pediatric intensive care room. At the moment of delivery the obstetricians would pass the infant immediately into intensive care, where it would be assigned a complete medical team. This would free the staff in the delivery room to care for the mother. Attached to the obstetric staff was a geriatrician. On the surgical floor there was also an adult intensive care unit with a dozen beds and a complete staff. As it turned out, there was no need for this facility.

The infant would remain in intensive care for four hours while it was tested. Blood and other fluid workups would be completed in laboratories attached to the unit. It was possible for some blood tests to be done in less than three minutes. Chromosome evaluations would also begin. If there were no apparent problems, the infant would then be moved to a transitional nursery, where, assuming there were no complications with the mother, the newborn would be joined by its parents. There were three complete units with this configuration on the top floor.

At the south end of the floor the engineers had broken through to the floor below. They had constructed four atmospheric chambers, each divided in half, much like a duplex apartment. The top portion of the chamber would be prepared to accept the newborn from each of the four mixed matings. The lower portion of the chamber would serve as housing for the expectant fathers.

If the newborn had dominant characteristics of the father, it would be immediately transferred, along with its own pediatric team, to the chamber. The chambers also had breathing apparatus and protective suits for the medical teams. Data regarding gaseous mixtures, temperature, pressure and humidity for the chambers had been supplied by Beam from the watership. But the engineers and scientists knew that they had to be prepared to turn and adjust these environments once the off-planet father arrived. The crucial adjustments would have to be made for the newborn if it was unable to survive under normal Earth conditions. Once the infant was born, the doctors and scientists would have but moments to analyze the situation before they made the decision to move the infant, or so they thought.

The second, or middle floor, contained the lower portion of the duplex chambers at one end. Then there were four completely staffed nurseries with a capacity to care for fifty babies. An additional pediatric intensive care unit and several laboratories were on this floor as well, just in case an emergency arose in the regular nurseries. The rest of the floor was devoted to examination rooms and housing for the parents.

The lower, first floor contained staff living quarters, the kitchen, housing for security people and a special apartment set aside for the President, complete with the communication equipment required to run the country should he decide to make an extended visit.

The top floor was painted green, the second floor blue and the bottom floor yellow. The plastic sealers, hidden in the walls and controlled by the chief of security, a Secret Service agent assigned by Benton Fuller, were bright red.

There was one other facility tucked away in the basement of the large hospital wing. Everyone prayed it would never be used. It was the pathology làb.

CHAPTER NINETEEN

They gathered in from Houston, Miami, Roscoe and Washington. Operation Earthmother's first phase was drawing to a close, perhaps more to a climax, that would bring the watership safely undetected to Earth, and the expectant parents to their special facility at the Johnson Space Center.

The meeting was scheduled to take place at the Omega Conference Center eleven floors belowground at the huge five-sided edifice of American military power, the Pentagon. This top-secret conference and command facility had been originally constructed after the Cuban missile crisis during the administration of John F. Kennedy. It was initially planned as a nerve center and communication switching complex for the President's military staff and political advisors who might remain in the nation's capital after a nuclear attack. As time passed, many Secretaries of Defense paraded through the Pentagon, coming and going with administrations, often fading rapidly when their military adventures failed. However, each secretary became enthralled with the Omega Center concept, many of them thinking that perhaps in the event of nuclear war they might be the one high-ranking official remaining to lead the country to victory. And so each somehow managed to appropriate funds to update and improve the center until it now boasted more computer and communication capability than the fabled War Room deep underground at SAC headquarters in Omaha, Nebraska.

Phillip Margolin and Alicia Sanchez had arrived

the day before yesterday and, along with Martin
LoCasio and Oscar Berlin, their two NASA staffers,
they had spent their time setting up the presentation
they would make in the Omega Center to the other
members of the Operation Earthmother group.

The hot, humid early June morning was a harbinger
of the Washington, D.C. summer that would officially
arrive in a few weeks. It was fast approaching that
time when the nation's capital emptied of government
functionaries, bureaucrats, legislators and administration staffers and filled proportionately with tourists
from the four corners of America who came to
observe the seat of their national government firsthand. All they found were monuments, cool empty
marble halls, a plethora of statuary ranging from the
great to the pitifully insignificant, expensive muse-
ums, enormous buildings stuffed with mountains of
paper—the flotsam and jetsam of bureaucracy tuned
to a fine art—and of course the brutal heat and
humidity, the hallmark of a Potomac Basin summer.

Alma and Joe Finley settled back in the limousine
that Secretary Mersky had sent to bring them to the
Pentagon. The traffic across the Key Bridge, stretching
from the massive Lincoln Monument to the entrance
to Arlington National Cemetery, flowed equally, in-
ward toward Washington and outward to Virginia.
Above the bridge, high on a bluff in the cemetery, the
monument, grave and eternal flame of the slain John
F. Kennedy was visible to the elderly couple.

"How long ago did we visit Kennedy's grave?"
Alma mused.

"It was 1970 . . . no '71."

"I'm still so sad about that. It was a terrible time."
She leaned back into the soft seat and found Joe's arm
waiting there for her.

"I suppose we wanted . . . expected so much from
him."

"It was a magic time," she said, rubbing her cheek
against his caressing hand.

"Camelot." He looked at her. "I love you, Alma, but I can't do it. Not yet anyway."

After dinner with Caleb Harris, Alma and Joe had returned to her hotel. They stopped for a nightcap in the oak-paneled bar of the Mayflower Hotel, and the conversation quickly came around to Mary Green's pregnancy. They'd been up talking for most of the night after that.

All the commanders knew about it. Alma wanted a baby, the baby she'd never had. She had spent her young life building her career, with no time for marriage or children. Joe had been her first marriage. It was his second. Somewhere he had an ex-wife and two daughters who'd been alienated from him decades ago. His experience with children was distasteful. They had talked about it, but Joe remained noncommittal. Until now.

"Do you want to tell me why?" she asked, leaving her cheek against his now immobile hand.

"I'm not sure I can. It goes deep. It was two lifetimes ago. There are emotions I thought I'd never have to confront again. Darling, I'm sorry. The idea of children, or being able to have children . . . now I mean, I'm just not sure I want it."

"But I do. I want it so very much, Joe."

"I know. I have to ask you to wait. Please. We have time. Perhaps forever. There's so much to do. And there are things we don't know."

"You mean why Bess miscarried?"

"Yes. It may have something to do with our being commanders. We just don't know. I want to be sure. I don't want you to be hurt the way Bess was." She took his hand in hers.

"Does that mean you want to have children someday?"

"If we can. If they will be . . . normal, then yes. With you, for you, yes." He kissed her hand and then her lips as the limousine exited the parkway and headed toward the Pentagon.

Mary, Ben and Dr. Kahwaji landed at Dulles International Airport at nine that morning. They were met by two other limousines, one from the Department of Defense with instructions to take the Greens directly to the Pentagon, and the other the Undersecretary's private car that would first take him to his office at the newly revamped Department of Public Health and Welfare, and then across to Virginia and the meeting in the Omega room. Since he'd been in Houston for the better part of three weeks, he had a desk piled high with documents that required his attention.

They parted company. As Mary and Ben began their journey to the Pentagon they reached out to communicate with Alma and Joe, but found their fellow commanders were blocking.

"They are near," Ben commented.

"We'll see them soon," Mary answered. She was tired and a little nauseous. She closed her eyes and breathed deeply.

"You okay, honey?" Ben asked, putting his cool hand on her slightly damp forehead.

"Just the old A.M. ills. You'd think that with all that physical processing I had morning sickness would have been eradicated."

Ben laughed. "I guess the Antareans never have that problem. There's not much nausea from a petri dish."

"Very funny," she answered, smiling weakly. "I'm not sure that isn't a bigoted remark." With that she transferred some of her discomfort to Ben, who became suddenly queasy.

"Thanks," he responded, "you're all heart, mother." Mary then cut off the discomfort, satisfied she had distracted him sufficiently. She had wanted to change the subject because when they had tried to contact the Finleys moments before and found them blocked, Mary had sensed something underneath Alma's block, something private. Something she understood. Fear. The very fear that Mary, who was also a commander, had about the baby growing inside of her. A baby being born to commanders. Would it be a baby like Bess Perlman's? They now knew that three healthy babies had been born aboard the watership. But their parents had not been commanders.

"What is it?" Ben looked at his wife, feeling her block.

"Just a private woman's moment."

"Oh. Well, why don't you lie back and take a nap? We've got another thirty minutes before we're there."

Amos had left Jack Fischer to watch over the Antarean probeship, since a Navy or police presence might be cause for suspicion. Jack would sleep aboard the *Manta III;* and now that Detectives Cummings and Betters had been removed from their surveillance, Phil Doyle brought the *Terra Time* down to Boca Raton, mooring it alongside the *Manta III,* thus affording even more protection to the submerged probeship. Only the old Greek aboard the fuel barge now watched these comings and goings with any interest. No one suspected he was aware of the probeship's existence.

The Navy Skyhawk Raider, piloted by Captain Thomas Walkly, banked for final approach into the small Naval air station at Annapolis. They came in low from the north over Chesapeake Bay. Amos Bright thoroughly enjoyed the ride.

"You'd make an excellent probeship pilot, Captain," Amos remarked as they skimmed above the marshes and wetlands.

"Thank you, sir," Walkly answered. "I'd sure like to take a crack at that aircraft of yours someday." He touched down gently on the blacktop runway.

"Just get older, Captain Walkly, and we'll see what we can arrange." A few moments later Amos and the Navy Undersecretary were in a Navy jet helicopter on their way to the Pentagon.

The President had come to the Pentagon earlier that

morning, ostensibly to be briefed on the new DOD weapons procurement budget. That is what the White House press corps had been told. It aroused little interest. In fact there had been little press interest in the activities of the people in the Earthmother group. The only close call had come when Sam Bixby, a veteran White House reporter for the Gannett Newspapers, had seen Alma Finley enter the White House press entrance with Caleb Harris. He'd come over to say hello to Alma, whom he remembered from her days as a news editor in New York. She was much older than Sam, a pleasant aging woman, he recalled, with a nice word for everyone.

But when he saw her she somehow appeared younger and quite beautiful. He'd said hello. She'd been cordial. When he was about to ask her what she was doing in the White House, Caleb Harris, who was not on Bixby's A-list, whisked Alma away with a weak explanation that "they were late for an appointment." Bixby's curiosity had been tweaked and he followed the couple, expecting them to exit the White House and leave the grounds. Instead, after they left the press area, they doubled back through the East Wing entrance, where they seemed to be expected. That entrance was used for guests and visitors to the Oval Office. Sam Bixby made a mental note to find out who Alma worked for these days, although he had the distinct impression that she had married someone in Boston and retired to Florida several years ago. His efforts were to prove fruitless.

After a perfunctory budget meeting in Defense Secretary Mersky's office, the staff was dismissed with the exception of Phillip Margolin. The President, the Secretary and Margolin then took a private elevator, an addition to the Omega Center by the previous secretary, fourteen floors directly down to the main conference room, where Alicia Sanchez and her two assistants were putting the finishing touches on their presentation.

Everyone arrived within ten minutes of each other. The last to arrive, Amos Bright and Captain Walkly, were delayed by heavy air traffic from nearby National Airport before they were finally cleared to descend into the heliport at the Pentagon. Up to the last minute the President and Secretary Mersky argued, as only old friends in those positions could, about whether or not to bring the Secretary of State into Operation Earthmother on the basis that unlike the Finleys and the Greens, Amos Bright was an emissary from another planet. He was in fact the first alien so far as they knew to be officially greeted by a government.

Gideon Mersky stubbornly argued against involving the State Department. "They'll fuss and flutter about with all that time-wasting, ineffective diplomatic crap. Meanwhile we've got a spaceship to land and a mess of pregnant octogenarians to handle." He was adamant. The President eventually bent to his point of view but withheld any final resolution of the correct protocol until the Geriatric Brigade was safely settled in at the Johnson Space Center Hospital.

As Amos and Captain Walkly descended in the main elevator, Ben Green spoke to the President.

"Amos Bright is on his way down, Mr. President." Press Secretary Margo McNeil and the assigned Secret Service agent moved ahead of President Malcolm Teller to the Omega Center's doorway. Margo had a 35mm Nikon camera with her to record the historic event. The door opened. Captain Walkly preceded Amos Bright into the room. After acknowledging the President he immediately stepped aside. Amos Bright then entered the room. The Antarean commander, a powerful and revered member of his own race, stood face to face with the President of the United States of America. Malcolm Teller stepped forward and extended his hand in greeting. Then, in an extraordinary moment, Amos Bright peeled back the protective humanlike skin covering his own hand, revealing the

Antarean's fragile opaque flesh and four tapered fingers. He extended his now exposed Antarean hand in greeting to the President, who gently took it in his own. The warmth, wisdom, honesty and genuine respect that flowed from Amos to President Teller was something the President would never forget. The others in the room sensed the importance of the moment. Margo McNeil was so enthralled she barely remembered to take the picture of the historic occasion and did so only after Amos Bright telepathically gave her permission.

He was then introduced to Secretary Mersky, Dr. Kahwaji, Caleb Harris, who had come over earlier that morning alone, Margo McNeil and the Margolin –Sanchez–LoCasio–Berlin team. They all then gathered to hear reports on the progress of Operation Earthmother.

Everything in Florida was secure. Benton Fuller and Gary McGill had Cummings and Betters in tow and were making the final security arrangements with trusted naval officers under Captain Walkly's special command. The transport from the watership to Houston, in the stages previously agreed to, was in place. They were prepared for any contingency. In addition, the captain proudly reported, a highly trained Navy Seal team had been brought in two days ago. Under the guidance and with the complete agreement of Amos Bright they had inspected the cocoon chambers. They had then plotted and inspected the underwater route that would be used in transporting the cocoons from the Stones to the parked watership. The Seal team, along with Jack Fischer, Phil Doyle, Madman Mazuski and the eleven Antareans aboard the watership supervised by Amos Bright would move the cocoons and load them for space travel. The estimate now, given good weather and a minimum of ship traffic in the area, was that the entire operation would take no more than two weeks, seventeen days at the outside.

"We toyed with bringing in a submersible like the *Alvin* that could handle up to twenty more cocoons per day. It could speed things up a bit," Captain Walkly concluded, "but that would mean also involving more personnel, vessels and equipment. At this point we feel we have an adequate, secure manageable, well-trained and enthusiastic group necessary to aid Mr. Bright in accomplishing his mission." The President thanked the captain, making a mental note to propose him for his admiralcy soon.

Dr. Kahwaji spoke next, outlining how far they had progressed with staffing and outfitting their wing of the Johnson Center's Space Medicine Hospital. He circulated five copies of a specially prepared briefing booklet that contained floor plans, photographs of the four duplex chambers and résumés of all the key staff now housed and secreted inside the secure hospital wing.

A team of medical specialists, along with state-of-the-art incubators complete with life-support systems, were being airlifted to Florida. "They will be there to meet the watership with us, Mr. President, and escort our visitors back to Houston," Dr. Kahwaji concluded.

A few moments were spent by the Secret Service agent discussing security for the President's apartment on the first floor of the hospital. He requested that Benton Fuller be allowed to inspect the facility before the President visited it.

Mary and Ben Green then communicated their own confidence in the facility and staff and praised Dr. Kahwaji and Dr. Yee for their marvelous work.

All eyes then turned to Phillip Margolin and Alicia Sanchez. The group had been informed that a viable plan, approved by Joe Finley and Amos Bright, had been devised at the Roscoe think tank. Everyone eagerly awaited the presentation that would show them how an alien spacecraft the size of the watership could be brought down from the moon to the targeted

South Florida waters and submerge there undetected by a world bristling with satellite and earthbound detection devices. The moment Defense Secretary Gideon Mersky saw they intended to employ and deploy SSP, the top-secret Solar Screen Program, he was on his feet protesting in the strongest terms.

"Mr. President, I am appalled." He turned to Margolin. "How dare you bring this material, this program to this meeting? Never. We cannot do this. Mr. President, I insist that Mr. Margolin's presentation cease immediately." Alicia Sanchez exchanged inquisitive looks with Phillip Margolin, both recalling their directive from the Defense Secretary some weeks ago. Had they misunderstood? Before the President could respond, Margolin confronted his boss.

"Excuse me, sir," he began politely, his voice controlled yet as forceful as Mersky's, "but our Earthmother directive, your directive, never excepted any programs, systems or facilities either operational or under development. SSP comes under that umbrella. I don't see where we've done anything improper."

"Idiocy," Mersky continued, addressing President Teller. "These 'yuppies' would have us compromise THE most secret project our military possesses. I'd resign sooner than reveal its existence to our enemies."

The Solar Screen Program—SSP—had been one of those far-fetched ideas that had been the brainchild of some long forgotten scientist back in the early days of the ill-fated Space Lab program. The basic theoretical idea was to develop a plastic, a plasticized metal or an ultrathin metal alloy that might be deployed in space to act as a shield against solar particle bombardment or even against meteors or other space debris that might someday endanger a space station. It was one of those innocuous items that just slipped along unnoticed into budget after budget. Then six years ago two NASA chemists, one involved in ozone layer studies and the other in development of specialized polymers, came upon the previously gathered data and theoretical work on SSP. Quietly they made rapid quantum leaps and finally in a breakthrough created a new technology, which they called vacuum deployment. Concurrently they developed a high-tensile, seamless polymer material that could be manufactured by combining chemical materials on site in the freezing temperature and total vacuum of space. There was theoretically no limit to the size and scope of the material. All that was required was the proper amounts of raw materials and a curious multinozzled spray machine that resembled the web-weaving organs of certain South American spiders.

Margolin and Sanchez proposed to use the technology and deploy two polymer shieldings of several square miles, high above the earth, in a configuration angled to mask the movement of the watership from the moon to South Florida.

"It's the only way we have to shield the watership's approach and landing," Dr. Sanchez maintained.

"It's out of the question," Mersky cut in, "if the Russians . . . if even our allies see we have this capability, it will scare the pants off them."

"And," President Teller responded, "if those same people saw a spacecraft enter our atmosphere and land in United States territory, that wouldn't scare them?"

"We have to find another way." Secretary Mersky was adamant.

"Sir, with all due respect, there is no other way!" Margolin stated firmly.

"And if I might be permitted to add," Amos Bright said softly, "there isn't much time either."

As the others watched, the President silently reached his decision to accept the plan and proceed.

More out of curiosity than concern, Alma Finley tried to reach into Mersky's mind to track his thought processes as he sensed rejection. She discovered herself blocked—completely blocked. Somehow Mersky was learning the commander's abilities. He would bear watching. Afraid that he might be able to intercept her own telepathy, she kept the discovery to herself, deciding to communicate to the other commanders when they were alone.

The matter was then closed to discussion. The President's decision was that a space shuttle would be readied immediately. There were three standing by now that could handle the mission. The announcement of the SSP test would be made at a presidential press conference to be called as soon as the watership was safely tucked behind the moon ready to descend to Earth. All he would say is that a new polymer solar screening device was going to be deployed by the shuttle science crew. It would be in two stages. The first screen would be deployed at an altitude of five hundred thirty-one miles and cover an area of sixteen square miles of space.

The second screen, thinner and thirty times larger, would be deployed at an altitude of two hundred fifty-nine miles. The screen's purpose would be announced as an ongoing program to protect the Earth's delicate ozone layer, which many believed was decaying from our extensive use of fluorocarbons, and thus protect the Earth from the invasion of harmful radio and ultraviolet waves produced by solar activity.

Any astute military planner, or for that matter any knowledgeable reporter, would immediately see the potential of those screens as they deployed out over hundreds of square miles of space. Although their stated purpose might make all the sense in the world, it would be obvious they could also be used as a radar and satellite detection shield as well as a deflector of ground- and aircraft-based radar. They could make satellite-launched missiles obsolete. Perhaps all other missiles as well.

The President complimented Margolin and Sanchez on their work. Before he adjourned the meeting, as long as Amos Bright concurred, he gave the final "go" for Operation Earthmother to proceed to landing. Amos Bright was delighted. After a phone call Dr. Sanchez confirmed that the shuttle *Remembrance* would be ready to launch and deploy the SSP in five days.

June 12, 3:15 A.M. was set as the watership landing date and time. Being on the water at night would add to the difficulty of the landing, but it was time to bring the expectant mothers and fathers and newborn babies home.

CHAPTER TWENTY

They crossed the Martian orbit on schedule. The Parman guides disengaged and the ion accelerator took over. The Antarean flight crew plotted their final approach to Earth, keeping the unusual silhouette of the watership blocked by the Earth's moon. They decelerated. Those who had been anatomically suspended, namely the Antarean cocoon recovery team and the four nonhuman parents, were awakened, processed and fed. Their organs were reactivated to normal function; their muscle tone was brought back to standard.

Panatoy joined Ruth in her cabin. They had not seen one another for nearly two months. They greeted and touched, embracing one another tenderly. Ruth's pregnancy, now in its seventh month, was a source of great joy to the tall blue Subax. He stroked her firm, distended belly. A broad, proud smile froze on his blue face. He kissed his mate, as she had taught him, and she in turn stroked the pale bare spot on the base of his spine in an erotic circular motion as he had taught her. His body was becoming alarmingly warm. It was time for Panatoy to return to the room next to Ruth's that had been adjusted to Subax atmospheric conditions. They parted physically but were able to see one another and communicate. On their next visit Ruth Charnofsky would go into his room, where she could, with protective clothing and breathing apparatus, spend more time.

The three other mixed couples were also having their long awaited reunions.

The female of the first couple was a human woman named Karen Morano from Mill Valley, California, who had been a widow and the cousin of a couple who lived at the Antares complex in Coral Gables. She happened to be visiting Florida when the Geriatric Brigade was formed. She and her cousins chose to join then and there, leaving their homes and worldly possessions behind. She had no family other than her Florida relatives. Her mate was called Tom. Tommachkikla, to be exact, but Tom it now was. He was a short, squat, powerfully built man, quite hand-some with a rugged bearded face. His planet, Destero, was in the Axian system near the star we call Castor. Its atmosphere is oxygen rich. Its gravity three times that of Earth. The average temperature on the giant planet, in the northern hemisphere where he lived, was 100 degrees Fahrenheit. Tom was a farmer whose spread had been in a place quite similar to the Australian outback—open, vast, deserted and lonely. He'd met Karen at the annual gathering on Destero when the Antareans arrived with their cargoships bringing off-planet goods to trade for the protein-rich Destero crops.

The next couple had to meet in a special chamber that the Antareans had hastily prepared. The female was from Wilmington, North Carolina. Her name was Ellie-Mae Boyd. Her involvement with the Geriatric Brigade came quite by accident. She had been a nurse for most of her life. She married and had six children. Her husband died in the Korean War and she raised the children herself. Ellie-Mae was a black woman. Her husband had been white. They had lived in common law because of the miscegenation laws in North Carolina. Her children all moved north with the exception of a daughter who had also become a nurse and worked in Florida. That daughter brought her aging mother to live with her, and to keep busy Ellie-Mae had taken a part-time job in a nursing home near Coral Gables. It was from that home that several of the Geriatric Brigade members were recruited, among them Betty, Bess Perlman's sister. Ellie-Mae had been the only person at the home who had been kind to Betty, who was the victim of a severe stroke. After Betty had been processed by the Antareans she found Ellie-Mae and invited her to join in the adventure. Although she was reluctant to leave her daughter, Ellie-Mae chose to join Betty and the others.

Ellie's mate was a doctor, a native of Betch, the sister planet to Hillet in the Alphard system near the star we call Hydra. In fact, Andrea and Frank Hankinson's friends, the Messinas and the Erhardts, both of whom had given birth aboard the watership, had conceived their babies on Hillet. The inhabitants of Hillet and Betch shared a common heritage and racial background. Betch, which is a seasonal water planet, supports a controlled humanoid population. At first glance, Ellie's mate, Doctor Manterid, might be mistaken for an American Indian or Eskimo. But closer examination would reveal pigmentation capable of rapid chameleonlike change, a genetic adaptation dating far back to the very origins of his species. His eyes were set wider apart than human, nearly reaching to the side of his oval, weathered face. His hair was jet black, coarse and braided. His mouth was also wide, with teeth set in two rows that interlocked and had been developed to make efficient use of the high cellulose vegetation upon which the people of Betch, called the Hillet, lived. On the nearby planet Hillet, which was colonized millennia ago, the people called themselves Hilletoros and were fiercely nationalistic about their planet and hard-won independence from Betch.

Dr. Manterid was a chemist. His atmosphere contained hardly any oxygen; it was nearly pure nitrogen. Earth atmosphere, which he barely tolerated, made him lightheaded. In order to spend time with Ellie-

Mae, he put up with the discomfort for as long as possible. Their room had been designed so that after an hour in her atmosphere, nitrogen was pumped in and the temperature dropped to frigid numbers. Within fifteen minutes, which were uncomfortable for Ellie-Mae, he was recovered. This way he could be close to his mate, whom he insisted on calling *wife*. It was a human word that he'd learned was important to Ellie-Mae. He had also questioned Commander Hankinson regarding Earth customs when he had decided to mate with Ellie-Mae. The concept of marriage was known on Betch. When the Doctor discovered that Ellie-Mae had not ever been legally married, he insisted on a full-blown wedding, Earth style. One of the Brigade, a retired Reform rabbi from Buffalo, performed the nuptials, which were a mixture of whatever Baptist ceremony Ellie-Mae remembered, a little Judaism, a sprinkling of Parman philosophy and some Antarean words to bless the Master's wisdom in this unique joining.

They were married. They were mated. They were deeply in love and, as the watership approached the moon, they were once again joined in a loving embrace.

The last of the mixed matings consisted of a human male and an off-planet female. He was Peter Martindale, a retired steelworker and union organizer from Ashland, Kentucky. Peter was eighty-six years old when his friend Paul Amato, a resident of the Antares condo, brought him into the fold. Paul knew Martindale from their common union connection to the National Board of the AFofL-CIO. Peter was a handsome man who'd kept himself in good shape. But before he'd been processed for space travel with the Antareans he was dying of lung cancer. The processing restored him to perfect health.

After his two years on Parma Quad 2 he chose to travel with an Antarean cargoship that was making a sweep of the Primary Quad in our galaxy. Their first planetfall was Turmoline, the fifth planet in the Spica star system in the constellation we call Virgo. The trip had been brief, less than a month, but during that time Peter Martindale concluded that space travel was not his primary interest. He found life aboard the cargoship boring, although he enjoyed the company of the small Antarean and human crew. On Turmoline, a lush water planet inhabited by a race of meat-eating humanoid hunters resembling humans very closely but living at a fairly primitive level as compared to Antares, Peter met Tern, a young female who served as planet liaison at the Antarean cargo port facility. He fell in love with the beautiful female. By custom he asked her tribal leaders permission for her to be his mate. They consented, which meant he had to work one Turmoline year in the service of the tribe before Tern was his.

Martindale's skill as a steelworker came in handy. On Earth he had been a melter, the man responsible for operating the huge electric arc furnaces that made specialized alloy steel. It was his job to bring the furnace, initially loaded with scrap metal, to the temperature required. When the metal was molten and red hot, he supervised the addition of other elements such as zinc, nickel and titanium in order to produce the alloy steel required. It was a highly skilled job with great responsibility. One mistake might ruin an entire furnace of molten steel. During his year of labor for Tern's hand, he built a small blast furnace and taught the tribe, the Penditan, to make hunting weapons superior to those they now used. Before doing this he had to ask permission of the Antarean envoy to Turmoline, since the improvement might be considered tampering with the normal development of a planetary population. The furnace was approved, because the Penditan already smelted metal and were sophisticated hunters on a planet that abounded in game and other fierce predators. It was also a fact that Turmoline skins and furs traded to the Antareans were coveted by many who populated other less bountiful planets.

After his year of servitude, Peter Martindale and Tern were mated. They lived together in Turmoline for more than a year after that and then traveled to Antares on a cargoship so that Peter might visit with Marie and Paul Amato, who were then living on Antares. It was on that journey that Tern became pregnant. When they arrived on Antares the other pregnant humans were gathering. Tern had the choice of going back to homeplanet to have her baby, staying on Antares or going to Earth with the others. She chose Earth, stating that her child was a mixed baby, and that her inner spirit voice, a feeling of deep religious significance to the Penditan, told her to take her baby to Earth to be born. "He is the seed of a new race," she told her mate, "but he must begin his life with the other babies of his father's kind." And so they joined the passengers on the watership, much to Peter Martindale's delight.

While the mixed couples had their reunions and the Antarean flight crew guided the watership to the moon's hidden side, the remainder of the returning Brigade met to discuss how to deal with the families some of them had left behind on Earth. They had received a preliminary report from Mary Green regarding her visit to her daughter in Scarsdale. The idea of her rejoining the family and their acceptance of her exceptional new life seemed to be a positive sign. But the fact that she hesitated to reveal her pregnancy weighed heavily on the others' minds now. Of the forty-two returning couples, nineteen had family on Earth. Jack Fischer had visited each family, bringing the news of their parents' and grandparents' journey into space as well as personal letters left behind by the travelers. He had assured them of the goodness of the Antareans and that the decision made by their loved ones was a free and rational choice. But of course there was no mention of return, much less pregnancy. The families had accepted their loss graciously and had each promised to keep the secret.

Now the group, along with the commanders aboard, wrestled with the problem. To contact their families —when and how. Was it fair, after saying good-bye in such a strange, abrupt manner, to rekindle those relationships? And what of grandchildren who had been without grandparents for five years? And how would sons and daughters in their forties and fifties take having newborn brothers and sisters? Emotions ran high, but in the end cooler heads prevailed. Bernie and Rose Lewis said it best.

"This has all happened very fast. There was a time when five years, the time we have been away, seemed forever. But now we have been out among the stars, we have sampled other worlds, other beings, and we have come to gather much wisdom. Now we return because something else has happened. Something new. Something that is common on Earth—birth, and something that is unheard of on Earth—birth from parents our age. There are many who would attach religious significance to this event. Many who would, because of their narrow point of view, look upon our return as some cosmic confirmation that the Earth stands at the center of the universe, when we know how primitive and parochial that thought really is. We are here to bear our young. That is the way of the universe we now have come to know. It is best that we go about our business first, that we have our babies, that we bring them into life with health and love, and that we are firm in our plans for their future. When that is done, then it will be time for each of us to decide what is to be told, or not told, to those whom we love and left behind those five years ago."

They had the word of the President that he would

arrange transport for their families to Houston whenever it was requested. Everyone agreed. Family contact would wait.

The conference room viewing portal was opened. Ahead, looming majestically, was the moon. Just beyond a blue dot was dipping below the horizon. It was the Earth. It was homeplanet.

CHAPTER TWENTY-ONE

Manta III bobbed about like a cork on the rough seas. It was nearly two A.M. and the wind had shifted from east to northeast, a harbinger of bad weather. Nearby, about one hundred yards off the starboard, *Terra Time*'s running lights were intermittently visible as it too was tossed in the ever increasing swells. Beyond the two sport-fishing boats, whose position was directly over the six-hundred-foot wreck, the rest of Captain Walkly's Operation Earthmother fleet waited in the ink-black night.

That morning, while Jack Fischer and Phil Doyle prepared for their part of the mission, President Teller spoke to the nation on the three TV networks. He announced that as he spoke the previously unscheduled launch of the space shuttle *Remembrance* was taking place. He then proceeded to outline the test of the Solar Screen Program, the SSP, that was to be made that very night along the eastern seaboard of the United States. He was questioned by the press as to why the test had not been announced and why it was being conducted now. The President stated that newly gathered data revealed considerable upcoming sunspot activity as well as a dangerous thinning of parts of the ozone layer. He also suggested that the moon was entering a waning phase and the sky would be darkest, enabling the NASA test instruments to study the highly reflective surface of the screens as they deployed. The program was of such a top-secret nature that no one in the press knew what questions to ask, and by the time they had conferred with their editors and science experts, the President had left Washington, ostensibly to observe the screen deployment from a naval vessel at sea.

Remembrance, one of the third generation of shuttles built after the *Challenger* disaster, had a flawless lift-off from the recently completed spaceport launch center at Vandenberg AFB in California. Previously the top-secret Air Force base had been used for military missile launches only, but since America had signed the treaty declaring space a nuclear-weapon-free zone, the money for the development of those weapons was put into a stepped-up shuttle and space station program.

The shuttle achieved its required orbit an hour later and one of the science teams aboard began their EVA, extravehicular activity, outside the craft as they prepared the delicate complex SSP deployment equipment. Inside the craft, the second science team began the intricate process of preparing the various chemicals that would eventually form the polymer screen in the vacuum of space.

The President's party, which included Margo McNeil, Secretary Mersky, Alicia Sanchez and Phillip Margolin, had left Washington aboard Air Force One, the President's plane, and had flown to Shaw AFB near Columbia, South Carolina. From there they had transferred to a Marine jet helicopter that flew them out to the Operation Earthmother flagship, the guided missile cruiser *USS Simi.* There they were greeted by Captain Walkly and Benton Fuller.

On a smaller naval craft, the frigate *USS Hapsas,* special agent Gary McGill watched over his charges, Detectives Matthew Cummings and Coolridge Betters. The two Coral Gables cops had been supposedly assigned as liaison for the massive drug sweep that was about to commence. They were impressed with the scope of the operation and the efficiency of coordination between what appeared to be Secret

Service, FBI and U.S. Navy forces. Earlier that morning, after they had been on board for two days, the *Hapsas* had left its mooring off Key Largo and headed northeast toward their current position. The two detectives were fed only bits of information, but they were privy to the coded radio traffic in the area and knew that at least seven other vessels, a submarine and four or five aircraft were involved in what was now called Operation Earthmother.

Cummings, a bachelor, had no difficulty being undercover. However, his partner had been married for forty-three years to a woman who worried about her husband more and more as the day of his retirement neared. Rather than tell her it was a dangerous drug operation, Betters lied and said he was going fishing with Cummings in the Keys for a few days on a friend's boat. As the weather worsened and the seas swelled, the two cops stayed out on the second deck just below the bridge. Neither was a sailor and both were on the verge of getting seasick.

"How the hell are they going to chase anyone in this ocean?" Cummings asked. His empty stomach grumbled.

"They have some big boats out here. And the choppers." Betters wished he had a bottle of Jack Daniels to settle his stomach.

"Why do I have this funny feeling we're being snookered?"

"That funny feeling is this damned ocean that won't stay still." Both men chuckled. Betters continued. "What do you mean, snookered?"

"It just feels too pat. I don't trust those feds."

"You're gettin' paranoid in your old age, Matt."

"Hey buddy, not me. There's a lot of expensive hardware out here. Big bucks. Now I ask you, why pull in two old farts like us?"

"Like the man said, we were on to his collar."

"Bullshit. Not those charter boat guys. I know

Doyle and Mazuski. Small-timers, if that. And that Fischer guy doesn't have the smarts for something this big."

"What about the old people?"

"Yeah. That's what's bothering me. Where are they? See, we weren't on to them . . . at least not after they gave us the slip. All we were doing was watching a couple of boats."

"So what's your point?"

"That maybe there is something more here than our FBI keeper or that other fed is telling us."

"The Navy guy seems okay."

"You know who he is?"

"Captain Thomas Walkly?"

"The same."

"I don't know . . . Spiderman?"

"Funny man. Not exactly, but close. He's the goddamned Undersecretary of the Navy."

"You're shitting me." Betters forgot his queasy stomach.

"I checked it out with our underwater snoop."

"Hans Leiter?"

"Yeah. He was one of those Seals before he went commercial. He knew Walkly as soon as I mentioned him. Seems the guy was heavy duty in Viet Nam when Leiter was in service there." Betters was beginning to feel uneasy.

"So what do you make of it?"

"I don't know, but let's keep our eyes open." The frigate *Hapsas* turned into the rising swells. Above them on the bridge deck, a seaman flashed a lantern semaphore message to another vessel off to port.

The ship that received the message was the NOAA research ship *Orca*, a seventy-foot steel-hulled vessel bristling with electronics and capable of supporting both submersible and free deep-diving scuba teams. The captain, Roger Hadges, a forty-five-year-old veteran of five round-the-world cruises aboard *Orca*, received his final instructions from his boss, Dr.

Caroline Macklow. She had been in Florida working with the special Seal team that was also aboard the *Orca*. The team was in civilian dress and was introduced as a new diving unit attached to the National Oceanic and Atmospheric Administration. Captain Hadges wasn't fooled. He knew military when he saw it, and these divers were definitely military.

"We will proceed to these coordinates now, Captain Hadges," Dr. Macklow explained, pointing to the position of the six-hundred-foot wreck off the Boynton Beach inlet. "I want to arrive there no later than oh-three-hundred hours." Hadges looked at his watch. It was one-thirty in the morning. He peered outside at the black moonless night and felt the swells rising underneath his vessel.

"We've got four-to-eight-foot seas now, and getting worse," he told the stateley Ph.D.

"We have to be there on time."

"Then I'd say it's time to get moving. I wish you'd have told me this sooner."

"We all have orders to follow, Captain Hadges."

"Those Navy boys of yours sure know how to do that," he said, unable to hold back the sarcasm from his voice.

"I beg your pardon?"

"That diving team. They're Navy."

"They told you that?"

"They didn't have to. I've been around those boys before."

"Well that's very interesting, Captain, but I think we'd best be heading up to Boynton Beach now, don't you think?" She gathered her chart, signaling the conversation was over.

"Whatever you say, Doctor." He turned to begin preparations to change course. The sailor on deck outside the bridge was returning the "hail" to the *Hapsas*. Dr. Macklow watched the captain carefully.

"I'm sorry if this mission is a bit strange, Captain. It's not my style to be secretive." He turned to face her once again. "All I can say is that in a few hours it will all be quite clear to you. And after that I can promise you some of the most interesting work you or I have ever done." She smiled. He believed her.

The high seas and dark night were going to be both helpful and difficult. The original plan to take the people from the watership to Elliot Key by helicopter had been abandoned at the last minute because of the high seas and the presence of a Soviet submarine detected in the area. Instead, the *Manta III* and *Terra Time* would be used to carry the visitors by water to the waiting helicopters now on the ground on Elliot Key. The fishing boats would be escorted closely by two Navy attack speedboats and, at a distance, by the destroyer *USS Metz*. The medical team from Houston, along with their hi-tech incubators and infant life-support systems, were aboard the speedboats.

Below the *Manta III,* ready to be jettisoned, the Antarean probeship with Amos Bright, the Finleys and Greens on board communicated with the watership flight bridge and the other commanders on board that craft.

Everything was in place. The Operation Earthmother flotilla began to converge toward the six-hundred-foot wreck off Boynton Beach where *Manta III* and *Terra Time,* their bows turned into the ever increasing swells, waited like two mice about to be pounced upon. From a distance the operation looked like a drug-running trap that was being sprung on the two charter boats.

The *Remembrance* reached the apogee of the first SSP release orbit at 11:17 Eastern Standard Time, 521 miles above Earth. The first solar screen was begun six minutes later. By midnight a polymer screen eleven molecules thick was spun and spread out over more than twenty-nine square miles of space, thirteen more miles than had been estimated. The sight was awesome and visible from Earth as a bright smear in the eastern sky. The world began to pay close attention to this scientific phenomenon, especially since they had been told that in another two hours a second screen, thirty times that size, would be manufactured twice as close to the Earth.

The dark side of the moon was also a beehive of activity. The Parman guides were comfortably at rest in their chlorine chambers rejuvenating their outer crystal layer, which always suffered some wear and tear from cosmic debris and dust as they pulled, hurled and guided Antarean spacecraft throughout the universe.

According to plan, two of the atmospheric storage tanks had been disconnected from the watership and brought down to the moon's surface to be stored. They were guided into a deep crater, fastened to the porous lunar rock and then camouflaged to escape detection from above.

The remaining tank, the one that would eventually carry the cocoons back to Antares, was brought up alongside the watership's main thruster unit and attached in a configuration that allowed for the smallest silhouette possible. Since speed was not a factor on their Earth approach, it was possible to present a very compact, almost spherical meteorite appearance, should the SSP fail to mask the watership's entry into the Earth's atmosphere.

Everything was ready at 1:30 Eastern Standard Time. All that remained was for the *Remembrance* to release the second solar screen.

At precisely 2:13 Eastern Standard Time, the second solar screen, manufactured in space to a thickness of three molecules, spread out across the moonless heavens covering more than one thousand square miles of the void above Earth. Every radar, every telescope, every military facility and research center in the world concentrated on the bright, shining oval-shaped cloud that glistened in the night sky.

The watership rose slowly above the rim of the moon. Ahead the bright blue and white planet Earth appeared and beckoned. The Antarean flight crew aligned their approach with the coordinates Amos Bright now telepathed, aligning the watership to make maximum use of the protective shielding the solar screen afforded.

After traveling to distant planets, galaxies and wonders never before dreamed of in human experience, the atmosphere aboard the watership was charged with excitement. All of the humans had but one thought as they observed their blue planet dead ahead. Home.

CHAPTER TWENTY-TWO

At 2:45 A.M. the thinner second solar screen's leading edge began to make contact with the edge of the Earth's atmosphere. The watership was safely tucked in above that screen and underneath the first screen. In effect it was the meat inside a polymer sandwich. But in this case the meat was unobserved from the Earth below and the various satellites above. As more and more of the thin polymer entered the atmosphere at the high speed it traveled, it began to burn and disintegrate. The fire spread across thirty miles of the atmospheric envelope, a truly spectacular sight as observed from the eastern seaboard and the Operation Earthmother flotilla below. As more of the screen entered the atmosphere the fire and debris grew more intense, and at a predetermined moment, when the fire was at its peak, the watership slipped into the atmosphere, its outer skin turning red hot at great speed, and hurtled down toward the rough Florida waters, impacting with a huge explosion thirty miles south and east of Elliot Key.

It was hoped that the burning screen would be a large enough diversion to mask the entry of the watership. From that point on it would appear to be a large meteor that punched through the debris from the burning screen. NASA made the announcement about the meteor and stated it had appeared suddenly and collided with the second screen, causing the test to fail as the screen was forced down into the atmosphere where it burned. The meteor had then plunged into the ocean waters off the Florida coast into deep waters.

Activities aboard the various ships involved in Earthmother heightened as the flaming watership dropped from the skies above and crashed into the sea twenty miles away.

Cummings and Betters stood on the bridge of the *Hapsas,* awed by the sight of the blazing sky above them and the fiery ball that lit up the rough waters around them before it crashed into the sea and disappeared. The small fleet was visible all around them. Then it was dark again.

"Did you see all those ships?" Coolridge Betters asked.

"I counted eight, maybe ten. What the fuck was that?"

"A meteor."

"And that fire in the sky," Cummings said, "did you see that?"

"Some kind of test. They were talking about it on the TV this morning." Gary McGill stood near them on the deck, but the fireworks had been so distracting that the two cops hadn't noticed him.

"I saw Jack Fischer's boat . . . and the other one too."

"Yeah. The *Terra Time.* But the rest of the boats were pretty big, huh Matt?"

"Too big to chase a couple of dopers."

The sea began to calm. It also began to glow with a yellow and white phosphorescence. McGill stepped forward. "You're right, guys." They turned toward the FBI agent as he put his arms around the both of them. "The moment for truth has arrived, or is about to arrive I should say." He indicated the brightened ocean around them as the watership began to emerge from beneath the sea.

Amos Bright had released from the *Manta III* at the moment the watership struck the ocean. He moved the probeship deep to the ocean floor, guiding the huge watership in toward the six-hundred-foot wreck. Excitement coursed through the cabin of the probeship as the Finleys and Greens anticipated their reunion with their fellow commanders.

The President's party aboard Captain Walkly's flagship, the *USS Simi,* were out on deck to watch the watership's landing. The sight was spectacular. In the excitement of the moment, Malcolm Teller forgot himself and hugged Margo McNeil in front of everyone.

"Jesus, Mary and Joseph," he had exclaimed, "just look at that fireball. There're Americans on board that spaceship."

"Watership," Gideon Mersky corrected. He remained outwardly calm, but inside, especially when he noted the nearly instantaneous deceleration of the Antarean craft just before it struck the water, his heart rate increased substantially. He contemplated the military significance of the technological secrets the Antareans and the Geriatric Brigade might possess.

"You want to tell me about it now, Doctor?" Roger Hadges asked after the fireball had submerged and Dr. Macklow had instructed him to head toward the meteor's entry point. The tall marine biologist nodded.

"To begin with, that wasn't a meteor."

"Part of that Solar Screen Program the President announced this morning?"

"No, not really. It's a spacecraft."

"Christ. Another accident?" Captain Hadges said softly, referring to the unfortunate *Challenger* disaster.

"No," she answered brightly. "This spacecraft is not ours."

"Russian?" he asked as he signaled for a new course and full speed ahead.

"Antarean."

"Where's that?" The bosun spun the wheel to port. Hadges noticed the heavy seas had subsided.

"In another solar system," she responded calmly, watching the wily captain as he studied her unflinching weathered face.

"You're serious, aren't you?"

Dr. Macklow moved nearer to him. She was a good five inches taller than the *Orca*'s master. She put her hand on his shoulder. "Roger, my good man, we are both about to have the adventure of our lives."

He didn't have time to respond. The seaman on forward watch hit the collision warning and the ship's Klaxon was bellowing out its warning. Up ahead the ocean was growing brighter. Something was coming to the surface. Something very large. The watership, having filled its atmosphere tank with seawater and adjusted itself to earthbound temperature, atmosphere and gravity, was now ready to discharge its precious cargo of life, which had grown by three since departing from Antares two months ago.

Ben Green left the probeship and passed through the watership membrane at a depth of three hundred feet under the sea. Ruth and Betty were waiting for him. They embraced. A moment later Mary entered the chamber and exchanged greetings with her fellow commanders. The Finleys would remain with the probeship on site until the cocoons were safely transferred. Amos Bright would return with the watership to Antares while the Finleys took the probeship to the port of Galveston, Texas. The watership continued to rise toward the surface, guided by the probeship and the Navy vessels above.

Jack and Phil were on the radio to each other as the water brightened below them. They saw the *USS Simi* heading toward them off the starboard while the *USS Metz*, the escort destroyer, moved closer in off their port.

"I hope those guys keep their distance," Phil said nervously as the big ships bore down on the two small fishing boats.

"Walkly said the President's on the missile cruiser. He's gonna say hello to the folks before we shove off."

"Well I hope he says hello from a distance." The two attack speedboats now appeared. One of them headed for the *Simi* while the other came up behind the *Manta III.* "I don't think that's in the cards, old buddy," Jack replied as he peered over toward the flagship.

President Teller, Gideon Mersky, Margo McNeil, Alicia Sanchez, Phillip Margolin and Captain Thomas Walkly were about to disembark on a forty-five-foot ocean yacht that had been brought aboard the *Simi* and was now being lowered over the side to join the speedboat that had now reached the sleek guided-missile cruiser. Benton Fuller and two other Secret Servicemen were already aboard the Navy speedboat. The ocean yacht, bearing the presidential seal and flying his flag, pulled away from the *Simi* and headed toward the *Manta III.* The sea was almost dead calm now and glowed a bright orange yellow.

The men and women from the Brigade prepared to leave the watership. Time was spent with farewells to the Antarean flight crew and the Parman guides. Beam and her medical team would be going to Houston. In the chamber inside the membrane was a domed room bathed in a deep blue night light to prepare the humans for their first exposure to Earth in more than five years. The excited passengers gathered as the watership continued its slow ascent to the surface. The three infants were brought forward. Ben and Mary asked to hold them and passed their feelings along to the Finleys.

The babies would be taken aboard the speedboat lying to port of the *Manta III,* where a pediatric team waited with three incubators. Beam and her two assistants would join them. The infants would be completely checked out by the time they reached Elliot Key.

Phil Doyle saw the President first. "Hey, Jack," he hailed over to his friend, whose boat was now within thirty yards of his, "it's the man himself."

"I guess we'll be on the A-list now," he joked, but he was nervous and proud to be a part of the operation. The President waved a greeting to Jack and Phil. They saluted back.

Matthew Cummings had trouble adjusting his binoculars. Betters was already absorbed as he watched the President greet their old adversary, Jack Fischer. Finally the senior detective, with some help from Gary McGill, focused in on the *Manta III* and the boats nearby.

"I'll be damned," was about all he could say. Then he saw the lights from the watership rising toward the surface. These were the same lights he had seen when the Brigade left Earth five years ago. Then he got angry. He put down the binoculars and glared at McGill. "So you guys knew all along that what I said to the DA was true." In the midst of the historic event unfolding before them, Cummings's remark was lost on Gary McGill.

"Say what?" The FBI agent had his own binoculars.

"I told the DA five years ago that they had some kind of a rocketship. It was just like that out there, just like I told them. And they said I was nuts. They said that if I started talking about spaceships and like that . . . that they'd have me off the force."

"I'm sorry about that, Detective Cummings. No one really did know."

"That Fischer guy and his buddies knew, and I told that DA so—"

Coolridge Betters cut his partner off. "Hey Matt, kick back. So we were right and they were wrong and no one gives a good shit about it now. Can't you see they let us in on it?"

"So?"

"So that's the payback, man. How many people you know are invited along with the President to meet some folks from outer space?"

Cummings chuckled and lifted the binoculars to his eyes again. "Not too many," he said as he scanned the horizon, checking out the *Metz,* the *Orca,* and the *Simi.* Then he peered back at the President's yacht, *Manta III, Terra Time* and the two speedboats. "Maybe two or three hundred from the looks of this welcoming committee out here tonight."

Malcolm Teller could only think of Herman Melville's description in *Moby Dick* when the great white whale, having sounded, rose from the depths, first just a tiny spot below growing larger and larger until he breached with all the power and majesty that that great leviathan possessed. He, too, peered into the ocean depths and watched the orange-yellow glow of the watership grow larger and larger beneath the ocean yacht. It was massive, covering the water beneath his boat, the two speedboats and the two fishing boats nearby. As it neared the surface the brighter lights emanating from it began to dim and a deep blue oval opening in the circular nose of the watership became clear.

The watership's flat dull white hull stopped thirty feet beneath the surface. *Manta III* and *Terra Time* were directly above the ship's membrane. The probeship popped to the surface and came to rest between the two fishing boats. From beneath the probeship a ray of white laser light shot down to the membrane and split into hundreds of separate beams, encircling the membrane opening. The beams then reflected back to the surface, forming a column of blue and white light. The water within the column drained out and the membrane was exposed to the night air. Then as the membrane parted, the first passengers, led by Ben and Mary Green, ascended to the surface on a walkway that rose up out of the watership's hull. At the same time Beam and her two assistants brought the three human infants to the surface on another walkway.

The President's yacht edged close to the walkway, as did the *Manta III*. Ben waved a big hello to Jack and then boarded the President's yacht, which was now side by side with the *Manta III*. Mary followed. They both greeted the President and his party. Then one by one, led by Ruth Charnofsky, the commanders came aboard, were greeted by the President and then filed onto the *Manta III*. At the same time Beam and her party boarded the medical speedboat.

Everyone aboard the vessels had been briefed on the mission that morning. No one, not even the most hardened Seals or the experienced Secretary of Defense, even Caleb Harris who had been aboard the *Hapsas,* was prepared for the sight that now appeared rising out of the membrane of the watership. Then all the married couples, people in their seventies and eighties, came to the surface, holding hands in the pale blue and white light. They were waving to the people on the boats that surrounded them. Many of the women sported rotund heavy bellies in which they carried the new generation of humans, conceived on other planets. Everyone cheered them and waved back. Even the sailors on the larger ships that stood off could be heard crying out their welcome.

The President had a few words of greeting prepared. He stepped forward onto the fantail of his yacht. The commanders stood behind him.

"I know that you still have a journey ahead of you tonight. A journey that will take you to the peace and safety you require. I will personally visit each of you very soon. So all I want to say now, on behalf of your country, of your fellow Americans, is a sincere and heartfelt . . . welcome home." He waved to the group and they applauded back. Then they quickly boarded the *Manta III* and *Terra Time* along with the commanders. Slowly the two fishing boats backed away from the watership, as did the speedboat carrying the babies. The President's yacht turned and headed back toward the *Simi*. The beams of light from the probeship retracted, and water once again covered the membrane. Then Amos Bright lowered his craft down to the opening of the watership. There, in the near darkness of the warm Gulf Stream current, the three off-planet fathers—Panatoy the Subax, Tom the Desteran, Dr. Manterid from Betch—and Tern, the pregnant female Penditan from Turmoline, each wearing special protective covering and encapsulated in pressurized containers built by the Antarean flight crew, were loaded aboard the probeship. Their journey to Elliot Key would be made as secretly as possible, for as far as those who had helped with the landing were concerned, the only passengers aboard the spaceship were humans returning for a visit.

As the probeship moved away the lights aboard the watership dimmed, and it sank quietly, settling on the ocean bottom just southwest of the six-hundred-foot wreck. The *Simi* and *Hapsas* remained on station. The *Orca* headed south to the Stones. It would be joined there by the probeship, and the difficult task of moving the cocoons to the watership would begin. The Presidential party returned by helicopter to Shaw AFB and from there to Washington, D.C. All the other craft were well on their way to nearby Elliot Key, where eight Marine helicopters would ferry the newly arrived visitors to Homestead AFB, and a waiting C-5A would take them to their new home in Houston.

Everything went like clockwork, a tribute to Captain Walkly and the people in his command. The C-5A was met in the early dawn by Dr. Kahwaji and his team, who now took over the responsibility of bringing new, perhaps alien life into this old and troubled planet.

CHAPTER
TWENTY-THREE

No one wanted to take the final decision, although in the end Dr. Kahwaji would be responsible. Beam told them that the off-planet beings, three males and a female, would be stable in their sealed environmental containers for another fifty-one hours.

"I don't have that knowledge," she told the Under-secretary of Health, "my training is medical. I can tell you what their basic requirements are, but I cannot tell you how to provide them."

He had called the meeting immediately after learning that the gas mixtures were unstable in the four living chambers constructed for the aliens. It was initially thought to be a computer malfunction, then a programming problem. Now it was unclear. The possibility of design and construction failures was now on the table as well.

"We had to make several decisions on short notice." The chief chemical engineer, a man Kahwaji had recruited from the Army's chemical, biological and radiological testing program at the Aberdeen Proving Grounds, spoke first. "The mixtures, the gasses we had to manufacture for these people were quite exotic. There just wasn't time to test every condition of temperature and pressure, so we went with the averages that the watership supplied."

"Yes," Dr. Yee interjected, "but these containers have gasses at variance with those in the chambers."

"They're small differences," Angela Lippman, the

computer specialist responsible for the program that controlled the total environment, said. "I think they'll be just fine in there."

"We are talking about life . . . lives here, Ms. Lippman. Think is not good enough." Dr. Kahwaji was firm. Beam received a thought from one of her assistants.

"There is one person here who can give us definite parameters for all the environments." Everyone at the meeting turned to the Antarean medical officer with complete attention. "Dr. Manterid, the mate of Ellie-Mae Boyd, is a chemist. An environmental chemist from Betch. He can give you all the information you require to be sure of the others' safety."

"But he's in a container himself," Angela commented.

"Yes, but it is factual that he has been able to survive for a reasonable period of time in this atmosphere. As we approached the Earth he was with his mate for some time."

"You're sure of that?" Dr. Yee asked Beam.

"Yes, sir. I am certain. We can confirm that with Mrs. Boyd." They did. An hour later Dr. Manterid was removed from his container. A scuba tank with pure nitrogen was supplied and that enabled him to work for the rest of the day with the engineers, doctors and chemists as they fine-tuned his living quarters first. Once that was controlled and functioning he was able to assist them in stabilizing the other three. The only unresolved problem was the intensity of ultraviolet radiation Panatoy required. Ruth Charnofsky, Panatoy's mate, who had lived with him on Subax, was asked to examine the room that Panatoy would inhabit. She was able to help by suggesting they graduate the ultraviolet across the room, thus producing different zones of radiation. When Panatoy was there he could tell them which was the most comfortable. They could then adjust the entire room accordingly.

It worked. With ten hours to spare, the living quarters were functioning, and the off-planet visitors were comfortably in residence with their mates.

Adjusting to their new environment was a different matter for the Brigade parents. The first order of business, after each couple had settled in, was to perform a complete examination on each woman to determine general state of health, the health and development of the fetuses, and the chronological birth schedule they might expect to have.

There were three complete and separate medical facilities on the top, or green floor, of the Space Medicine Center. For these early tests those units were converted into nine completely outfitted examination rooms. Each was staffed and equipped to perform the general examination as well as ultrasound, which at the state of the art enabled the doctors to observe the fetus in minute detail. On call to the facility were four of the best highly specialized fetal surgeons in the country. Their skills enabled them, by using sophisticated, high-resolution ultrasound, to do actual lifesaving surgery on a fetus while still unborn within the amniotic sac.

Mary Green, who was now barely four months' pregnant, resisted taking up residence with the others. She had conceived on Antares just before the probeship left for Earth. She believed her time would be better spent working with the other commanders. Ben was insistent, but Mary resisted. Then, while waiting for her first examination, she was visited by Bess Perlman. The two women had not had a chance to be alone until now. Mary's room was bright and sunny. The President had sent a bouquet of a dozen roses to each woman, and their sweet scent permeated the tidy room.

Because time had been short, little attention had been paid to decoration. The rooms were Spartan but neat. A bed or beds—the couples had the choice of a large single bed or twins. They all chose the single bed. Simple furniture and fixtures, a bath with tub and shower, and a dining and living area were supplied. The Brigade traveled with little luggage, just personal items and uniform clothing. Their work on different planets required such a large variety of clothing that it was impossible to travel with all of it. Every place they had been, their garments and personal items had been supplied by their guests. Payment for such things was absorbed by the Antareans.

One of the amenities offered by Kahwaji's staff had been to bring in a large variety of clothing for the returning humans. For many of the women it was the first time they had been shopping in five years, and even though the clothing was complimentary, there was excitement in picking and choosing the new fashions. But much of it was maternity clothing along the lines of what the staff thought seventy- and eighty-year-olds would want to wear. Life out among the stars had changed all of that for the Brigade. The latest hi-tech fashions were exchanged for the more conservative wardrobe offered. That made maternity wear easier to obtain.

"You'll have to start wearing maternity clothing soon," Bess Perlman commented as she watched Mary Green cross the room. On her way to get more coffee, Mary stopped and sniffed her roses. So many things they had been without for all these years now tasted and smelled wonderfully strange.

"I know. This guy is going to be a buster."

"A boy? For sure?"

"I hope so."

"Well, they can certainly tell you that with all the equipment they have here."

Mary poured more coffee from the carafe supplied by the kitchen on the first floor. There was a printed menu. The visitors were served either in their rooms at any hour or in a central dining room during fixed hours. But room service was twenty-four hours a day.

"I don't want to know. Ben too. We want to believe it will be a boy. You know we lost a son in Viet Nam?"

"Yes. Scott, wasn't it?"

"Yes." Mary sat down across from her old friend. They had not seen one another in more than three years. Telepathing was not the same as being face to face. "We should get a Mah Jong game going here," Mary continued, recalling how the four of them, Bess, Rose, Alma and she sat for hours playing the ancient Chinese game that had been strangely adopted by Jewish women in the 1930s.

Bess smiled, remembering those long ago days herself. "What if it's not a boy? Will you be disappointed?"

"No. Maybe. I don't know, Bess. It's not really important." Mary had avoided talking about Bess's miscarriage. Now she felt stupid worrying about the sex of her baby when Bess had lost hers.

"It's very important that you take care of yourself, Mary," Bess said softly. "I wish I'd been able to get here . . ."

"I'm so sorry about your losing your baby."

"It couldn't be helped. But please don't be foolish. Don't take chances. We . . . you came to mother-planet to have your baby. Betty and Rose and I will care for the others. And the men have things well in hand. You have to promise you'll listen to the doctors. Please." There was fear in her voice, a voice Mary had not heard for so long, but remembered well. She smiled at her old friend.

"Okay. I promise."

"Good."

"Do you think we might not be able . . ." It was hard for her to say. Bess Perlman understood the question. Besides herself, Mary Green and Ruth Charnofsky were the only pregnant commanders. And Ruth had mated with an off-planet male, so her case might be different altogether.

"No. I think it makes no difference. I lost my baby

because it was not meant to be. As Beam said, it was not part of the Master's plan. I accept that now. You just relax and let these doctors take care of you."

"Thank you." Mary reached across and touched her friend's hand.

"And be sure that Beam is involved too. She seems to have definite ideas about why all of this has happened to us, to the Brigade. Her people, the Antarean council, sent her on a special mission . . . aside from the medical aspect."

"Did she tell you what it is?"

"Only that the Antareans believe these children are very special. They call them a new race. A becoming race in the Master's plan. If it is true, then it is one of the most powerful signs the Antareans have that they are chosen among many races to execute the Master's grand plan."

For a moment there was silence in the room as both women stared at one another. It had been a long time since religious thoughts had been discussed openly. That the Antarean council considered such things about the Brigade was special.

"Do the others know this?" Mary asked.

"No. Beam said she will tell when she is asked."

It took two days for all the expectant mothers to be completely tested. All of the fetuses were viable and appeared normal. The three human mothers who had mated with off-planet males and the one pregnant off-planet female, Tern, also appeared to be carrying normal human babies. The only abnormal event occurred when Dr. Yee requested a second amniocentesis from Ruth Charnofsky. The obstetrician performing the procedure was Dr. Fogel, a woman from Columbia Presbyterian Hospital's world-renowned Obstetric and Pediatric Clinic. When the long needle was inserted into the amniotic sac and fluid extracted for the second time in so many days, the fetus, a Subax-human that was being observed ultrasonically, suddenly turned and grabbed at the intrusion in its warm, safe fluid world. Dr. Yee observed the baby's unexpected movement at the same time Dr. Fogel turned her attention to drawing out enough amniotic fluid. Dr. Yee, his instincts still razor-keen despite his aging body, quickly reached over the examination table, firmly grabbed Dr. Fogel's hand and extracted the long needle just as the fetus grabbed at it.

"What the hell?" Dr. Fogel shouted. Ruth Charnofsky, who had felt the needle being withdrawn quickly, immediately went inside Dr. Yee's mind and understood what he had done.

"The baby was grabbing the needle," he snapped back. "I had no time. It just had to be done." Dr. Fogel understood.

"He's very fast, isn't he?" Ruth asked the aging Oriental doctor, who had already informed her the baby was a male. The identification had been made visually the day before during the first amniocentesis.

"And smart. He doesn't want us poking into his nice little home," Yee answered as he motioned for Dr. Fogel to clean off Ruth's stomach, apply a bandage and end the procedure.

"How soon before you can tell me about the genetics?" Ruth asked. Dr. Yee hesitated, calculating how much time the geneticists would require and then how long it would take for Beam to assess her own input as well. The Antarean knew much about Subax. Her opinions would be invaluable but she had to learn how the human geneticists worked. Dr. Fogel finished and Ruth raised herself up from the table.

"Give us a day or so. There's no rush. You have at least six weeks before you come to term."

"On Subax six weeks is only about three weeks Earth time," Ruth told him as she stepped gingerly onto the floor. The tiny wounds made in her stomach wall and uterus were already healing. It was one of the benefits of being processed for deep-space travel. Her remark disturbed Dr. Yee, but he showed no emotion.

"Three weeks, six weeks . . . what's the difference?

I said a day or two. No more." But he was concerned and Ruth knew it. There had been all manner of materials and cells never before seen by the geneticists in her amniotic fluid. What was especially disturbing was the complete lack of antibodies and white blood cells normally present even in minute amounts. "Just give us a little time. Beam is helping too. Everything will be just fine. Now you go back to that big blue husband of yours and have a rest." The nurse helped Ruth into a wheelchair and took her back to the special Subax-human duplex. Dr. Yee remained behind to discuss things with Dr. Fogel.

Everyone settled in and rested after their long journey and the two days of tests. The staff met and were confident they could perform their mission. Other than the unknowns that might present themselves in the mixed matings, everything else looked good. The three newborns were healthy and appeared normal. Their blood was extraordinary. Exactly like their parents, like all the Brigade members—no disease, perfectly formed red cells, maximum organ function and efficiency and the ability to repair cell and tissue damage immediately. The physical state of all their guests was excellent. The prognosis, the same.

What they didn't know, and something that the commanders agreed to keep secret, was that the mental status of the newborns was far from normal. The Messina girl and the Erhardt twin boys were communicating, telepathing with each other in a language none of the commanders nor Beam and her assistants understood. But beyond communicating with each other, the commanders strongly suspected the infants were also communicating with the unborn fetuses as well.

CHAPTER
TWENTY-FOUR

The DOD, NASA and the White House had their hands full with inquiries from the press, complaints from foreign governments including NATO, and outrage from the Soviet Union about the SSP experiment. The party line was simply that the test had been for peaceful purposes, namely "An added protection for our rapidly deteriorating ozone layer . . ." NASA announced that the program looked promising, but there was much yet to be developed. They stressed that when the meteor strayed unexpectedly into the larger solar screen and pulled it into the atmosphere, thus destroying it, the test was over and their data inconclusive. Margo McNeil briefed the White House press corps the morning after the "Fire-in-the-Sky Show," which is what the media had dubbed the SSP. She followed NASA's lead and only added that the President was "disappointed and has asked for a review of the entire SSP project." He felt, she went on, that we launched too soon even though it was an unexpected event, the meteor, that ruined the test.

But the Secretary of Defense had a different problem to handle. His counterpart, Marshal Pavel Kuzkonin, was on the hot line to the Pentagon early the morning after the test. Their hot line was not a telephone, as many believe, but a sophisticated series of word processors, translators, teletype machines and printers. The printed word is a far better tool when discussing details at a high level.

"Good morning, Mr. Secretary," the Russian message began. "We send greetings. The purpose of our contact to you this morning is to voice, in the strongest terms possible, our dismay and displeasure at your unauthorized use of international space last night between 0100 and 0330 hours Eastern Standard Time. This is a clear violation of the International Space Treaty accords signed by the United States of America and the Union of Soviet Socialist Republics two years ago in Phoenix, Arizona. Specifically the use of space for weapons, or weapons defense research. The grave consequences of this flagrant violation are being discussed today at the highest levels of our government."

The message was clocked and answered: "Received —please stay on the line." Gideon Mersky was prepared for the Russians to be annoyed, but this was very strong language. As prearranged with President Teller, he responded.

"Good evening to you, Marshal Kuzkonin, and greetings as well. To go straight to the point, we do not believe our SSP test yesterday was a violation of the Phoenix accords. In fact, we can prove they were in keeping with the stated purpose of the treaty, namely the peaceful exploration of space for the benefit of the entire planet. The Soviet Union is a major user of fluorocarbons, which research shows has a damaging effect on our precious ozone layer. The SSP is designed to protect the Earth. It is in no way a weapon or a defensive tool. The test was done on short notice because perfect weather conditions in the test area suddenly emerged, and because our scientists are predicting severe sunspot activity in the next six-month period. I trust this information will satisfy your government. In addition, may I now formally invite you and your staff to be my personal guests if and when we attempt another such test. As I am sure your scientists have reported, our test last night was a failure, due in part to the unexpected arrival of a meteor in the test zone. My best wishes to your family."

The communication was answered: "Received. Good morning."

The return trip aboard Air Force One had been jubilant. Alicia Sanchez and Phillip Margolin were congratulated several times by the President and Secretary Mersky. By the time they landed at Dulles International both young people were floating on a cloud of success.

"I want to see you two tomorrow afternoon in my office," Gideon Mersky had commanded in a friendly, fatherly voice. "We've still got to get that watership launched and out of here in a few weeks."

"Yes, sir," the young scientists had said in unison. They stood next to the DOD limousine as Mersky closed the door and ordered the car to take him to the Pentagon. It was six A.M. The second DOD limo waited for Margolin. He and Dr. Sanchez walked slowly to the waiting stretch. They were euphoric.

"I can't sleep," she said. "It was the greatest night of my life."

"It's not over," he replied, looking at his watch. "The boss said he wants to see us this afternoon. Why not keep the flavor going?"

"What do you have in mind?"

"How about breakfast at my apartment, and we take it from there?"

"To where?" she asked as they got into the limo.

"That," he said, "as Shakespeare wrote, is not in ourselves, dear Alicia, but in the stars." The car began to slowly pull away as the driver waited for instructions.

"You've got that backwards," Alicia responded.

"I hope so," he answered. "The Watergate apartments," he instructed the driver. Then he kissed her. She put her arms around him and kissed him back . . . hard.

* * *

Orca and the Seal team were stationed over the Stones. The *Manta III* with Jack, Phil Doyle and Madman Mazuski aboard was anchored fifty yards off the *Orca's* stern. The probeship with Amos and the Finleys aboard was on the bottom, just south of the first cocoon chamber. The ocean floor was ninety-seven feet at this point. It slowly fell off from here as you traveled north toward the submerged watership that lay on the bottom nearly four nautical miles from the Stones at a depth of six hundred feet near the Boynton Beach wreck.

The plan was for the Seals, along with Amos and the Finleys, to operate as two teams.

The Seals, using scuba gear and supported by the *Orca,* would bring cocoons up to the *Manta III,* which would then transport them to the waters above the watership. Aboard the *Orca,* Dr. Macklow would supervise their activity. But her primary function was to monitor the seawater taken aboard the watership to see that it remained chemically consistent with the water around the Stones.

The *Manta III* would appear to be a fishing vessel trolling for sailfish and other pelagic fish. Jack had the outriggers spread and four baited lines ready to go. Four of the eleven Antareans remaining on the watership would take the cocoons from the *Manta III* and bring them down to the waiting storage tank, which was now filled with seawater.

The other team, Amos and the Finleys, would also remove cocoons and take them to the probeship. They would then transport the cocoons underwater to the watership and turn them over to the remainder of the Antarean crew. Since the Antareans and the Finleys did not require any breathing apparatus, they could operate in this manner.

Between the two teams, it was estimated that fifty to sixty cocoons could be moved each day. At that rate Amos estimated the watership would be loaded and ready to depart in nineteen days.

Although they were well within the United States

territorial waters, operating at night would be dangerous and risky. There were reports of Russian and NATO submarine activity nearby. Ostensibly the foreign subs were tracking on the "meteor," which NOAA announced it was trying to locate and bring to the surface. That explained the presence of the *Orca.* During the day reports that observation satellites had readings of a large metallic object off the Florida coast increased speculation that the meteor was large and intact. Farther out in the Gulf Stream the *USS Simi,* the *USS Hapsas* and the *USS Metz* remained on station, keeping the area clear of nosy ships. Their presence was explained as drug traffic interdiction and patrol.

On the first day of operation both teams were able to move and store only forty-one cocoons. It now looked like thirty days would be a more realistic departure date and Amos so informed his council back on Antares.

Matthew Cummings was now a part of the team. Betters, McGill and he had the responsibility of keeping the operation secure when the *Manta III,* with the probeship attached to its hull, was in port. It was also anticipated that the *Orca* would have to make at least two visits to Miami harbor for supplies. Their security would also be handled by the two Coral Gables cops and their FBI cohort. After witnessing the arrival of the watership and finally understanding what had happened five years ago, there was an unspoken, half-spoken, continuing conversation going on between Cummings and Betters. It always ended short of answering the question that was never directly asked.

"Those folks sure looked good, didn't they?" Betters would say.

"Like kids. Imagine, being parents at that age." Matthew Cummings had never married. Betters had no children.

"They seemed happy too," the black detective murmured.

"And young. Those guys we saw with Fischer? They haven't aged in five years, I swear."

At noon Alicia and Phil shared his dark blue tile and glass stall shower. He reached around her and rubbed her smooth firm stomach with a soapy pink washcloth as he held her close against his own body. She leaned back and let the warm water hit her face as it rested on his shoulder. The water ran down her neck and between her perfectly formed breasts as Margolin slid the washcloth up along her belly. Then dropping the washcloth, he caressed her nipples with his soapy fingers. She felt him growing hard against her buttocks.

"More?" she murmured.

"I'll never have enough of you."

"That's my boy!" She turned and faced him, then pulled herself up onto him, spreading her legs and wrapping them around his soapy hips. He was a short man, but he was strong and took her weight easily. Twenty minutes, he figured. Then they would have to dress and head over to see Gideon Mersky. Of course, he then thought, there's always tonight.

Their meeting with the Defense Secretary was brief and to the point. They had done a wonderful job and he wanted them to work on a plan for the watership's departure. When they suggested they would head up to Roscoe again, he rejected that idea.

"I want you two down in Houston with the visitors."

"Isn't that a busy place right now?" Margolin asked.

"I'll have Kahwaji set you up on the first floor. I want you there for another reason."

"Yes, sir?" Sanchez questioned.

"You two got along with that Finley guy. He's operating down in Florida on the cocoon matter. I want you to get friendly with some of the other leaders . . . what do they call them?"

"Commanders," Margolin responded.

"Right. I want you to get to know them . . . get to

work with them a little. Find out what their plans are after all these babies are born."

"I thought they were leaving after the babies were born." Alicia Sanchez was surprised Mersky didn't know that.

"Yes, they say that, but I have a feeling they might be convinced to stay, at least for a while. Just do your work and get friendly. It can't hurt. Okay?" They both agreed. As they were leaving the office he asked one more favor of them. "If you hear anything . . . any plans they might have? Don't call me or anything like that. I'll have you flown here once a week or so and we can talk about it here. For now let's just keep that part of your mission within these four walls."

Sanchez and Margolin left the Pentagon confused. Then they realized they would be working alone together for the next month or two, and they couldn't wait to get back to Margolin's apartment and celebrate their good fortune.

Later that night at 11 P.M., while the two lovers were asleep in each other's arms, Gideon Mersky placed a call on the scrambler phone to Colonel James "Jimmy" Smith, commander of the 1159th Light Infantry Brigade, which was stationed at Fort Campbell, Kentucky.

"Jimmy. How the hell are you?" the Secretary began, his voice cordial. He knew he had roused the colonel from a warm, but not empty bed.

"Very good, sir. How are you?"

"Just fine, Jimmy, just fine. You keeping busy these days?"

"We're alert, if that's your question." The colonel's voice grew sharp, attentive. He sensed a special mission. He lived for special and preferably dangerous missions.

"You still keep that special company . . . what'd you call it?"

"The creamers, sir. The cream of my crop. Yes, sir.

I've one hundred of the best Americans this country has ever produced and trained."

"Well that's good to hear, Jimmy. You do me a favor and keep that cream right on top for the next thirty or forty days. Okay?"

"Consider it done, sir."

"Thank you, Colonel. Sorry to disturb you. Good night."

"No trouble, Mr. Secretary. My pleasure. Thank you, sir. And good night." The colonel had been seated on his king-sized waterbed. He hung up the telephone and looked over at the short blonde hair of the WAC captain he'd taken home that night. She was about to get awakened by an aroused, excited American fighting man.

Back at the Pentagon, Gideon Mersky also felt excitement course through his body, but it wasn't sexual. It was the sweet taste of power.

CHAPTER TWENTY-FIVE

The first sign of trouble came in the middle of the second week when Marie Amato's husband, Paul, was awakened by his wife at three in the morning. She was in labor. The doctors had told them the baby was due in eight weeks. He pressed the medical call button, wisely installed in every room. In moments an emergency team was at their door. The team chief, an obstetrician from the Mayo Clinic, sized up the situation immediately. He ordered Marie taken directly to prep and at the same time ordered delivery complex Alpha staffed and readied. The team rapidly deployed. The ruckus awakened everyone on the top floor. There was deep concern and at the same time anticipation that the first Earth-born child was on the way.

It was a girl, perfectly formed and appearing to be a full-term baby. But all the tests, and confirmation of the time of conception with the Amatos, pointed to a birth two months hence. If this was a premature birth, then why wasn't the infant underdeveloped? The baby was kept in the pediatric intensive care unit for the maximum four hours allotted, then released to the transitional nursery, where Marie nursed her. They named her Beam. Her namesake, the Antarean medical officer, was delighted.

A staff meeting was called by Dr. Kahwaji as soon as things settled and returned to normal. The senior staff would have to reevaluate their schedule. Reexamination of all the expectant mothers, with careful attention to changes indicating time of birth, was prescribed by Dr. Yee. He thought back to the incident with Ruth Charnofsky when the fetus seemed to grab at the intruding amniocentesis needle.

"We will have to face the fact that these babies might be something more advanced than other human children. If they are coming earlier, and that certainly seems to be the pattern—you recall the births in space were also premature—then we must be ready. I want all the women, including the mixed couples—all of them—to be scheduled for ultrasound first. I think we'd better have a closer look at those fetuses."

The commanders also met that morning. During the night, just before Marie Amato went into labor, Mary Green had been awakened by someone calling to her telepathically. It had happened before to all of them, but their minds were able to block a disturbance when they slept. There were ways to awaken one another if the situation was critical. But this intrusion into Mary's subconscious was different.

"It came from within," she told the others. They had gathered in one of the large examination rooms on the top floor.

"I heard something too," Ruth Charnofsky admitted, "but I couldn't understand the message."

"It woke you?" Frank Hankinson asked.

"Yes. I think so. I may have been awake before . . . a moment before. I'm not sure."

"What did it sound like?" Ben Green asked his wife.

"A voice . . . no, voices, talking. But in a strange tongue. Yet I thought I could understand. It was like the time when we had just arrived on Parma Quad 2. We knew the Parman language, but other than the guides, we had never actually met any of them."

"You mean the dialects," Bess Perlman suggested.

"Not exactly," Mary Green answered. "I mean the way they spoke to one another sometimes. The lost language, they called it . . . something like that . . ."

"The ancient language," Betty Franklin remembered. Bess's sister had been one of those who stayed behind on Parma Quad 2 after the two years. She had come to know their culture as well as any of the Antarean ambassadors who lived there. "It was the way of communicating before their race changed to a complete crystalline form." An uneasy feeling passed through the room. Bernie Lewis spoke next.

"I believe we are all thinking the same thing. What woke Mary and Ruth was from within."

"The babies," Rose said aloud. "The babies are calling to us."

"No," Ruth said firmly, "not to us, to each other. Somehow they know about each other. They are speaking from the womb in a language we have long forgotten."

"We have to reach them," Mary stated matter-of-factly.

"Or they have to reach us," Ben replied.

Alicia and Phil had settled in on the first floor of the hospital. Their equipment and computer hookups were completed in a few days. The problem of getting the watership off the planet with a minimum of detection was now before them. The size of the space vessel alone posed a problem. Electronically its mass would be detectable from anywhere on the planet. The data given to them by Amos Bright and the watership flight crew suggested that it would take several moments, perhaps twenty to thirty seconds, for the watership to reach a speed where it would appear only as an anomaly on radar screens and satellite tracking systems. To launch it from American, or even NATO territory would alert the Russians and Chinese. The problem was difficult.

Their sleeping quarters were adjoining. For some inexplicable reason they gravitated to Alicia's room each night. It became their love nest, and there was no mistaking that they were deeply in love. That was how they became friendly with the commanders.

It happened the fifth day they were in Houston, just a week before Marie Amato gave birth. Ben Green was working with the pair, trying to compute the overall mass of the watership in relation to the amount of seawater it displaced. They were slowly coming to a conclusion that the watership, once loaded and ready to depart, would have to be moved from its present location to a more remote launching area.

Ben, who had made love with Mary earlier that morning, began to pick up on very strong feelings of love in the room. He misread it as Mary calling to him. He telepathed to his wife, who told him she did love him, but hadn't called to him. Ben then realized the emotions he'd picked up were coming from Alicia and Phil. As a gesture of understanding he silently reached out to them and wished them well. Both the young scientists turned toward Ben at the same moment. Somehow they had heard him, somehow they understood what he had done. He tried to be nonchalant as they stared at him.

"Yes?" he asked, "did you say something?"

"Did you?" They said in unison, looking at Ben and then at each other. "I . . . we heard you say something . . . about us," Phil Margolin said first.

"About our love," Alicia said proudly. It was very strange because they both had agreed to keep their affair a secret and now she was blurting it out to a stranger. But was he a stranger? That was the interesting part of it. Both Alicia and Phil were suddenly comfortable with Ben Green as though he had been an old friend. Ben understood their thoughts and feelings. He made his second mistake by thinking that and not blocking his thoughts. They read him again.

"You're talking without talking," Phil said slowly, incredulously.

"You can hear me?" Ben asked aloud.

"We can," Alicia answered. "How?"

"Telepathy," Ben responded. "Humans are capable of it. Most of the Brigade have the capacity. We . . .

the commanders have a slightly different ability. But we were only able to do it after we were prepared for space travel."

"But we heard you, and you heard us. Can you teach us how?" Phil said.

"Yes. Jack Fischer was eventually able to learn to receive and send, but never consistently."

"Was that when the Antareans were first here?" Alicia asked.

"Yes. Shall we try some more?" Both Phil and Alicia immediately agreed without speaking. For the rest of that morning they communicated without words. It was difficult for Alicia to do directly with Phil, but with Ben joining in, acting like a medium, they could read each other's thoughts clearly.

Later that day Ben reported the event to the rest of the commanders. It was then that Alma Finley, who was under the sea at the time, told them about Gideon Mersky's ability to block and read them as well.

The work at the Stones was going well. Dr. Macklow was now diving with the Navy Seal team. She had stabilized the seawater in the container that housed the growing number of cocoons. They were nearly finished emptying the first of four cocoon chambers. Two of the Antarean flight crew now joined them and the Seals became fast friends with the Antareans. They called them Ants, a nickname that spread to Houston as well.

Amos was concerned about the time it was taking to move the cocoons. There were three chambers to go. This first one had been the smallest, containing only 217 cocoons. He'd noticed that toward the end of their work in that chamber the cocoons left were not as viable as those taken earlier from the same chamber. He discussed this with Dr. Macklow, suspecting it had something to do with their exposure to the fresh ocean water. He was correct. There was an increase in the amount of caustic chemicals and sewage in the water. Amos came aboard the *Orca* when she did the final tests confirming the change.

"In the past three days it has increased eleven percent," she told the Antarean leader.

"That is alarming. The last time we were here we found the cocoons had been damaged. I fear the situation has gotten worse."

"Just locally and within the past few days."

"Are you certain?"

"Fairly certain," the tall marine biologist responded, her steel-grey eyes revealing a mind actively at work. "What I'd like to know is where it's coming from."

"What?" he asked. He liked Dr. Macklow and passed kindness to her.

"The pollution. It has to be local. Either an illegal sewage dump or maybe passing ships." She leaned over her charts and computer printouts.

"There is a water planet near the star you call Pollux in the constellation Gemini. It's known as Chexis Quad 3. On this planet there is a life form that must reproduce in the water . . . salty mineral water like your ocean. There is only a special time when they can breed, when the water is not poisoned. That is when the clean water comes from springs very deep in their seas. It rises up along fixed routes. These creatures, they are called Mellis, can follow the spring water just by tasting a few molecules. They can find it, they know when it is coming . . . they know where it is coming from."

"We have a species like that on Earth," Dr. Macklow interjected, "called salmon."

"I was fascinated with this ability," Amos continued, "so I experimented, with their approval of course, and was able to discover the means by which they could find the clean water. I converted that to instrumentation. Perhaps . . . I was thinking, if we could take some of this pollution and feed it to my electronics, maybe we could track it down . . . find the source as you say."

"I have a sample right here," she said, picking up a jar of seawater.

"Then, Dr. Macklow, may I have the honor of inviting you aboard the probeship?"

The second medical examinations were completed in one day. There was no doubt about it now. With the exception of the mixed babies, all of the fetuses were six to eight weeks advanced from the normal growth pattern of human embryos. Their size was deceiving. They were all small, but their development was advanced. During the ultrasound tests another strange phenomenon occurred that gave the doctors pause to reflect. It didn't come out until all the testing was over and senior staff went over the results. This time they invited Beam to join them. After they had finished with their briefing Dr. Yee asked Beam if she had ever witnessed this kind of change in a species' birth pattern.

"No, we have not," she answered forthrightly. "But this is the first we have processed a species as though they were Antarean. It was not our doing originally, as you know. The men found our equipment and used it. They changed. All of them changed. Many of their functions have also changed . . . been enhanced. But the return to reproduction was a surprise for all of us on Antares."

"Well," Dr. Kahwaji concluded, "we must assume that this is now a fact. A full-term baby for these people is just short of seven months. We should make our plans accordingly."

"The births also seem to happen rapidly and easily," Dr. Yee said, looking for confirmation from the other obstetricians in the room. The others agreed. "And something else," he continued. "These tests today . . . the ultrasound. I watched all of them. Did any of you feel anything special when you were conducting them?"

For a moment there was silence in the room. Then Dr. Fogel, the specialist from Columbia Presbyterian, spoke up. "I'm going to say something foolish."

"I don't think so," Dr. Yee said.

"Very well," Dr. Fogel continued hesitantly, "during the ultrasound I did on the six women assigned to my team, I had the distinct impression that I was being watched."

"There were others in the room, Doctor," Dr. Kahwaji said.

"No, sir. Not that way. It was as though . . . Christ, I hate to say this, you'll think I'm nuts. Well, it was as though the fetus—the baby—was watching me as I was studying it on the TV screen."

"Yes," Dr. Yee announced. "I felt . . . I saw that too."

"They were speaking to me," Dr. Fogel admitted, encouraged by Dr. Yee's words.

"Me, too," the obstetrician from the Mayo Clinic said. "I thought I was imagining things. We've been working long hours here and . . ."

"It is true," Beam then said. "I have seen it, I have heard of it before. There are species that communicate with their young before birth."

Dr. Michelangelo Yee leaned back in his leather chair and smiled. "Well," he said, "now if we can find a way to get those little beggars to help us, to talk to us somehow, our job here will get a whole lot easier."

Alicia could not sleep. She watched Phil Margolin peacefully resting next to her and, though tempted to wake him, she resisted. Something was gnawing at her. Something bad. Then she heard a voice. "Protect us. You must protect us." It was a child's voice, far away, tiny. Then it was gone. She got out of bed and took a hot shower. When she returned to the room Phil Margolin was awake, sitting up in bed with the light turned on. He was writing on a pad he always kept next to him.

"An inspiration?" she asked, toweling herself off and sitting next to him. He kissed her shoulder.

"It makes no sense. I was sleeping, dreaming I guess. Then I was up. I heard you in the shower and thought maybe that's what woke me. Then I began to hear strange voices." Alicia felt a shiver pass down her spine. "They sounded like little kids . . . no, maybe like . . ."

"Angels?" she asked.

"A choir maybe. Young, clear voices. No words. Just thoughts. Probably some backlash from that telepathy we were doing with Ben Green."

"I heard them too, darling," she said, leaning over to see what he had written. "Protect us. Protect us," she read aloud.

"Protect who?" he asked.

"The babies."

"From whom?"

"Gideon Mersky, I think." They both dressed quickly, calling out to Ben Green silently as they did. He met them at the door to Phil Margolin's room.

CHAPTER TWENTY-SIX

There were two distinct sources of the pollution around the Stones. The worst of it came from a phosphorous-processing plant in Lake Worth. They produced fertilizer and had had a breakdown of their waste-material filtering system. While it was being repaired, the plant, recently acquired by a Japanese consortium, continued to operate under the orders of the new Japanese plant manager who brought with him a fierce desire to improve the bottom line. He simply stored the caustic waste material during the day and then ordered it dumped into the ocean at night. After all, he reasoned, this ocean was a long way from Japan. The most important thing was that his company succeed.

It was an easy matter for the probeship to locate that culprit because Amos and Dr. Macklow had to track the source at night. The probeship was too valuable moving cocoons during the day. When they found the plant's location they sent Cummings and Betters up to Lake Worth the next day to have a good look around. The manager proudly showed the two detectives that he was storing the waste material. At the same time Captain Hadges, aboard the *Orca*, notified the Florida office of the Environmental Protection Agency of the violation. That night, as the plant spewed its killing waste, they were caught redhanded.

The sewage was more difficult to trace. It took three more nights, but eventually they discovered a barge leaving a trail of sewage just off Jupiter Beach. They did not know where the barge originated and they were sure it was, at best, an intermittent thing. All Amos could do was to notify Captain Walkly aboard the *USS Simi.* The captain dispatched the *USS Metz* to intercept the barge and put the fear of the U.S. Navy into whoever operated it.

The sight of a Navy destroyer bearing down on them in the middle of the night was frightening enough, but when the *Metz* loudly hailed the errant barge with a warning that they were polluting a government area and could be fired upon, the crew aboard the barge came out of the deck cabin with their hands high in the air. The *Metz* came to a stop and turned on her bright searchlights. The forward machine guns were manned, aimed at the three quaking men. Satisfied, the *Metz*'s captain turned abruptly and put a wash across the deck that soaked the barge operators. They were not seen again in the area.

That night, on the way back to the *Orca,* Amos Bright explained how the sensing device worked. Dr. Macklow listened intently. She was not sure if she could duplicate the electronics, but she did understand the basic theory behind it and knew it could prove to be a powerful tool in tracking water polluters all around the world.

In Washington Gideon Mersky, who had begged off accompanying the President, called Phillip Margolin in from Texas for a meeting. It was to be a quick overnight visit. He wanted Margolin back in Houston the next day when the President arrived, ostensibly for a planned visit to NASA. His real purpose, of course, was to meet personally with the space visitors at the hospital. Both Margolin and Sanchez were scheduled to brief the chief executive on their progress in developing a plan for the watership's departure.

It was Friday afternoon and Washington was emptying out for the weekend. The Defense Secretary kept

Margolin waiting for nearly an hour. When Mersky finally emerged from his office he was with a tall, severe-looking man who Margolin immediately pegged as military even though the man was dressed in a tan summer suit.

"Phillip Margolin, I'd like you to meet an old friend, Jimmy Smith." Margolin, who was quite strong himself, tensed at the viselike grip of Smith's handshake.

"Very nice to meet you, Mr. Margolin."

"My pleasure, sir." Smith released Phillip's hand and smiled. He then reached a softer handshake to the Defense Secretary.

"Good to see you, Mr. Secretary. You all take care now. And don't worry about that problem. I'll be able to handle it."

"I'm sure you will, Jimmy. I'll be in touch." Smith left, and Mersky signaled Margolin into his office. After a moment Margolin, who had developed the beginnings of a plan to launch the watership as secretly as possible, began to present his ideas. The Secretary listened intently, but made no comment until Margolin finished his presentation.

"The plan sounds fine, Phillip. I think it needs some refining, but you've broken its back for sure."

"Dr. Sanchez and I both worked on it."

"Of course. It's good. I'm sure the President will like it. I'll be talking to him in the morning before he leaves for Houston." Mersky shuffled some papers on his desk. He had no idea that Phillip Margolin was, in a very crude manner, trying to reach into his mind, to read his thoughts. Ever since he'd discovered the Brigade commanders were able to telepath and auto-suggest, Mersky had practiced and sharpened his own abilities to block their intrusion. He never believed or accepted Alma Finley's contention that they were not permitted to interfere with people's actions by mind control. But now, not suspecting that Phillip Margolin had been developing his own telepathic abilities with the commanders' assistance, the Secretary was not blocking.

"That's encouraging, sir," Margolin answered, knowing their meeting had an additional agenda. Mersky continued playing with the papers for a moment, then looked up.

"How're you doing with those commanders?"

"Very well, sir. I've become friendly with Mr. Green and Mr. Lewis. Dr. Sanchez has also met them and gone out of her way to become friendly with their wives. Of course, with the birth schedule moved up things have been pretty busy for them."

"So I understand. How many born so far?"

"Ten, I believe. Dr. Kahwaji says they're not really premature either."

"Yes. Interesting. It seems these babies take only seven months to develop instead of the normal nine."

"They're special."

"More than you know." Margolin was inside Mersky's head, but his exact thoughts were difficult to read. The Defense Secretary was excited. "That man you met before . . ."

"Mr. Smith?" Margolin said, unable to hide the slight tone of sarcasm in his voice.

"That's really his name. He's a bird colonel down at Fort Campbell."

"One hundred and First?"

"No. A newly formed light infantry brigade." Margolin knew about those new brigades. They were part of the RDF—Rapid Deployment Force, a product of the need for the military to respond quickly to trouble spots on a global basis. The unit could move on a moment's notice. From a single squad to the entire brigade, they were always combat ready. They airlifted by jet transport with all their equipment. From that point on they operated with a minimum of support and a maximum of deadly force. Gideon Mersky continued. "I'm concerned about the safety

and security of those people down in Houston."
Margolin knew he was lying now.

"They seem secure in the hospital," Margolin offered, putting a certain naivete in his voice.

"Well, they're not. I'll be giving Colonel Smith the task of relocating our visitors to a more remote and secure facility."

"What about the babies?"

"The babies? Of course we'll take the babies."

"No, sir. I mean what about the medical attention they need, and the ones not yet born?"

"Oh. We're not planning any moves until all the births are finished. The last thing I want to do is run a hospital. No. In a few months."

"Will the President be telling the visitors about that on this trip?"

"No. This is extremely confidential. He's approved it, of course, but he wants time to develop the plan so when he does present it the . . . ah . . . visitors will have all the information and understand our reasoning. These are Americans. They need perhaps to be reminded of that fact. What they know . . . what they can do . . . it's all very important to the nation. I'm sure you understand that, Phillip." Mersky was lying again. Margolin still couldn't read all his thoughts, but he knew it was a lie. Oh, he was sure Mersky believed that part about it being important to the nation, but he had no intention of allowing the visitors their freedom to choose where and how they wished to live. At least there was time before Mersky made his move.

"Now tell me more about these commanders, Green and Lewis."

Margolin talked innocently about them for another fifteen minutes. He explained they were the leaders and had developed certain abilities beyond the other Brigade members. He talked a little about their adventures on Parma Quad 2 and gave the Defense Secretary a brief explanation on how the Parman guides were used for deep-space travel. He knew that kind of talk would tweak Mersky's curiosity to know more. That way, Margolin assured himself, he would be asked to continue his spying assignment. But he told Mersky nothing of the commanders' plans. That was the last thing Gideon Mersky should know about now that it was clear he intended to hold the Brigade by force.

The President arrived in Houston ostensibly to review the progress of the NASA Office of Exploration, a position created by President Reagan to put men in space. Some time after the *Challenger* accident the government began to realize that it had stopped pursuing the dream of exploring space. Instead they were just running a transportation and hardware-hauling business. President Teller took that realization one step further in his first inaugural address when he stated, "The time has come for all of us on this planet to get up off our tails and put them out among the stars." Prophetically, that was only a few months after the Geriatric Brigade had begun their journey to Parma Quad 2.

The meetings at the Johnson Space Center had the normal press coverage, but nothing special. The President then went on a private tour of the sprawling NASA facility with his last stop being the newly renovated Space Medicine Center Hospital.

His arrival coincided with another birth. The baby, a boy, was born to parents who originally lived in New York City and were old friends of Ben and Mary Green. President Teller was delighted to personally witness the birth from an observation room above the Beta delivery suite. Dr. Fogel was the chief obstetrician. She delivered the baby easily. Dr. Kahwaji, who guided the President while he visited the hospital, commented that the births were the easiest he had ever witnessed.

"They seem to all leave the womb in a similar

manner. There is very little labor and the infants emerge at the correct angle and position. One of our doctors maintains they come out with their arms extended as though they were asking to be held."

While the President visited with the Brigade parents and parents-to-be, Margolin and Sanchez met with the commanders who were in residence at the hospital. The Finleys were still on site with Amos, transferring the cocoons to the watership. Margolin reported on his meeting with Mersky. He had tracked down Colonel Smith's unit before he left the Pentagon.

"It's an elite group. Highly trained. This Colonel Smith is one of the best. And I'm certain the President has no knowledge of their plans."

"Let's assume he does," Art Perlman suggested. "That way we can use his ignorance to our advantage. Let him be surprised when Mersky makes his move."

"*If* Mersky makes his move," Ruth Charnofsky said. "I personally think we have to make our plans to leave before it comes to a confrontation."

Ben Green agreed with a reservation. "We will still need help to reach the mothership."

"On that subject," Bernie Lewis interjected, "I think we'd better contact Amos and have the mothership leave for Earth as soon as possible." They all agreed and telepathed their concerns to the Antarean leader.

"We have to present our plan for the watership to the President in an hour," Alicia Sanchez said. She had filled the commanders in on how they proposed to have the Antarean craft depart Earth. "But," she continued, "I think that Phil and I should begin to develop a plan for your own departure as well."

"We assume you will need special arrangements for the children," Margolin suggested. For a moment the commanders linked their thoughts, blocking all others.

"We will need to discuss that with Beam and the off-planet parents," Bernie Lewis answered, "but for now we must assume everyone here, other than Alicia and Phil, are involved in Gideon Mersky's plan to hold us against our will. Anything we plan must be kept secret."

"Do we have a departure date we can aim at?" Margolin asked.

Betty Franklin, Bess's sister who had been assigned the task of liaison with the still expectant mothers, spoke. "As best we can determine it will be two months and three weeks. Let's say mid-October to be safe. Mary will be the last according to Dr. Yee's new schedule."

"Of course we can't be certain about the mixed babies yet," Ruth chimed in. On Subax a pregnancy might last as long as a year, depending on the time of conception and weather conditions.

The newborn baby was transferred to pediatric intensive care as standard procedure. The initial tests and examinations showed another perfectly formed, healthy and extremely alert baby. The President, accompanied by Margo McNeil and Benton Fuller, visited the nurseries on the third and second floor next. There were six infants still in the transitional nursery near the intensive care units. The procedure was to move them down to the second floor after five days. As soon as the President arrived at the top-floor nursery the babies awoke and became quite active. Down on the second floor, in the main nursery, the older infants stopped their activity and suddenly became quiet and still. It gave the chief pediatric nurse quite a scare. She immediately signaled for an emergency unit, but when they arrived they could find nothing wrong. All of the babies, nine of them, lay in their bassinets on their backs, eyes open, staring up at the ceiling. Their breathing was normal.

Back at the commander's meeting Alicia Sanchez suddenly stood up. She covered her ears with her hands, her face contorted in pain. Phillip Margolin's body stiffened, his feet shooting out under the table as he gasped.

"Jesus!" he exclaimed.

"What's wrong?" Ben Green asked. He reached into their minds but he was blocked.

"The children," Alicia said, "they want us to come to them . . . now." She relaxed, as did Margolin. Everyone stood up.

"No," Phillip Margolin said, "they only want us."

President Teller stood among the bassinets in the second floor's main nursery admiring the calm but alert babies. Yet he was uneasy. He watched Margo McNeil as she held one of the infants who had been handed to her by the chief nurse. That baby, in fact all the babies, seemed to be staring at him.

Sanchez and Margolin entered the nursery. All the babies turned their attention toward the couple. The baby being held began to squirm, and Margo had to put her back in her bassinet.

"Hello, Mr. President," Margolin said.

"Ah, the two geniuses from DOD. How are you?"

"Very good, sir," Sanchez answered.

"Quite a bunch we have here. They seem so alert, so healthy."

"They are, Mr. President," Margolin answered. Then he heard the voice. So did Sanchez. They spoke rapidly, alternating with each new thought. Alicia spoke first.

"These are the children of the new race."

"These are the children of mankind off-planet."

"These are the children who will teach for the Master."

"These are the children who must be protected."

"These are the children who will serve all races."

"These are the children who will lead you to peace."
"These are the children of the beginning."

Alma Finley heard the voices deep beneath the ocean as she swam outside the watership's flight bridge. She was carrying the cocoon of an Antarean commander at the time, guiding it toward its berth within the cargo container. She swam past the green translucent bubble that housed the Parman guides. They were sealed inside, replenishing themselves with chlorine. They transformed the gas into an absorbable crystalline form. At first she thought it was coming from the Parmans. Then she realized it was coming from the cocoon she carried, which was pulsating a reddish light from within. Amos swam up next to her.

"Can you hear it?" he telepathed.

"What is it?"

"The children. They are calling to us. They are announcing their arrival in the universe. Today the fifteenth baby was born. Their power increases geo-metrically as more join them."

"This sleeping commander also hears them," she thought as she touched the glowing cocoon.

"Yes. I think perhaps the entire universe hears them now. I must send for the mothership immediately."

Phillip Margolin brought the President back to their work area on the first floor. The shock of what had happened in the nursery remained with everyone, but they had not discussed it yet. Sanchez prepared the preliminary presentation for the watership's de-parture, but the President told her not to bother.

"Secretary Mersky filled me in on everything. It sounds just fine to me. You coordinate that with him." The work area was one large central room with four computer terminals, TV monitors, two laser printers, a FAX machine and a teletype link to the Pentagon Communication Center. Maps and charts, mainly of the mid-Atlantic Ridge, a chain of huge underwater mountains that stretched from Greenland down past both North and South America to the Antarctic. Two smaller rooms off the main room were used as offices. LoCasio and Berlin, the two assistants who worked with Margolin and Sanchez, occupied those offices now. President Teller indicated for Benton Fuller to close the doors to the offices.

"What happened up there?" he then asked.

"I'm not sure, sir," Sanchez answered.

"Those things you said about the babies. Who told you?"

"Again, we're not sure, Mr. President," Margolin said.

"When I first met Alma Finley, she was able to . . . well, sort of hear what I was thinking. Afterward I talked to Caleb Harris and he told me they, these commanders, that they can put thoughts into your head too."

"I wasn't aware of that, sir," Alicia lied.

"Well," he continued, "whose voice did you hear telling you to say those things?"

"We don't know," Margolin said quietly. "Perhaps it was the commanders." The President was disturbed. He had a sense that things were out of hand, that he had somehow been duped by the commanders, that he was being used. He didn't like it.

"It sounded to me like someone was warning me about something."

"Did it sound that way?" Alicia asked, "or did you feel that?" President Teller didn't answer. But Alicia knew she had hit the nail on the head.

In four weeks they'd completed moving half the cocoons into the watership. Bad weather and the pollution problem had slowed them down. Now another storm system was moving into the area and they would have to stop work for three or four days. The *Orca* put into the port of Miami for supplies and fuel. None of the crew or the Seal team left the vessel for security reasons. Jack Fischer brought the *Manta III*, with the probeship attached to its hull, into his dock at Boca Raton as he had every night since the operation began. He stopped at the fuel barge to fill his twin gas tanks. The old Greek serviced the boat and watched Jack and Phil Doyle carefully. They had come and gone each day, but without the submarine. The probeship had remained out at sea next to the Stones. Now he noticed the *Manta III* had the submarine attached to it again.

"You for to use gasoline in that boat too?" he asked, pointing with his bent cigar to the waterline of the *Manta III*. Jack didn't understand what he meant.

"Yes. I use gasoline in this boat."

"You want me to fill up?"

"Yes. Both tanks." Jack went back to his conversation with Phil Doyle.

"Where is gascap?"

"What? You already have the caps off."

"Not these caps, Jack. I for to mean the cap for your submarine under the boat. I need to know how to put gas." Jack and Phil understood immediately what the old man meant. He had seen the probeship. Jack made light of it.

"Submarine? That's not a submarine. It a special fishing thing . . . a sonar . . . like a fish finder."

"It's a big one, huh?"

"Big finder for big fish." Jack laughed. Phil laughed. The old man turned away to serve another customer. Okay, he thought to himself . . . "you want for to get your gas somewhere else . . . that's your business." But he was annoyed that Jack felt he had to lie to him. Below, inside the probeship, Amos Bright heard the conversation. His mission was to get the cocoons safely home to Antares. Nothing could stand in the way of accomplishing that. He decided to have a talk with the old man at the same time he spoke to Cummings and Betters. Perhaps the Brigade could use some more members.

* * *

Leaving Earth was never a question. The Brigade had come to homeplanet for births, nothing more. But the question of what they might do with the babies could not be answered until they knew exactly what these babies were. It was clear now that physically the babies were human in every way. They all had inherited the disease-free blood, organ and muscle tissue their parents had as a result of the Antarean processing. The preliminary tests showed no genetic abnormalities. There was a question about what the effect of two new sets of chromosomes present in the infants meant. And their growth rate could not yet be determined. The chief pediatrician needed at least six weeks to hazard a guess as to how rapidly these infants might develop. He would base his estimate on comparison with a group of human babies being born in Houston Children's Hospital during the same time period. Until that data was in, the decision as to how soon the infants might be able to travel would have to be deferred.

Two days after the President's visit the mothership left Antares. Its route would be similar to that of the watership. In fact, if the cocoon retrieval went according to schedule, the mothership and watership would rendezvous near the first-magnitude star Vega, in the constellation we call Lyra.

But for now, as requested by Amos Bright, the mothership had brought aboard the means to process and cocoon the infants for space travel. How long they would have to remain in suspended animation was not known, and Beam was deeply concerned that this might prove a dangerous, if not impossible task.

"We have processed our own kind this way. We know that for us, cocooning works. But for humans . . . for ones so young . . . who can say?" Her apprehension was disconcerting to the commanders. But they had little choice at this time.

At a meeting of the Brigade in the dining room, the

commanders informed their comrades about the potentially hostile plans of the Defense Secretary and the problems they might have to solve.

"We will have to see what condition the infants reach in the next month," Beam told the gathering.

"And we will need to see what surprises the mixed babies bring to us as well," Ruth added as she felt her own baby move as if in response to her observation.

CHAPTER TWENTY-SEVEN

Paige Betters thought her husband had finally lost it. When he decided to tell her the story, he began by going back five years to the chase up Red Lake Canal when his speedboat was lifted from the canal, hurled across the manicured lawn of a wealthy Coral Gables resident and dumped into the man's green and red tiled swimming pool. Detective Coolridge Betters's wife listened patiently as they sat alone in the Florida room sipping cool white wine spritzers. When he got to the part about seeing the President of the United States, she knew he'd gone mad.

"Stop right there," she insisted, getting up from her chaise, hovering over him as he lay prone on his own lounge chair. "The story was good, damned good. One of the best you've told. But just what do you think I am? The President? Give me a break."

"I swear, honey."

"Don't you swear about those lies. You've been with Matt too long. Both of you have carried around this condo story from five years ago like heavy baggage. Now that retirement is near I guess Matt wants to clean up old business. But that doesn't mean you have to be involved."

"Honey. Please," he begged. "Everything I say I can prove. It's not the story that matters. It's what we want to do about this offer . . ."

"Someone offered you a job after you retire?"

"Sort of . . . like that. But it involves you too." She

walked over to the wet bar they had built in the corner of the tropical room and fixed herself another drink. They had both worked hard for this house. It was in a good section of Kendall. They had paid sixty thousand dollars twenty-two years ago. Now it was worth over two hundred seventy thousand. It was their equity. Paige was extremely proud of the house and loved her husband dearly. Police work, even in the Coral Gables sheriff's office, was dangerous. They'd had no children. Once, after they were settled in the house, they discussed adoption, but were told they were too old when they finally applied.

"I want you to listen to me, honey." Betters's voice was serious. She came back to the chaise and sat down.

"Okay. I'll listen." And she did, although she didn't, couldn't believe a word of what he said. Yet she had never seen him so insistent and as far as she knew he'd never lied to her. They were up most of the night until she decided that if—and she used the word *if* advisedly—the story was true, then she would go if he wanted it. He said he did. She was suddenly frightened, realizing either way her life would change radically. If he were lying then it was obvious he was ill, Alzheimer's perhaps. And if he were telling the truth, then they were about to begin a life she couldn't comprehend.

They met at the *Manta III* dock before dawn. Cummings had brought a small suitcase, but Amos told him to leave it behind.

"You'll have plenty of time to gather personal things before the watership departs," he told the aging cop. Then he welcomed Paige Betters and suggested they board the *Manta III*. They found the Finleys, Phil Doyle and the old Greek, Gabriel Sorukas, on board having breakfast in the spacious cabin. Introductions were made. As they cast off, Gabe—the old Greek asked to be called Gabe—smiled a toothless smile.

"They say I will for to grow teeth again," he said to

Paige Betters. Then he laughed. "And maybe babies too. Many babies." She was frightened now. Could this really be happening? Alma Finley understood her panic. She telepathed comfort to the sixty-seven-year-old black woman, a retired schoolteacher who was on her way to an unimaginable life. Then she spoke softly to her.

"It's a little disorienting, isn't it?"

"I don't know what's happening. I listened to my husband all night. I had to come . . . I wanted to come. But is this really true?"

"Yes," Alma assured her. "It is true. The decision to ask you and the others came from Mr. Bright. He is the only one who can invite us—human beings—to join the Antareans on their voyages."

"It is true, isn't it?"

"Yes. And wonderful."

"Well," Paige Betters then said, taking a cup of coffee that Jack Fischer offered to her, "I always believed that life didn't end on this Earth of ours, that there had to be something beyond. I guess I'm about to find out that's true."

Eighteen babies had now been born. The first three who were born on the watership were more than two months old. The pediatric nursing staff was growing because the mothers had taken the decision to stop nursing their infants. And it was clear to the parents and the commanders that the babies were controlling their feeding and general care by calling telepathically to the nurses' subconscious. It wasn't clearly manipulation, but the parents were comfortable with the thought that their babies understood why they had gone to bottle feeding at this time. Two reasons caused the decision.

The first was that it seemed clear the parents would have to separate from their children at some point in the near future. Unless it was deemed safe for the babies to endure space travel with the Parman guides, which seemed highly unlikely, they would have to be sealed in life-support cocoons and demetabolized until arrangements could be made for them on an Earth–type planet. It was certain that their young bodies could not be processed with the Antarean equipment used on the Brigade five years ago. The processing only worked on human bodies that had passed their peak and were well along in the aging process.

The second reason was that since the mothership was now on the way to Earth to pick them up, it was time for those who had families in the United States to visit them if they wished. Of the humans who'd returned to Earth, only thirty-one, less than half, had become parents and had any family they knew how to reach. Of these, twenty-seven wanted to pay a visit. Dr. Kahwaji mentioned this to the President, and he arranged for military aircraft to transport those who wished to see their relatives.

Before they left it was decided that nothing would be said regarding the babies or the location of the hospital. A deadline was set for the return of everyone to Houston six weeks hence. They were to check in by telephone weekly. In early August those who wished to see their families began to travel out into the country. They all listened to Mary Green's story of what her visit had been like. She counseled them to be positive and to resist telling too much detail about the other worlds they'd seen.

"It will only cause them worry and runaway imaginations. Try to make it sound like a long vacation overseas. Use that analogy. And little white lies about harsh weather, poisonous atmospheres and hostile inhabitants is in order. Remember, especially with the kids, their image of life on other planets is limited in great part to the horror and fantasy movies they see."

Ruth Charnofsky put it another way. "We know how much we have changed and how fortunate we are. They do not, will not, have that same opportunity.

They do not understand death as we now do. They do not accept the gift of life as we have learned to accept and cherish it. Be kind and loving, as we all have become, but do not let them peer too deeply into your heart and mind, and likewise respect theirs as well."

Three days after the twentieth human baby was born, Tern went into labor. The female from Turmoline didn't awaken her husband, Peter Martindale. Their specially prepared living quarters were kept at a temperature of ninety degrees Fahrenheit with a humidity level close to eighty-five percent. The air was oxygen rich and filtered. This approximated the jungle conditions where Tern's tribe, the Penditan, lived and hunted. She felt the onset of birth and left her husband sleeping in their bed.

She prepared a corner of their living room for the occasion. She rolled back the carpet. She picked fresh leaves from the lush house plants provided to make her habitat more familiar and comfortable and gathered them in the corner, placing them on the floor to form a nest. She then removed the uncomfortable human clothing she'd been supplied. Naked, she squatted over her nest and began to bear down, helping her baby into the world. It took thirty minutes. The boy dropped onto the leaves without a whimper. Tern gathered him up and began to clean his pink body. She blew into his tiny mouth, and he began to breathe. His skin and hair was lighter than a Penditan baby. His milky eyes looked as though they might be blue someday, like his father's. Tern was pleased that the child was a male and that it resembled the other human babies she'd seen in the nursery. After the infant was clean she bit the umbilical cord and tied it in a knot. In the center of the knot she placed a curved bone amulet with markings of her tribe inscribed along one side and the symbol of their deity, three circles in a line. The center circle was black. Standing, she placed the infant at her full breast and it began to suckle. Her milk flowed easily. She walked proudly back to the bed and got back into it, still holding the nursing baby. Later that morning when Peter Martindale awoke, he rolled over to say good morning to his wife and found he had a new son.

It took all morning for the doctors to convince her to let them examine the baby. Martindale's coaxing finally prevailed, but Tern insisted on staying with the infant in her sight at all times. The baby was healthy and vital. He was larger and heavier than the other babies. He did not cry as long as he felt his mother's presence. When the medical team moved him to the transitional nursery, he became agitated. There were four new babies in there at the time. Tern heard her baby cry and rushed to take him from the nursery. As soon as she had him out of the room the crying stopped. The doctors tried to put him back in the nursery one more time and the same thing happened.

Downstairs, Alicia Sanchez was working on the final details of the watership's departure. She was suddenly uncomfortable, agitated. She heard the voices of the babies inside her head. One of them was frightened, calling out for help. Then the cry was gone. Then it came back, this time stronger. She left her work and went up to the top-floor nursery. When she saw Tern, Martindale and their new baby, she understood.

"He has to stay with you for a while," she told the parents. The doctors were annoyed, but knew that Dr. Sanchez was on the President's personal staff and carried weight in Operation Earthmother. "He's not in tune with the other children yet," she explained quietly to Martindale. Rose Lewis arrived on the floor. She had also been touched by the new baby's cries. She understood his discomfort and suggested that Martindale take Tern and the newborn back to their duplex.

"He needs the warmth and humidity. He needs his mother's smell and touch. He wants her breast. Go ahead," she commanded gently, "I'll speak to the doctors." But instead she turned to Alicia. "Did you hear the child too?"

"Yes. He was afraid of the others."

"He will have to learn to communicate with them. The fact that he can hear them is good."

"I wish we could tell them about him, that he's different. That there will be others soon that will also be different."

"Maybe there is," Rose said. "Maybe if we allow them some time to absorb the differences they will learn." The idea of newborn infants being able to learn complex social structure telepathically among themselves was too much for Dr. Sanchez to fathom. But there was enough conviction in Rose Lewis's voice for the NASA scientist to respect her theory. Rose was the one commander who seemed to have a special way with the babies. Rose understood them, and they responded to her presence.

Back in their quarters Tern and Martindale comforted their new son. The baby was content to nurse and sleep in his mother's embrace. Once in a while the baby would awaken, as though called by a voice. It would listen, its tiny brow would wrinkled once or twice, and then it would go back to sleep. Only Rose Lewis knew that the other babies had understood the new baby was different. They were trying to communicate, but this time they called to him one at a time and gently.

The morning of the Martindale birth, Bernie Lewis had boarded an early flight from Houston to Nashville, Tennessee. From there he rented a car and drove northwest across the Kentucky border to the Fort Campbell Military Reservation. Bernie's wife, Rose, was the niece of Ruth Charnofsky, the chief commander. He too was a commander. Bernie was a veteran of World War II. His brother Marty had been killed on Okinawa and he had been with the first units that entered Auschwitz, the Nazi concentration camp.

He was a much decorated soldier and active in the Jewish War Veterans Association.

It was easy for Bernie to get onto the post. He showed his veteran's ID and said he was looking for the son of an old buddy who he'd served with in Europe.

"Smith," he told the MP at the gate. "He's a bird colonel, I think."

"With the 101st?"

"No, I don't think so." Bernie put on his doddering old man act. "Infantry. I think it's that new infantry."

"RDF?"

"Yeah. That's it." The MP checked his officer roster on the computer screen in the guard post. He found it in a minute. "You'll want the 1159th Light Infantry. That's in a restricted zone so you'll have to go to base headquarters and call him from there." The young Airborne MP politely gave Bernie directions. As Bernie drove away he thanked the soldier. The young man snapped to attention and saluted. "My pleasure, sir. Welcome to Fort Campbell."

The commanders had discussed the propriety of Bernie's visit to the Army base. After Phillip Margolin revealed Gideon Mersky's plan to put the Brigade under the military "protection" of Colonel "Jimmy" Smith's elite company, Bernie and Ben wanted to know firsthand what they might be up against. The last thing they wanted to do was get into a power struggle with innocent soldiers, not to mention the possibility of hostility around their newborn babies.

"Having a look wouldn't hurt," Ben argued.

"I'm a veteran. An old man. I'm just visiting to say hello. These soldiers love to put out for old guys like me . . . to show that they are as tough and ready as we were way back then." Bernie was persuasive.

His wife's Aunt Ruth finally agreed, but warned him. "No interfering, Bernard. Stay out of that colonel's mind."

A man can have a head without a mind, Bernie thought to himself as he waited in the post headquarters dayroom. The OD, officer of the day, was a portly major whose uncle had served in Europe at the same time Bernie was there. He called Colonel Smith's headquarters and left word that the colonel had a visitor at post headquarters. Bernie had told the major he wanted to surprise "Jimmy," so the message only requested that Colonel Smith come as soon as possible. He arrived twenty minutes later in combat dress, having been in the field preparing a night exercise with the firing range officer. The major brought Colonel Smith into the empty dayroom. As he came through the doors Bernie jumped into his mind with the impression that his was a familiar face.

"Mr. Lewis," Colonel Smith said, beaming as he approached Bernie. "What a surprise." He extended his hand. The major stood nearby smiling.

"Jimmy," Bernie began, "I'm sorry to bother. I was going to be nearby and I promised your dad I'd stop in. He says to give you a hug." Bernie opened his arms and embraced the colonel. As he did that he was back into the soldier's mind, exploring the subconscious. Colonel Smith's father was retired in Arizona. His mother was dead. Bernie peeled some more layers and found the secret place where Gideon Mersky's mission against the Brigade was stored. He absorbed it in an instant and stored it away to be examined later. While he did that, which took a matter of seconds, he blocked the other commanders. Aunt Ruth would have cause to yell at him until he told her what Gideon Mersky was planning to do. Bernie spent the next hour passing the time pleasantly with Colonel Smith. They discussed his father at great length and the days they'd spent together in the "big war." After Bernie left Fort Campbell and was on his way back to Houston, the autosuggestion he'd left with Colonel Smith occurred. At the start of the night firing exercise for an inexplicable reason, just as Colonel Smith began briefing his staff, he urinated in his pants, wetting his camouflage fatigues and steel-plated, spit-polished, paratrooper jump boots.

Three days later the third cocoon chamber was empty. The teams began work on the fourth and final chamber. Amos estimated that if the weather held they would be ready to leave Earth in six days, maybe less if Cummings, Mr. and Mrs. Betters and Gabe were able to help with the loading. Their processing was nearly complete.

Ellie-Mae Boyd, the black nurse and close friend of commander Betty Franklin, went into labor five days after Tern gave birth. In her case it was quite a different story. Her mate, Dr. Manterid, the chemist from Betch, could not help her. He had to remain in his controlled environment, a nitrogen-rich atmosphere, high humidity and moderate temperature. Ellie-Mae was familiar with the signs of labor. She'd given birth to six children in her previous life in North Carolina. But these pains were acute. At first she and the attending doctors joked nervously about the pain. They said a woman of her age should expect a little reminder that some time had passed since her last pregnancy. Beam did not see the humor. She was concerned. This baby was not coming as easily as the others had.

After two hours of labor, they all agreed something was terribly wrong. Her cervix had dilated, her contractions were normal and strong, her muscle tone perfect. They decided to try a mild drug to stimulate more contraction. That only caused more pain. The medical team was anxious. Beam tried to telepath and relax Ellie-Mae. But something, someone was interfering. The two other Ants, as the Antareans had come to be called, recalled the birth procedures of the Hillet, Dr. Manterid's race on Betch. It was very similar to human birthing. There was no answer there.

Another hour passed. The doctors began to discuss doing a cesarean section. The father was given a breathing source, rich in nitrogen, so he could be with his wife. He was terribly excited and concerned. His anxiety and Beam's worry forced the medical decision. They prepped Ellie-Mae for surgery.

The cesarean section took only a half hour. The baby, a female, looking very much like a Hillet, only darker, was removed from her mother's womb. During the surgery it was noted that the placenta had an unusual growth on it. It resembled a small starfish and was attached to the umbilical cord where it joined the placenta.

After the cord was cut, the baby was rushed to the pediatric intensive care facility that adjoined the operating room. It was kicking and screaming. It was immediately apparent that the baby was in trouble. She began to gasp and turn crimson. Beam, satisfied that Ellie-Mae was recovering, came into the intensive care room. She was struck by the crisis atmosphere surrounding the newborn. Then an idea occurred to her. Beam rushed back into the recovery room where Dr. Manterid sat with his wife. She took his breathing apparatus from him and rushed back to the baby. The moment she exposed the baby's face to the nitrogen-rich mixture, it responded. It nearly reached for the breathing mask, trying to pull it down to its face.

"Get Dr. Manterid back to his chamber," she ordered aloud to the staff. "And let's get this little girl down there too. I don't know how we missed that." Later they learned that the nursery had been bedlam during Ellie-Mae's labor. It only calmed down after the baby girl was safely in her father's native atmospheric conditions.

The medical team was exhausted and slightly embarrassed. This became more acute when the Ants reasoned that the baby didn't want to be born. The prolonged labor was caused by the little girl refusing to leave the safety of her mother and enter an atmosphere that was unbreathable. The small starfish-shaped organ that had been attached to the umbilical cord proved to be an oxygen converter.

It was, the Ants finally remarked, genetically a giant leap forward. "It is known that species interrelate and interbreed. But this mating was radical. Yet the human body adjusted. The infant survived and flourished in the womb and had the good sense to resist entering a lethal atmosphere."

"It was trying to tell us, and we were not able to understand," Beam said.

"But somehow you did," Dr. Fogel remarked wistfully. She was feeling inadequate at the moment.

"I was moved to do it . . . by those infants who sleep on the floor below, I think." Beam reflected.

"Or," said Rose Lewis, "by the Master who is always above."

The cocoons were loaded aboard the watership on schedule. Dr. Macklow made a final dive aboard the probeship to the chamber filled with seawater and checked the quality of the water with a sample taken from each chamber before they'd begun work. The salinity, temperature and viscosity were correct. The cargo chamber was sealed and put on automatic control. Final plans for lift-off were computed and the flight crew did a thorough check of their massive spacecraft. Lift-off was scheduled for eight days hence, but they had some underwater traveling to do before then.

The Finleys would take the probeship to a safe anchorage that Ben Green had located in the backwaters near Galveston Bay. At the last minute Amos Bright decided to come too. They would all say their good-byes to the commanders and the Brigade people that were to remain behind. The Finleys, Perlmans, Hankinsons and Betty Franklin would return with Amos Bright via military aircraft to Homestead AFB.

They would then be driven to the *Manta III*. Jack Fischer and Phil Doyle would take them out to the watership. And by then Matthew Cummings, the Betterses and Gabe would have cleaned up their earthly business and be aboard. The rest of the Geriatric Brigade, which was scattered all across the universe, needed their commanders.

The commanders gathered in a meeting room with Amos Bright, Beam and the two Ants. It was the first time they'd all been together in nearly eight months. The mothership was on the way and, as approved by the Antarean council, a rendezvous was scheduled near the star Vega. The discussion centered mainly on the babies and their future. Mothership would bring the means to cocoon the infants and secure the mixed babies and off-planet parents as well. Bernie Lewis assured the commanders that there would be no trouble with Gideon Mersky once the President was informed of the Defense Secretary's maverick plan. Ruth Charnofsky, as leader of the commanders and the only human with Antarean citizenship, spoke last. She thanked Amos and Beam for their kindness and help in Operation Earthmother. Then she surprised everyone by putting forth a new idea that had been formulating in her keen mind for several days.

"There is no doubt that Ellie-Mae's infant girl will have to return to Betch," she began, her voice talking to no one in particular. It was almost a stream of consciousness. "And of course we must anticipate the other mixed babies might be faced with the same imperative. But these others . . . these human babies of ours . . . I have been watching them, listening to them. They telepath to one another, you know. Yes, you know that. They seem to always speak to Rose and those two nice young people downstairs. I think we must consider a very hard decision. I think it is possible that we might have to leave our babies here on Earth. I think this may be the place where they will grow the best and become whatever God has brought them to us to become . . ."

But before the others could comment, Ruth Charnofsky gasped and doubled over in pain. It was not a labor pain. Something was radically wrong. Bess's thought passed to all the others. Ruth was the chief of the commanders. Was this the proof that because of the special processing and adaptations done to them, the commanders could not bear children?

CHAPTER
TWENTY-EIGHT

Ruth and Panatoy's baby had been developing well inside the ninety-year-old chief commander. At her last examination, five days before the pain began, everything looked normal.

"Ultrasound is a great tool," the young doctor, Robert Chollup, from New York's Albert Einstein Hospital, said to Beam and the medical team assigned to Ruth Charnofsky's case, "but you have to know what you're looking for." His arrogance was exceeded only by his amazing, almost legendary skill as a fetal orthopedic surgeon. Fetal medicine had made slow but substantial progress in the past decade with the advent of high-resolution ultrasound examination procedures and genetic research.

"No one can be faulted for not noticing these changes, Doctor," Beam told him. "The baby's skeletal structure, especially the legs, developed at an abnormal rate in the past four days."

"Yes," Dr. Chollup agreed, nodding as he examined the ultrasound videotape recording of the fetus taken the week before. "I give you that. But I would have anticipated some additional growth near term just by examining the father. His bone structure is quite different from ours. As you can see, the fetus is now growing toward a pattern more in keeping with the ah . . . what is it?"

"Subax," Beam answered. "Can you do anything to alleviate the problem?"

"I can't stop the fetus from developing, unless . . ."

"Unless what?" Dr. Yee asked.

"Unless you want to terminate the pregnancy."

"That is an option of last resort," Beam suggested.

"Well," the young surgeon said, peering once more at the row of illuminated X-rays displayed on the wall next to him, "let's have a look again."

Beam knew the man had an answer to Ruth's problem, but she let the surgeon play out his game. "I think we can take a shot at something here. I look upon a fetus as a patient separate from the mother. I treat it as though it were out of the womb. But in this case I think the relief will be temporary. If the fetus continues to develop the way I think it will, we'll be back in the same boat next week, maybe worse."

"Then, Doctor, may I suggest you take care of the short term," Beam answered curtly, "and I'll see what I can do about the longer-range problem." Dr. Chollup smiled at the attractive female Antarean medical officer, acknowledging her with a patronizing tilt of his head. He was unaware her human appearance was only a protective skin covering. Had he any idea that she was reading his thoughts, understanding that the exterior bravado covered his insecurity about this case, he might have put aside the pretense. But that was his way and Beam knew it. Let him be what he must, she thought. He is skilled regarding the human body. That is what Ruth needs now.

The Subax are a tall race living on a dark, cold planet rich in minerals and medicinal fungi. Their bone structure has evolved to accommodate the high gravity of the huge planet. Notably, their legs are long and muscular. In particular, their femur, the large upper leg thigh bone, and tibia, the main lower leg bone, are twice the weight of human bones and a third to twice the length. The development of these bones in Ruth's baby had crowded the Subax-human fetus inside a human womb. The bones were pressing on the base of Ruth's spine, pinching nerves and threatening paralysis.

Dr. Chollup prepared Ruth with a local anesthetic. That relieved the pain and relaxed her. He then entered the amniotic sac with delicate instruments guided by a miniature video camera and light at the tip of a needle. The progress of the surgery was followed closely on the high-resolution ultrasound TV monitor. The baby reacted to the intrusion immediately, reaching for the needle and twisting violently in its warm safe fluid world. Dr. Chollup withdrew his instruments.

After carefully examining the blood flow and heart rate of the fetus, he decided sedation was necessary. "She's not going to let us in without a fight," he commented coldly as he inserted the needle again and with cool precision injected the fetus with a mild cocaine derivative. The baby had spasms, then relaxed. Dr. Chollup then moved quickly to reinsert his instruments and operate. He placed tiny metal pins in the femur and tibia of each leg. Then, in a display of incredible manipulation, he stitched a thin, sterile wire between the pins. When he tightened the wire the baby's legs bent backward in a froglike manner. When they were bent at about forty-five degrees, he tied off the wire and withdrew. Beam was impressed.

"That was quite something," she said with professional admiration in her voice.

"Thank you," he answered, his voice and manner much calmer now. He knew he'd done a good job. His concern was now for the future. "The longer term is now in your hands, Doctor." That was the first time anyone had called her doctor on Earth. She felt accepted.

"It's being taken care of, even as we speak." Her thoughts then went to the main nursery on the floor below where Alicia Sanchez and Phillip Margolin were trying to communicate with the more than twenty infants in residence there. But they were having no success. The babies didn't understand what the images Alicia and Phillip were trying to project to them meant. Rose Lewis was also in the nursery. More and more, she was the one with whom the babies communicated. Perhaps because she was the only female commander who remained who was not pregnant. They loved when she held them. The older ones were now capable of smiles and laughter, especially when she telepathed love to them.

"They don't understand what we want," Rose told the two young scientists. Then she hit upon an idea. Telepathing up to Beam, she asked if Ruth was recovered enough to be brought down to the nursery. Dr. Chollup said okay.

A few minutes later Ruth Charnofsky was wheeled into the main nursery room, a large pale blue facility with bassinets and cribs in five neat rows concentrated in the center of the room. Along the walls were all manner of emergency equipment, ranging from incubators to complete life-support systems, specially engineered for infants. Off the main room were two laboratories for blood workup and immunization testing as well as genetic follow-up studies. The hospital was gathering quite a mass of data on these special infants.

"Put her in the middle of the room," Rose commanded, sensing the babies were beginning to understand they had a chore to do. She then spoke to her leader, the chief commander. "Ruth, honey. How do you feel?"

"Better. What are you trying to do?"

"I want to see if we can get these little ones in here to talk to your daughter in there," she whispered, stroking Ruth's distended belly.

"To tell her what—stop growing?"

"No. To tell her to stop moving around so much, that she's hurting her mother."

"If they can do that, tell them I'll give them all lollipops tomorrow."

"It's going to have to be a three-way conversation. Open yourself up to them. They're really quite delightful. But no words—they don't know many words yet. Give them images. Of Panatoy, of the Subax long legs, of your pain—whatever you can send them to tell the story."

"And then?" Ruth asked, whispering back to her fellow commander.

"And then they will send their thoughts to your baby . . . I hope."

Ruth began to reach out mentally to the babies around her. At first she felt nothing. Then, after a moment, she experienced the most delightful lightheaded sensation she'd ever had. Her mind was full of light and laughter. Everything was clean. There was joy within her heart. She was in the children's minds and they, in their innocence and love, came into hers too. She told them a picture story of the baby inside her and the problem they were having. She sent images of what the doctor had done to keep the long legs away from her spine. Then for a moment it seemed that the children left her conscious mind. Then they were back, but only one came forward. It was the first-born girl, the daughter of the Messinas, whose name was Melody. Ruth felt her baby stir inside her. She then heard a stream of language that could only be described as tongues, the babble that some possessed people, caught up in religious fervor, spew forth. The conversation flowed through her. It became a two-way conversation. Her daughter was communicating with Melody. Then it ended. She had the sensation of her baby turning, adjusting her body. Then a voice.

"In one week take away the wires. She will lie still and not hurt you after that." Beam explained to Dr. Chollup what had happened. At first he didn't accept the fact. But when Beam continued her story without speaking words, he understood that the universe held many secrets and wonders beyond his ken.

They arrived above the wreck and it was time to say thanks and bid good-bye to Jack Fischer, Phil Doyle and Madman Mazuski aboard the *Manta III.*

"This time we are not as rushed to say farewell," Amos told Jack after embracing the young charter boat captain.

"And no Coast Guard choppers tryin' to shoot me down either," Madman said with a chuckle.

"Hey," Jack said, extending his hand to the Finleys and then the Perlmans, "you guys take it easy now." He hugged Betty Franklin and the Hankinsons. "Go in peace."

He turned back to Amos Bright. "And then next time you're coming, give us a little notice. We'll get you some decent digs." The visitors began to slip over the side and swim down to the watership six hundred feet below. Amos embraced Jack again.

"I am forever in your debt. May the Master watch over you always."

"Thanks, Amos. My pleasure. You just remember we've got a date in about forty or fifty years."

"That was and is my promise. Good-bye." He dove over the side and was gone.

A short while later they were ready to begin the journey home. It was fitting, Amos thought, that Ruth should be well again as they were leaving. This was her idea. Now, light years across this Milky Way Galaxy, an entire planetary civilization on Antares waited to welcome home their brothers and sisters who had been sleeping in their cocoons for over five thousand Earth years. The mission that had brought him back to Earth was finally going to be completed.

The final job to be done before departure was to bring the Parman guides inside from their chlorine chambers atop the flight deck. The cargo container, filled with the sleeping Antarean cocoons suspended in seawater, was safely tucked under the watership. Three of the flight crew helped the last of the glowing green Parman guides into the main deck. There were six of them, alert and satiated, ready to bring the watership to Antares, or rather Antares to the watership, depending on how one defined travel with Parman guides. In a brief ceremony before leaving their ocean bottom mooring near Boynton Beach, Amos introduced the Parman guides to the new passengers aboard. Having spent years on Parma Quad 2, the Finleys, Perlmans, Hankinsons and Betty Franklin knew their race to be wonderful, open and giving beings. But for Cummings, the Betterses and Gabe, although they'd been processed and their senses enhanced, Parmans were only the second alien life form they'd encountered. The Antareans had shed their human coverings a few days ago and the new space travelers had adjusted to their ephemeral appearance. The translucency of their skin and lack of facial features was overcome by their strong presence.

But the Parmans were another story. They were crystal-base beings with the green quartzlike covering and amorphous shape common to crystalline structures on Earth. But they did have language and from them emanated great waves of friendship and trust. Gabe reached them first. He smiled, newly budding teeth popping through his now pink gums.

"Calimera," he said.

"Calimera," the Parman nearest to him answered.

"Hey," Gabe chirped out, "these guys for to speak Greek."

"They will speak any language, if you will teach them. They enjoy learning," Amos said to the newcomers. "We always play a game with them. We give them a new thought, a new idea for us, and they give us one back."

"I never thought I'd ever talk to a crystal," Coolridge Betters said aloud.

"Nor I a policeman," the Parman nearest to him answered.

"I think you all look beautiful," Paige Betters said.

"We cannot look the way you do. But we know of your beauty from within."

"I never thought I'd be traveling in space," Matthew Cummings said to the largest and oldest Parman guide.

"You are not yet," it answered, "and if we do not depart promptly, this old rock will need another feeding." Amos laughed. As he removed his four molecule thick human covering he gave the order to the flight crew to begin the journey. Ahead of them, the nuclear submarine *USS Schulman* also moved east, running a mile or so in front of the watership. It would keep an eye and ear out for unfriendlies that might detect the hugh Antarean craft under the water. Above, the *USS Hapsas, USS Metz* and *USS Simi* also got underway, heading due east toward the mid-Atlantic Ridge.

Two days later, after being shadowed by the Soviet submarine *Pomorze* and its companion guided-missile cruiser *Novosobirsk,* the watership cover fleet reached its destination. Throughout the journey the American and Russian vessels played a game of cat and mouse. But instead of the American ships and submarine, the Russians were interested in the huge metallic mass that filled their sonar screens. Playfully the Antarean flight crew electronically changed the shape of their craft. At times it was another submarine, then a mountain ridge, then a school of blue whales and at times it disappeared. It had the Russians confused and concerned. They reported back to fleet command that the Americans had developed a new sonar jamming device.

The watership took leave of its escort, bidding Captain Walkly farewell. The Navy Seal team had been transferred from the *Orca* to the *Simi*. Amos Bright thanked each of them personally. The watership then dove rapidly into the depths of the ocean. Three and a half miles below they found the mountain peaks of the midocean range. They continued diving deeper until they reached the valley floor and the midocean rift, an area of tremendous volcanic activity and geothermal upheaval. This was the place where two enormous tectonic plates met. The watership followed the rift north, steadily increasing speed, slowly engaging the ion drives. The pressure outside the spacecraft was hundreds of thousands of pounds per square inch, capable of crushing almost any manmade object. But the watership was built to withstand pressure many times this load. It moved through the ocean depths as though it were air.

As they neared Greenland the volcanic activity increased. They turned northeast, skirting Iceland, up into the Greenland Sea, then under the thinning summer pack-ice, due north toward the magnetic north pole. At the predetermined time and place calculated by Margolin and Sanchez, the watership engaged its ion engines and sped toward the surface. It exploded through the pack-ice and soared into the bright arctic summer sky. The flight crew overdrove the ion engines so that an excess of negatively charged electrons flooded the atmosphere behind it. It sped away from the Earth at incredible speed. By the time human detection devices recorded it, it was gone. All that remained was a negatively charged image, an anomaly. The Russians chalked it up to electric disturbance. The Chinese listed it as a solar disturbance that activated the Earth's northern magnetic field. The American observers on station in Greenland and along the Canadian DEW line filed a variety of reports. Among them, one young Air Force lieutenant with an active imagination suggested it was a UFO.

By September first three more babies had been born. Everything was normal. The nursery was flourishing. Ruth Charnofsky and her unborn Subax

daughter were on good terms. Dr. Chollup had removed the wires and pins, and to his amazement the
fetus had remained stationary. Studying the human-
Subax female with extremely high-definition ultrasound, a machine he had specially flown in from New
York, he watched in fascination as the baby flexed and
toned its own muscles in her mother's womb. But the
baby never stretched or pressed near Ruth's spine or
other organs. As it grew larger it huddled tighter into
the fetal position, moving slowly and deliberately and
only when necessary.

The parents who had gone out to see their families
began to return. For most it had been a magical,
wonderful time, seeing children and grandchildren.
None of the couples went to see any old friends. What
could they say to them? There was no more processing
room, no way to take them along into their future.
Many came back to Houston ahead of schedule. They
said they missed their babies. In fact they did, but
they also wanted to escape the dreadful reminders of
what life on Earth for many really meant. Television
was filled with poverty, the homeless, brutality, war,
religious and racial hatred—a world that had not
changed since they left. A world that seemed intent on
destruction and hatred compared to the other worlds
they'd seen.

Marie and Paul Amato had gone to see their son in
Boston. He was a speech and English professor at
Tufts. After the initial reunion with him, his wife and
their two grandchildren they decided to take a week
and drive into the New England countryside. It was a
beautiful trip. "We've missed so much," Paul told Ben
Green. "We've left behind a lifetime."

Marie saw things differently. "Our life is changed
forever. This planet is our homeplanet, but it can't be
our home anymore. The steps we've taken, the places
we've been . . . the long life that lies ahead . . . I can't
relate to Earth anymore. I feel as though I'm just a

visitor. It's the same way we felt on Hillet. Just a visitor."

"And our family?" her husband asked, unhappy with her because she wanted to leave their son and grandchildren earlier than planned.

"Our family is the Brigade. Our family is lying asleep in that bassinet on the second floor." She had tears in her eyes. "Our family is now traveling to every corner of the universe."

Another couple, who had gone to Denver where both their married children lived, told Beam the same things in a different way. "We became intolerant of our children and grandchildren. Probably much the way they were intolerant of us as we grew old and set in our ways. But now we've stretched, expanded. We can never be what we were before. When we left this planet, we left it forever."

"Not exactly," Beam answered. "You are back here for good reason."

"But not to stay," the couple answered. "We can never live here again, not after what we have seen and done out there."

No one was sure just where the idea was coming from, but several of the Brigade, after returning from their family visits, began to have doubts about cocooning the babies. Even Beam was not convinced that was the best course of action. The closer the parents became to their children, the stronger the fear and doubt grew.

Peter Martindale's mate, Tern, asked the question as she held her son while he slept in their tropical quarters. "Are there no places on this planet where it is warm and wet like on Turmoline?"

"Many," he answered.

"Then why take the child so far? This is homeplanet for you. I am your mate. I can stay here with you and hunt."

Besides being a steelworker in his former life in

Kentucky, Peter had enjoyed teaching others. He had dreams about taking his new son fishing and hunting in those Appalachian Hills he knew so well. He had thought about asking the commanders to allow him to stay behind. Many other parents, especially those who had no family to visit, were having similar thoughts. And no one was happy with the idea of putting the babies in suspended animation for such a long period of time.

Ruth, Beam, the Greens and Lewises sat with Alicia and Phil in their office on the first floor. LoCasio and Berlin, the two NASA assistants, had gone back to their regular jobs in the Johnson Space Center. Rose Lewis had called the meeting. She had news.

"Some of the babies are communicating in English," she began.

"Three can speak the language of the Penditan, Tern's tribe," Beam interjected.

"And the language of Betch as well," Ruth added.

"We know they communicate with your Subax too," Mary added, glowing with her own pregnancy. Her baby was due in less than a month. It would be the last born.

"May I say something?" Phillip Margolin asked.

"Of course," Ruth answered. She too had the magic aura of motherhood surrounding her. The daughter she carried continued to grow rapidly. Ruth sensed birth was imminent.

"Alicia and I have been talking. This may be way out of line, maybe none of our business, but if you're not sure about how cocooning or space travel will affect the children, why do it?"

"What other suggestion do you have?" Bernie Lewis asked.

"Stay here," Alicia answered.

Bernie laughed. "I'm sorry. It's just that the memory of that gung ho mindless colonel is still a fresh memory. Look, part of this government means to hold us against our will. That Mersky fellow knows a lot.

Alma told me he can block, and he is on the verge of understanding how to get into our own heads. You know that, Phil. You know how dangerous that can be."

"All I'm saying," Margolin continued, "is that we might explore some alternatives."

"Such as?"

"Such as staying here." Alicia picked up where she'd left off. "Staying here on Earth in a safe place." Everyone considered the idea carefully. "The President isn't like Mersky. He would understand."

"He's a politician," Bernie said quickly.

"He's a good man," Margolin answered.

"Good men come and go. Governments change. The mothership is on the way," Bernie remarked to no one in particular.

"The children don't want to leave," Rose said suddenly.

"They told you that?" Ruth asked.

"No. I sense it. I think it would be a mistake to take them from here."

Beam had listened patiently. Now it was her time to speak as Amos had instructed her. "The custom of bearing young on homeplanet is very old. Most of the traveling races, like our own, like you would become, always try to avoid the uncertainties of alien environments for the newborn. Until the young mature no one can know what they are, what they can be. Here on homeplanet, the genes are safe. Later it will become clear which are the travelers among this new race of human beings."

"And what about the mixed babies?" Ruth asked the Antarean medical officer, knowing that through Beam she was speaking to Amos Bright as well.

"They are special. The Master mixes many kinds in the universe. Each is the beginning of new life, new possibilities. We will have to see what these are, and how they must be nurtured. So far the Penditan woman has a child that can live on this planet. The

Betch baby cannot. It must be taken to where it can survive naturally. But the others, the human babies, they can live here."

"And if we stay," Rose asked. "What will become of us?"

"If you mean do I know if you will grow old and pass on," Beam answered, "I do not. The processing we did was to prepare you for space travel, to be like us, to move through the void as universal particles. The other changes—this ability to reproduce again, to be free of disease—we have no idea what maintaining that status on Earth entails."

"So we are faced with the same challenge again," Mary Green said. "Do we stay or leave?"

"Not exactly," Rose answered. "Who says that all of us must remain? It is only the children who may need to stay, who seem to want to stay."

Alicia and Phillip had the same thought at the same time. "We could care for them, teach them, protect them." The commanders and Beam read their strong thoughts instantly. They all knew of the love the two scientists had for each other. It was also apparent they shared a deep mutual love for the Brigade children. And the children responded to them in kind.

Maybe it was the children who put the thought in the minds of those in that meeting. Maybe they knew something about their future that their parents did not.

CHAPTER
TWENTY-NINE

Dr. Chollup stayed around the NASA hospital until Ruth gave birth. From all indications it would have to be a cesarean section because of the size of the baby. She went into labor at the moment of the Autumnal Equinox. It had no significance other than the child was named Autumn, although Skye would have been more appropriate. She was pale blue when born and appeared to have blonde or silver hair covering most of her long, muscular body. When the pediatricians and nurses had cleaned the infant and dried it, it became apparent that the hair was a soft, downy fur. Autumn's features were human, but her body was Subax.

Panatoy viewed his daughter's birth on a closed circuit television hookup in the environmentally controlled apartment he shared with Ruth.

The baby was healthy and vital. Mary Green was relieved since Ruth was the first commander to deliver a child. Mary sent the word out to the other commanders, now light years away being transported by their Parman guides toward Antares. Those commanders in turn sent forth the good news to Antares, where Ruth was an honored citizen, and beyond to the rest of the now scattered Geriatric Brigade.

Ruth recovered rapidly from her surgery. Her healing powers, common to the commanders, were phenomenal. Within a few hours she was joyfully asking to see her child to feed her. Dr. Chollup was not so happy. He had a proprietary interest in the beautiful blue downy infant. And something was wrong. The child's demeanor had changed. She was quiet. List-less. Her eyes, originally dark and clear like her mother's, were now glassy. Her temperature was normal. The blood tests were normal; they matched the other all human babies. Dr. Chollup asked that the child be kept in intensive care while he stayed by her side, pondering the slowly deteriorating condition.

When Ruth asked for the baby he immediately brought the infant to its mother. Ruth held the now listless girl to her breast, but the child would not nurse. Beam took the baby and examined it.

"It is warm," she said to Ruth.

"Normal temperature," Dr. Chollup said.

"What does Panatoy say?" Ruth asked.

"He has not held the baby yet," Beam answered.

"Then take her to him. Quickly." Ruth's voice was firm. Dr. Chollup stopped Beam as she reached to take the child from her mother's arms.

"You can't put that child in such a frigid environ-ment. It will kill her."

Beam hesitated. "We will wrap her in blankets."

"Hurry," Ruth begged. She was still weak, but her fear was apparent. Beam rushed out of the room with the baby. Dr. Chollup and two pediatric nurses fol-lowed close behind.

Panatoy held the child in his strong blue arms. He bent his face close to his daughter, parting the layers of blankets to see her face. His room was ice cold. In deference to the baby he had lowered the ultraviolet light necessary to his survival to the minimum level he could tolerate. Beam and Dr. Chollup, both dressed in heavy fur-lined Air Force parkas with hoods, stood nearby at watch with great interest. The Subax spoke to Beam in his language, which she understood and spoke.

"The child is ill. Do you know what is wrong?"

"No, Panatoy," Beam answered. "She was functioning normally at birth."

"How long has she been like this?"

"Nearly three hours. I'm concerned."

The Subax stood. His height and deep blue coloring made him an impressive figure. Dr. Chollup stepped back a little.

"Is this the medical officer who helped Ruth while she carried my daughter?" he asked Beam.

"Yes. He is a doctor. He is very skilled and has my respect."

"He is ignorant about the Subax. You, an Antarean traveler, should know better yourself." Panatoy began to remove the blankets and clothing that had been put on the baby in intensive care. He threw the warm, bulky coverings aside, scattering them like a stripper in high-speed motion.

"He'll kill that baby!" Dr. Chollup shouted, moving to take the newborn from its father. Panatoy turned and faced the doctor as a huge grizzly bear mother might confront a hunter who'd come between her and her cub.

"Tell him to stay away," Panatoy warned Beam. But she didn't have to tell the arrogant surgeon. Panatoy's glare and offensive body language were universal. Words were not necessary.

Panatoy, stripped little Autumn naked. He turned up the ultraviolet light source to maximum and held his daughter close to the source of the light. Steam began to rise from her body as it cooled to the below-freezing Subaxian temperature.

"He'll kill her," Dr. Chollup moaned. The baby was his patient.

Then the improbable happened. Once the baby stopped steaming it began to move. It wriggled in its father's arms, reaching for the deep purple light source. Then it laughed. Not a small chuckle, but a gurgling sound of total joy. Panatoy brought the naked

baby down to his face and kissed her. The child
grabbed at her father's face and thick long white hair.

"She is hungry," Panatoy told Beam. "Can you
bring Ruth to us?"

In all his days in medicine, Dr. Chollup would
never forget the sight of a woman over ninety, wearing
protective eyeglasses, nursing her naked blue furry
newborn in subzero temperature, dressed in a fur
parka with special holes cut into it in order to expose
her nipples to the baby's hungry mouth. Panatoy
remained close to his family, as proud as any new
father had ever been.

As her daughter suckled, Ruth Charnofsky's
thoughts went out to Ellie-Mae Boyd, who was also
nursing her new baby in the environmental duplex
next door. Ellie had to wear breathing apparatus since
her mate and infant required an oxygen-free,
nitrogen-rich atmosphere.

Both women knew their babies could never live
naturally on Earth. Both would have to be returned to
their father's homeplanet.

The NASA security people and the Secret Service
detail assigned to the hospital by Benton Fuller were
extremely efficient. There had been not one breach of
security since the Brigade arrived. When the Army
colonel from Fort Campbell arrived and presented his
authorization papers, personally signed by the Secretary of Defense, they were checked, double-checked
and certified. He was allowed access to the first and
second floors. Only special visitors with escorts were
allowed on the critical top floor.

Bernie Lewis saw Colonel Smith first. He was on his
way to meet with Alicia Sanchez and Phil Margolin
when he perceived a familiar presence in the hallway.
Bernie ducked back into the doorway to the kitchen
staff quarters and watched. Colonel James "Jimmy"
Smith was reconnoitering the hospital, making mental notes on various doorways and facilities. He was

especially interested, as Bernie Lewis learned when he read the intruder's mind, in the location of the security people and their housing quarters.

Bernie Lewis called up to his wife, Rose, who was in the main nursery on the second floor. He alerted her to the problem and suggested that the floor be closed to visitors.

"Use any pretense. We don't want him near the children," Bernie proclaimed.

The commanders met again, this time in Rose and Bernie Lewis's apartment. Sanchez and Margolin were also there. Bernie was adamant this time.

"That Mersky son of a bitch has the arrogance to send his puppet soldier into our midst. We can't afford to wait any longer." He wanted to confront Gideon Mersky immediately.

Ruth had been confident that the attempt to imprison the Brigade and their babies wouldn't be made until the last birth had occurred. But now that she was a mother, in spite of her wisdom and extensive new abilities, she reacted protectively as any mother anywhere in the universe might.

"I think you're correct this time, Bernard. But I also think before we confront this problem, we'd better have a solution to the larger question. What are we going to do about the children?"

The night before, just for a change of pace and scenery, Sanchez and Margolin had gone into Houston for a first-class seafood dinner at Kaphan's and some laughs at the Comedy Workshop. On the spur of the moment they decided to take a hotel room for the night, winding up with a posh suite high above the glittering ribbon of nighttime traffic on the Southwest Freeway. The suite had a hugh four-poster bed. The bath was a pink marble tub with gold fixtures. As they sat naked side by side in the warm scented water, sipping wine, relaxed and satiated, he asked her to marry him. She said she would.

Now, at the meeting with the commanders, the

young couple announced their intentions. Everyone was delighted.

"We didn't tell you this just to garner some good wishes," Margolin said.

"No," Sanchez continued, "we've been giving the problem of the babies in space some very serious thought. We have a plan . . . well, just an idea—"

"But it can work," Margolin interrupted. "I . . . we know it can work. It might be the answer to everyone's concerns."

They continued the meeting for hours, listening carefully to the plan the two young scientists proposed. After they were sure Colonel Smith had left the premises, they all went down to the office to look at the computer models Alicia had prepared.

"I think it can work," Bernie said after the plan had been completely exposed, "but it will require exquisite timing."

Ben and Mary Green weren't that positive. "It will have to be put to a vote," Ben suggested.

"Many of us are concerned about taking the babies into deep space," Mary added.

Ruth had listened silently. She was recovered from her operation and enjoying motherhood. She knew her daughter would have to travel to Subax and that she would go too.

"A vote may not be the proper way," she finally said. "That is to say, *our* vote. The children have a voice too—we all know that. Rose speaks to them. They communicate with her."

"And with us," Margolin added.

"Yes. That too. The plan these two young people have devised is brilliant. I think we need to know more facts. And we have to complete the births."

"That's only three to four weeks away," Bernie Lewis reminded her.

"I know," the chief commander answered. "The mothership is coming. We are here for it. We can develop two plans . . . one to leave and another to stay. Much will depend on what Bernard finds when he confronts Gideon Mersky in front of the President."

"The children will want to have a voice in the decision," Rose said.

"Yes," Ruth answered. "But for now we must proceed on the basis that we are all prepared to leave with the mothership. Bernard will go to Washington. Will you accompany him, Ben?" she asked the remaining father-to-be. "If you want to stay here with Mary, I'll understand."

"No," Ben answered. "We have time. She still has three weeks to go. I know Bernie is a little long winded," he joked, "but even he can't talk for that long."

"All I need is ten minutes with that sleazy Mersky character," Bernie answered, not finding humor in Ben's remark.

"Good," Ruth said. "I'll ask Jack Fischer to pay us a visit to get things moving on the other end."

After the commanders had left, Sanchez and Margolin went over their plan one more time.

"Are you sure it can be done?" Margolin asked his new fiancée.

"Theoretically it works. But until we try it, we'll never know." There was confidence in her voice. He took her in his arms.

"I love you," he whispered softly in her ear. "I want to have many children."

"Me too," she answered, caressing the back of his head. "And perhaps they'll have more playmates than they'll know what to do with . . . ."

There were now only six human couples and one mixed couple awaiting the arrival of their babies. It was mid-September. The staff had been cut back and only one delivery room and intensive care team was on call. Everyone was confident that the births would go smoothly. In the next two days two women went into labor and delivered healthy baby boys. They were moved without incident to the main nursery, which had become the busy center of the hospital. There were now twenty-two babies, ranging in age from four and a half months to four days, in the nursery and three in the environmental duplexes.

Were the staff able to hear the communication Rose Lewis monitored and joined in between the babies, they would have been shocked. These children were learning at a rapid rate from each other, from their caretakers, from Sanchez and Margolin and most of all from Rose herself. The older ones, those born on the watership as it came to Earth, were now absorbing information from the commanders aboard the watership by using Rose Lewis as a conduit. The Erhardt twins and Melody Messina were also in touch with Amos Bright and Beam.

It was now apparent to the Antareans that this special race of humans, created in part by their cocoon-processing equipment, was destined to be a far-ranging instrument of the Master. The children, no matter where they were reared, required an education of universal range and scope.

The watership was approaching its rendezvous with the mothership. Decisions would have to be made about the future of the children and the Brigade. Amos communicated his thoughts in the Antarean language to all the commanders and Ruth Charnofsky.

"Our race has traveled the universe for millennia. You know we have chosen to reproduce our own kind at homeplanet. We have improved our race genetically ourselves, with science and time. Most of the traveling races tend to do that. But the humans are sudden travelers, thrust upon the universe with abilities of a high order. With the abilities of Antarean commanders. Your offspring are unique. In the universe there are a myriad of beliefs regarding the existence of life, its purpose and its future.

"Many of the races keep to themselves, as we Antareans have. Many mix and interbreed, forming new races, new possibilities. They are in the majority. They believe this is the grand plan—that life will mix and blend until there is one that encompasses all.

"There are many who believe we are all one now, that we come from the common universal seed placed among the stars by the Master . . . the Being . . . the God.

"Who is to say which is correct? Perhaps they are both one and the same.

"The great civilizations, the unwritten laws, the overwhelming respect for life—these great truths have all been given to us by the mixed races, by the blending of the common DNA and genetic matter with the universal spark of life itself.

"These children are a new race. They are to be protected. They are to be taught. I will confer with the Antarean council from the mothership and pass along their opinion as to a plan of action."

Jack Fischer arrived back in Houston a week after Autumn was born. He had met with Mr. DePalmer at the Coral Gables Bank and located several promising situations that fit into the alternative plan Sanchez and Margolin had developed. The final decision would be made after the Antarean rendezvous near Vega, and after Bernie Lewis and Ben Green returned from their mission to Washington.

A baby girl was born to a couple from New Orleans. It was the only child that had been conceived on Parma Quad 2. When the Parman guides on the watership learned of the event they asked the flight crew to request that the child be granted citizenship on their planet. Amos sent the message and the parents accepted with gratitude. The girl was named

Parmabelle. Now only four mothers were still pregnant.

September was drawing to a close. Bernie Lewis and Ben had flown into Washington that morning after requesting a meeting with the President and the Secretary of Defense. Ben looked back at Arlington National Cemetery as they crossed the Key Bridge in a taxi. His only son, Scott, killed in Pleiku during the infamous Tet Offensive, lay buried under one of the thousands of snowy white markers that covered the rolling Virginia hillside behind him. Then, as they drove past the somber Viet Nam Memorial, upon which Scott Green's name was joined by fifty thousand more, Ben's thoughts went out to Mary with an inner silent prayer that their new baby would be a son.

Bernie Lewis understood his friend's emotions. He'd been a soldier, he'd seen his friends die in foxholes next to him. He remembered the mass graves and still smoking, skeleton-filled ovens at Auschwitz. Both men understood they were about to confront a man who was bent on using military force to control their lives and the destinies of their children.

Somehow, passing by all these monuments to the dead, which symbolized the senselessness of war and oppression, gave strength of purpose to both commanders.

"It's going to be all right," Bernie said to his friend as they approached the White House reception gate.

"Yes," Ben Green answered, "and this time, I believe, life is going to be the winner!"

"Amen!"

CHAPTER THIRTY

Bernie Lewis and Ben Green had requested that in addition to President Teller and Secretary Mersky, Caleb Harris, the NBC Washington News Bureau Chief, Captain Thomas Walkly, the Navy Undersecretary, and Doctor Kahwaji also be present at the White House meeting. They all now gathered informally in the Oval Office, the place where President Malcolm Teller first learned about the Geriatric Brigade from Alma Finley. Only Gideon Mersky was absent. He'd called earlier that morning to say he would be late.

"Mrs. Finley sends her greetings, Mr. President," Bernie began. "She is now aboard the watership rapidly approaching the star called Vega."

Caleb Harris was surprised. "She never called to say good-bye," he said wistfully.

"There was little time and a great deal of work to accomplish," Ben answered. "The Antareans are eternally grateful to all of you for your efforts that enabled them to bring their cocoons home after five thousand years."

"They are entirely welcome," Malcolm Teller said. "And please let them know they are always welcome in America." A momentary uncomfortable silence gathered in the room. Tension filled the air. Bernie and Ben knew it was something else.

Ben Green let his mind open while Bernie blocked. Gideon Mersky was nearby. His mind entered Ben's consciousness. So he's learned to do it, Ben thought to himself, masking the revelation. He sensed the Defense Secretary groping to make contact.

"That's enough." Bernie Lewis's abrupt thought cut

into Mersky's own mind, jarring his concentration. "Come in here now," Bernie commanded.

"What's enough?" the President asked, unaware that he had not heard the words said aloud. At that moment Gideon Mersky entered the Oval Office. He quietly sat down in one of the blue armchairs.

"Our stay here on Earth," Bernie answered, nodding politely to Mersky. "The time grows near when we must also depart."

Malcolm Teller was clearly surprised and disappointed. He glanced over at Gideon Mersky with a questioning expression.

"I thought you were going to stay," the President said. "Didn't you tell Secretary Mersky's people that the babies were too delicate to travel, that you were going to keep them here on Earth for a while until they were stronger?"

Ben Green now riveted his concentration on Mersky as he spoke to the President.

"No, sir. That was just a suggestion your medical staff made. It was never a firm decision. Dr. Kahwaji can confirm that."

"That is true," the Undersecretary of Health told the President. "We believe it is dangerous for the infants to be subjected to the rigors of space travel as it was described to us by the Antarean medical officer, Beam. The children would have to be put into a kind of suspended animation. The Antareans believe that such a procedure with ones so young might be unwise."

"Nevertheless," Bernie Lewis said, "we've made the decision to leave. There is an Antarean mothership scheduled to arrive within the next three to four weeks. The time has come to begin our preparations for departure."

"I'm sorely disappointed," the President remarked. "Secretary Mersky was confident you'd stay. He told me he'd prepared a special living area, a secure compound, for you out west somewhere. In Arizona, I believe."

"That's correct." Mersky spoke for the first time.

"I'm sure he did," Ben Green said sarcastically. "But it's time to end the power games. The lives of our children are at stake." Ben's tone of voice confused everyone except Bernie Lewis and Gideon Mersky. He sounded belligerent, threatening.

Before the President could assess that there was a serious problem, Gideon Mersky stood and began to address the chief executive. It was a power play designed to force the President to make a decision in Mersky's favor. Both commanders now sensed that Colonel Smith was outside the Oval Office. He was armed.

"Mr. President," Mersky began, his tone of voice even and measured, "you will recall several months ago, when these senior citizens returned from their adventures in space, I took the position that they were obligated as Americans to share their knowledge and special talents with the rest of their countrymen. The woman, Mrs. Finley, insisted otherwise, and, in my opinion, used her extrasensory powers to persuade— no, that's the wrong word—to force you to give them everything they needed to secretly have their babies and get those cocoons, whatever they were, out of our territorial waters."

At any moment it was possible for either Bernie or Ben to stop Mersky, but they chose to let him continue. Mersky's voice grew stronger now as he came to his conclusion.

"At your insistence I put military facilities, manpower and equipment at the disposal of these people. Undersecretary Walkly informs me the Navy budget alone was more than three million dollars. I imagine the NASA figures might be twenty times that. We have spent the taxpayers' money. We have been party to a conspiracy to perform secret activity within the borders of our own country. Now we are being told thanks and good-bye. For me, as a government official and as an American, that is just not good enough. Deny it or not, these people are Americans. The others, the aliens that travel with them, are in this country without a visa. They all come under United States law. I believe the time for accountability has arrived. I believe they are manipulating us. I believe they have subtly forced and coerced us into supplying and fulfilling all their needs without once offering anything in return."

"What do you want?" Bernie Lewis asked calmly.

"The list is long," Mersky replied immediately. "To begin with, this talk about leaving in a few weeks has got to end. Your country has need of the technology you and those aliens possess. We want to learn how to use telepathy as you use it. We want—"

Ben Green cut him short. "This has gone far enough. Mr. President, it was explained to you months ago that we no longer consider ourselves Americans. We are human beings from planet Earth. We are universal travelers. We have come home to bear our children. That is now our natural way of things—"

Mersky cut in. "You're back in America! We have our own way here!"

"BE SILENT!" Bernie Lewis commanded. His authoritarian voice stilled the room. An unheard emotional shock Bernie sent through Gideon Mersky's mind stunned the Defense Secretary.

"Now just a minute," President Teller began.

"There are no more minutes, Mr. President," Ben Green answered quickly. "Outside your office door right now, an armed American Army colonel is prepared to harm Mr. Lewis and myself."

"What?" The President was visibly shaken.

"He's only there if these two don't listen to reason, Malcolm," Mersky said, having recovered from the jolt Bernie sent through him.

"There will be no gunplay in this office!" The President was incensed. "Just who the hell do you think you are, Gideon?" This is the office of the President of the United States, not some back alley for kidnapping." He stood and went to his desk. He rang his reception secretary. "Midge. Is there an Army colonel out there?"

"Yes, sir," was the reply on the speaker phone.

"Please send him in here immediately."

"Yes, sir." A moment later Colonel James Smith entered the Oval Office. He started to walk toward the end of the office where everyone was seated.

"That's far enough, Colonel," the President said. Smith stopped and stood stiffly at attention. He saluted.

"Yes, sir."

The President approached him. "Colonel Smith, what were you doing in my outer office?" Smith glanced over at Mersky. "I'm asking you a direct question, Colonel, and as Commander in Chief I'm ordering you to answer me. Now!"

"Yes, sir. I was ordered there by Secretary Mersky."

"For what purpose?"

"This is difficult, sir."

"Answer me, Colonel, or you'll answer a General Courts Marshal."

Gideon Mersky stood up. "Answer the President, Jimmy."

Malcolm Teller spun around and pointed his finger at Mersky. "You sit down. This officer is under my command, not yours." He turned back to Colonel Smith, who had turned pale. "I'm waiting, Colonel."

"Yes, sir. I was there under orders from Secretary Mersky to be prepared to take those two gentlemen into custody." He pointed toward Ben and Bernie.

"How?"

"By force if necessary."

"If they resisted?"

"I was to shoot to maim and subdue them."

"I see," President Teller said softly. "Is there anything else you want to say?"

"Well, sir, my command, the 1159th Light Infantry Brigade, is under orders to take charge of that wing of the Space Medicine Center at 0230 hours tomorrow morning." The colonel gazed down at the rich blue carpeting. He was standing in the center of the presidential seal.

"Surrender your sidearm," Malcolm Teller told the officer. "I am now ordering you to place yourself in the custody of Mr. Fuller, the chief of my Secret Service detail. He is in his office adjacent to my secretary. Good-bye, Colonel."

Smith unsnapped his holster and placed his silver-plated .45 on the coffee table nearby. He then saluted the President and left the office. President Teller turned to Captain Walkly. "Tom, please get on the horn and notify the base commander—where would that be, Gideon?"

"Fort Campbell," Mersky said quietly.

"Yes. Of course. Notify General Packlaw of the 101st that I'm ordering the 1159th confined to barracks until further notice." Walkly left the room to do as the President ordered.

"Now," the President continued, "let's get a few things straightened out here . . ." He proceeded to explain to Gideon Mersky that he was the President, that the Geriatric Brigade, the Antareans, the other off-planet parents were his guests and guests of the United States under his executive protection. He made it clear that their space vehicles, Operation Earthmother, and the removal of the cocoons using military personnel and equipment were done as a direct order from the President.

"No one forced me, Gideon. No one got into my mind. No one coerced me. I know what these people are capable of doing. But not once did they resort to violence or coercion. But we did, didn't we? These people are correct when they say we still live in caves. I am ashamed. I want your apology for what you've attempted to do, and I want it now."

"I apologize," Mersky said unhesitatingly. "I only thought I was doing what was best for the country."

"That, thank God, is my job." The President then ordered Mersky to cooperate with the commanders. "If you can't, then I'll have your resignation."

"They'll have my complete cooperation," Mersky answered. "And you can have my resignation whenever you wish." Ben and Bernie knew Mersky was beaten.

"Good. Now let's help these folks get to wherever they have to go. Dr. Kahwaji, is there anything we can do to help them protect those babies in space?"

"We just don't have that kind of technology."

"The watership will rendezvous with our mothership shortly," Bernie said. "We are confident they will have a solution to that problem. Now, what we'd like to discuss is the plan Mr. Margolin and Dr. Sanchez have devised to get us all up to the mothership." He explained that the mothership was far too large a vehicle to bring to Earth unnoticed.

Caleb Harris, who had been quietly watching the events in the Oval Office had a new thought. "You know, Mr. Green, this visit—everything that has happened—well, it just won't remain a secret forever."

"Yes, " Ben responded. "We understood that from the moment we knew how many people would have to be involved in Operation Earthmother. We have begun to release staff from Houston and take over the care of the children ourselves. Some of the medical data, videotapes of the births and of our off-planet guests are missing or have been copied. We expected that. Perhaps it is time that the human race knew they are not alone in the universe."

"May we tell them?" Caleb asked.

"After we are gone, we expected you to do just that."

"But for now," Bernie Lewis interjected, "it would be much better if we kept a lid on things until we are gone."

"Agreed," the President said.

After they had coordinated the departure plan and finalized areas of responsibility, the meeting began to break up. Mersky had been quiet during most of it, answering only when asked a question or if he saw a flaw in the plan. There were few such times. Sanchez and Margolin had done their homework. The President had a few more questions to ask Ben and Bernie before they adjourned.

"There is no way we could convince some of you to stay for a while?" he began.

"I'm afraid not," Bernie answered.

"What if Secretary Mersky's plan had worked?"

"You mean if you had taken us prisoner?" Ben asked.

"Yes. Would you have fought the soldiers?"

"We would not. Neither would the Antareans. The others—the off-planet beings—I think they would respect our wishes."

"But what if we threatened to separate you from the babies?" Caleb asked.

Bernie Lewis spoke. "I'm seventy-eight years old. Most of us are pretty old by Earth standards. If you tried to hold us here against our will, then I believe we would die. We know what it is to grow old here, and we know what it is to face the prospect of a long, long life out there among the stars. The idea is that no one can own another, no one can enslave another or imprison them. You can have the body in chains, but the soul can always be free. Threatening a life, a body, is the way of this planet. I have not been away that long that I've forgotten war and death. But we've learned out there that when you threaten another, when you kill senselessly out of petty hatred or greed or fear, then you only succeed in destroying yourself."

"But you didn't answer Mr. Harris about the babies," President Teller said.

Ben Green then spoke. "That is true. Bernie speaks only for the Brigade. The babies can only speak for themselves. Perhaps someday they will answer that question for us. But if you want my opinion, if the soldiers, if anyone tried to imprison us, or them, they would protect themselves."

"How could they do that?" Caleb asked.

"I wouldn't even venture a guess," Ben answered.

"I wouldn't want to be around to find out," Bernie stated flatly.

CHAPTER THIRTY-ONE

Tommachkikla, "Tom," the farmer from Destero, held his son proudly above his head, spinning and dancing with happiness. His wife, Karen Morano, formerly of Mill Valley, California, delighted in his joy. Their living quarters were divided into a hot and oxygen-rich room for Tom to match conditions on Destero and a normal Earth atmosphere room for her. The infant was comfortable in both environments, but seemed to prefer his father's most. The baby boy was the last of the mixed matings. It was October first.

Nine light years from Antares, drawn along in the solar orbit of the first-magnitude star Vega, the mothership dwarfed its companion watership as the two spacecraft rendezvoused and linked. A special team of scientists and medical officers had come from Antares aboard the mothership to inspect the cocoons and travel back to Antares with them. A huge celebration was being planned for the homecoming with special accolades for Amos Bright. Also aboard were cocooning experts who studied the data available on the human and mixed babies back on Earth. It was decided that the risk was not as great as Beam had feared. The infants were growing physically and developing mentally at an astounding rate. Most of the experts concluded that they would survive the journey to the oxygen-water planet in Quad 2 that had been graciously set aside for them by the Parman civilization. The Antarean craft then detached, and each went on its separate journey with the blessing of the Antarean council.

One more Brigade woman gave birth. A son. Three days later another boy was born. Now Mary and Ben Green were the only occupants of the top floor left to become new parents.

During his years on Parma Quad 2 Bernie Lewis had been a translator and lived with the Parman guides. Because they were to be used aboard the Antarean spacecraft, Bernie had to learn everything he could about the various Antarean space vehicles. He could fly any of them.

Now Bernie Lewis spent most of his time teaching Jack Fischer, Phil Doyle and Madman Mazuski how to fly the probeship. They made several practice trips under water and above water, barely skimming the surface, from Galveston Bay to a small cove called Sea Feather Bay on the British Crown Colony of Cayman Brac in the Caribbean. Jack, with the aid of Mr. DePalmer, had purchased a defunct hotel and forty acres including the sequestered cove.

The hotel was in disrepair, but sat high on a bluff that commanded a view of the whole island and surrounding crystal-clear waters. With local workmen straightening things out, Jack estimated the place would be livable in two weeks.

By October 6 all of the Brigade parents who wanted to visit their families had returned to Houston. Most of the staff was gone. The care of the infants was in the hands of the Brigade, Beam and the two Ants. Mary Green knew she would not have time to see her family again, but she hoped that the baby would come in time for Ben to make a fast trip to Scarsdale. In all the time they'd been back, he hadn't had a chance to see them.

Alicia Sanchez and Phillip Margolin were married on October 8 in the multidenominational chapel at NASA. Then, after one final meeting with NASA and the Defense Department staff to coordinate the movement of the Brigade to the mothership, the young married couple said their farewells and left on their honeymoon. They were honored guests of Jack Fischer at his newly refurbished hotel on Cayman Brac.

Everyone now anticipated their departure. On instructions from the mothership, which was fast approaching our solar system, the babies were prepared for spaceflight. Their food intake was reduced. They were kept in a cool environment that lowered their body temperature. Drs. Yee and Kahwaji were still worried.

On October 9 Mary Green went into labor. With her husband at her side, Dr. Yee and Beam delivered a beautiful baby boy and placed him on her chest. Then and there, she and Ben named him Scott in honor of their first son, who was born and died on this Earth. "The soul never dies," Beam reminded them.

President Teller came to Houston for the last time. He was optimistic about the safety of the children and about seeing the Brigade people again. Bernie Lewis spoke for all of them.

"We have contacted the others in the Brigade and told them about the babies. They now know they are welcome on their own homeplanet."

"Will we see you again?"

"In this universe, anything is possible," Mary Green said as she held her newborn son in her arms.

"Just remember that governments change," the President said.

"So do people," remarked Gideon Mersky, who had accompanied the chief executive on this trip. He had never been to the hospital. He had never seen the babies. "At our last meeting in the Oval Office," he said to Bernie Lewis, "I apologized for my actions. I am truly sorry. Now that I see these children, I know how special they are to all of us. I can feel their strength and the power of their future."

For reasons known only to Bernie Lewis, later that day he took Gideon Mersky aside and asked the

Defense Secretary if, when he'd grown old enough, he might contemplate joining the Geriatric Brigade.

"At a moment's notice," was the enthusiastic reply. Bernie left the conversation there, making no promises.

When Ruth Charnofsky asked him why he'd done that, Bernie replied, "Just planting seeds that might bear important fruit one day."

The next day Ben Green made a fast trip to New York and spent five happy hours with his family in Scarsdale. Their farewell was teary. But the knowledge that Mary and he could reach out to them from across the universe with thoughts of love tempered the sadness of the parting.

On October 14 the mothership entered our solar system, disengaged her Parman guides and decelerated along a trajectory plotted to intercept Earth's orbit in eleven hours, when they would then anchor and wait on the dark side of the moon.

That night, under the blanket of darkness, the hospital was abandoned. They divided into three groups. The first and largest consisted of the Brigade parents, led by commanders Mary and Ben Green.

Next a smaller group traveled in special steel cargo containers with the required controlled atmospheric environments: Panatoy and his daughter, Dr. Manterid and his son and Tommachkikla and his newborn son. Their human spouses led by chief commander Ruth Charnofsky traveled with them. Beam and her two assistants, the Ants as they had been fondly nicknamed, also traveled with this group.

The last group were the babies. Each was encapsulated in a plastic container with life-support systems attached. They were an adaptation of the intensive care incubators Dr. Yee had originally supplied when the watership first landed months ago in the Atlantic. Traveling with the babies were Peter Martindale, Tern and Bess Lewis.

Bernie Lewis traveled along to the secret anchorage of the probeship. At the proper time, according to the plan left behind by Sanchez and Margolin, he would join the others for the trip to their new home.

The three groups boarded separate military aircraft and flew off to their designated locations.

Early the next morning Margo McNeil called the three television networks and requested a White House hookup for a special announcement. At noon, Eastern Standard Time, President Teller announced the three separate and consecutive launchings of the American space shuttles *Liberty, Freedom* and *Brotherhood*.

CHAPTER THIRTY-TWO

The first launching was from Wallops Island, Virginia. The space shuttle *Liberty*, with the Brigade parents, lifted off in the early dawn just as the sun rose on the horizon to the east. The passengers nestled comfortably in the cargo bay aboard a specially sealed and life-supported container that could be released intact into space. It was painted a deep red color.

At the same time President Teller stood at a podium in the Lincoln Room and smiled out at an audience of bleary-eyed reporters. He read from a prepared statement.

"The United States," he began, "is about to take a first step in the development of a long-range deep-space exploration program . . ." He went on to detail that there would be three shuttles launched within a few hours of each other, that they would rendezvous in a high orbit and deposit the initial materials required for the construction of a huge space platform from which future space exploration would evolve.

There was nothing new in the plan or program. The surprise was that it had begun suddenly, without announcement or press coverage of the launches. An irate media fired questions about the secrecy at Malcom Teller. His answer to each attempt to obtain an answer was the same.

"The exact reasons for our decision to launch and commence platform construction will be made public at a later date. At this time I can only say that they are compelling reasons and I am certain that the American public will concur with my decision."

Angry reporters, who had become used to the game of embarrassing, baiting or badgering American presidents at press conferences, began to fire questions that bordered on arrogance and disrespect for Malcolm Teller. He responded in a calm manner, in the manner of a man who knows he has all the cards in his hand.

Later that day the opposition party would call for Congressional investigations into the matter. The President just smiled. In a few weeks the fantastic visit of the Brigade parents and their friends would be known. The world would have proof that Earth was not the center of the universe, that a myriad of life existed beyond our troubled, rather backward planet and that if we ever had hopes of joining the rest of God's living creatures, we'd best clean our own house and put it in order.

Freedom, the second shuttle, lifted off from the brand-new NASA launch facility on Padre Island, Texas. It was an hour after the first launch, just before dawn reached the south Texas coast. Aboard, nestled in the cargo bay in their specially sealed and life-supported container, which was painted blue, were the Antareans and three of the four mixed couples. Peter Martindale, Tern and their infant son were aboard the third shuttle.

Bernie Lewis guided the probeship out of Galveston Bay as *Freedom* separated from its booster rocket tanks high above. He kept the sleek craft submerged for several miles until he'd cleared the last of the offshore oil-drilling platforms that dotted this part of the Gulf of Mexico. Surfacing, he slowly rose into the air at subsonic speed. Climbing to a commercial airline altitude of 30,000 feet, he circled his craft back toward the Texas coast. The sun was rising. He began to climb and gather speed over the west Texas desert. Then, as *Liberty* reached orbit and *Freedom* was well on its way to joining her sister shuttle, Bernie fired the ion drive and rocketed the probeship into a parallel trajectory with *Freedom.*

Caleb Harris sipped coffee on the patio of his Georgetown home. He'd been up all night, writing the story of his career. The sky was blue and the weather crisp. He gazed up toward the heavens and whispered good-bye and good luck to his friend Alma Finley.

Brotherhood, the third shuttle, had its launch delayed for fifteen minutes. A gasket was leaking in the special white cargo container that housed the babies, Rose Lewis and the fourth mixed couple. It was located and resealed. The lift-off, this time from Vandenberg AFB in California, took place an hour and fifteen minutes after the Texas launch. The babies were all safely nestled in tiny containers that would absorb the stress of lift-off. Rose, seated among them, listened to their excited chatter. They knew they were leaving the Earth. They knew the plan.

The dark, predawn California sky lit up as the powerful solid rocket boosters lifted *Brotherhood*'s precious cargo into an orbit that would coincide with that of *Liberty* and *Freedom.*

The Antarean mothership slipped out from behind the moon and drifted toward the planet Earth, glittering before it as a bright sapphire in the black velvet void. On the flight deck the Antareans monitored the progress of the primitive human Earth craft as the three shuttles closed on one another in a orbit more than 20,000 miles above the blue planet.

Bernie Lewis shadowed *Freedom* and communicated with the commanders as well as the mothership.

Five hours after the launch of the third shuttle the three converged at the apogee of the polar orbit. They presented a large radar target. The world was watching. The mothership aligned with Earth, keeping the shuttles between it and the magnetic north pole. It closed in on the shuttles as they now orbited in formation.

Bernie Lewis departed from the trio and flew up to the fast-approaching mothership. He entered the huge craft through a cargo membrane and parked the probeship. He then proceeded to the flight deck where he greeted and embraced many old friends.

At the predetermined point, *Liberty* opened its cargo bay doors and released its red cargo container into space. Moments later *Freedom* did the same. Its blue container floated in a tumbling orbit, slowly drawing away from the shuttle formation. Finally, with what was the most precious cargo of all, *Brotherhood* released the children in their white container. For the first time in months the Brigade was free of its motherplanet Earth.

The mothership descended rapidly toward the shuttle's orbit. As it approached the now floating, tumbling cargo containers, a long extender arm plucked each from the void and retracted it into the mothership through the same cargo membrane that Bernie Lewis had used earlier. The containers were safely aboard. The mission was a success.

Speaking from the flight deck, Bernie thanked the American shuttle crews for their excellent work. Then the Antarean mothership slowly turned away from the trio of empty shuttles. The Parman guides were set in place above the flight deck. The membranes were sealed, and the mothership sped away toward deep space, leaving the empty shuttles behind like a huge bumblebee deserting flowers from which it has drunk all the nectar.

Those back on Earth, aware of what was happening, felt a deep sense of loss. Yet they knew they had experienced something truly wonderful. They had met beings from other worlds, and had, for a brief moment, a glimpse of what their own race might someday become.

EPILOGUE

The shuttles remained in orbit for three more hours, then separated and commenced their individual descents toward Earth.

As the *Liberty,* the first one home, approached its landing strip at the Kennedy Space Center on Cape Canaveral, the mothership slowed down and eventually came to a dead stop in Venus's orbit. The cargo membrane opened. The probeship sped out and away from the huge host vessel.

As the *Freedom* glided safely onto the runway at NASA's Padre Island launch facility, something that appeared to be a large meteor streaked across the now darkening Caribbean skies. Bernie Lewis, with his wife Bess in the co-pilot seat, guided the probeship through the Earth's atmospheric envelope in a fiery descent.

As the *Brotherhood,* the last of the shuttles launched that morning, came to halt on the five-mile runway in the dry, hot desert of Andrews AFB, the Antarean probeship plunged into the dark, cool waters of the Caribbean some five hundred miles south of Miami.

A few hours before dawn, the powdery white sands of Cayman Brac glistened like silver ribbons below Jack Fischer's newly renovated hotel. On the balcony overlooking Sea Feather Bay, the newlyweds, Alicia Sanchez and Phillip Margolin, held hands and breathed deeply of the sweet predawn air. Peter Martindale and Tern joined them as the sky to the east lightened.

In the lush rain forest below the hotel, Jack Fischer,

Phil Doyle and Madman Mazuski finished covering the probeship with camouflage netting. The sun rose on that part of the Earth in a clear pink and blue sky.

On the top floor of the hotel, now renamed the Butterfly, Bess and Bernie Lewis tucked the last of the Brigade infants into their cribs. The Lewises, the Martindales, the Margolins and Jack and his friends would all share in the care and upbringing of these very special human beings on homeplanet. Through the commanders, their education would be universal in scope, but their mother Earth would nurture them. Time would tell what they would become.

The children were silent, their eyes open toward the heavens above. They all heard the same message beamed from the mothership as it left our solar system in Quad 3 of the Milky Way Galaxy.

"Serve the Master as we do.
We are joined to you forever.
Grow in peace.
We love you."

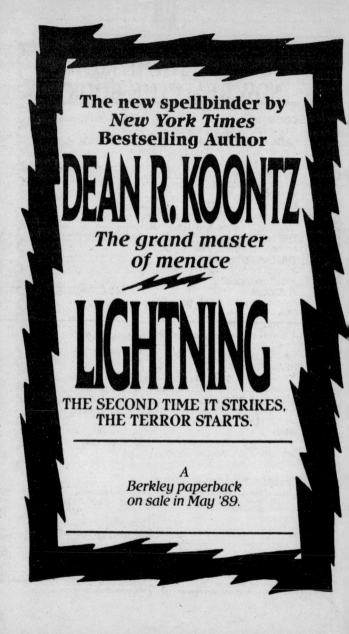